TAKING BACK CONTROL

A Tracy Wright Novel

Meg Hallam

TAKING BACK CONTROL

A Tracy Wright Novel - Book 1

MEG HALLAM

CHAPTER 1

May 1994

Tracy walked out of class and into the grey dark corridor with a gleaming smile across her face. *I've done it*, she thought to herself. She'd finished her first year of A-Levels and had eight weeks of the summer holidays to look forward to.

She hadn't admitted it to anyone, but taking English and Psychology was much harder than she had envisioned. Midway through the year she had started to doubt her choices and was still unclear about what to do when she finished college. But that was now a problem for next year.

Apart from working in the village café, she was determined to make the most of the summer. For this summer was likely to be the last her friends were all together, as next summer they would either go off to university or start working full time.

Tracy walked out of the college building and into the car park. She was instantly greeted by still humid air and the sun's heat on her face, causing her eyes to squint as she got accustomed to the brightness.

The early summer heatwave was predicted to last for several more days, until the forecasted rain arrived, putting an end to the glorious weather.

"Tracy," shouted a familiar voice across the car park, breaking Tracy's thoughts.

Her best friend Emma was waving and shouting her name from the open window of her dark green Mini.

Tracy had known Emma for years. They had first met and became friends when they had started school together at the age of five.

Emma was tall with an athletic build. She had beautiful long straight red hair, bright green eyes and always felt more comfortable wearing sports clothes. And she was popular amongst both boys and girls.

Emma was the first of her friends to pass her driving test and was lucky enough to have her parents afford to buy her first car. A ten-year-old dark green Mini with a white roof for her seventeenth birthday.

"Want a lift?" said Emma.

"Sure." Tracy replied.

It gave them the opportunity to discuss their summer celebration plans for Friday night, and saved Tracy the trauma of catching the college bus home.

On Friday night they were heading to the Viper nightclub in Portsmouth. A popular establishment amongst students. Known for letting those slightly underage in without question and for serving cheap drinks. It was to be their end of year celebration and was set to be the event of the year.

Portsmouth was fifteen miles away from the leafy village of Toddington, where Tracy and Emma lived. Proving to be a logistical challenge for nights out into town.

Travelling into Portsmouth before nine p.m. was never usually an issue as busses ran every hour. Although two busses were needed to get to the centre. Coming home on the other hand was different, public transport was not an option and they had to rely on parents for picking them up.

Their parents generally took it in turns to ensure their safe arrivals home. However, it usually meant a one a.m. pick up, when the atmosphere in the club was still going strong. But they had no choice other than to comply, they simply couldn't have gone out in town on a night out without their parents' generosity.

They also had to limit how much alcohol they drank. One

night, earlier in the year, their friend Simone drank way more than usual and ended up throwing up in the back of Emma's mum's new Jag. After that night, Emma's mum refused to pick the girls up, and they all made sure to be careful and not drink too much.

It was not yet an option to stay close to home and go out in Toddington. It was a small village where everyone knew each other and most of the girls were still underage.

Friday was going to be different. Driving was still a novelty to Emma, who had only passed her driving test the previous month. She had offered to drive the girls to and from the Viper club. Happy to sacrifice her vodka red bulls for the evening, opting instead, for showing off her shiny Mini and newfound freedom. Tracy understood. Having had a couple of driving lessons she could not wait to drive but was six months younger than Emma and was far from being ready to take her driving test.

With Emma driving it meant that for the first time there were no curfew and the other passengers; Jo, Simone, Francis, and Tracy didn't have to limit how much they drank.

Emma pulled into Tracy's Street, a cul-de-sac containing fourteen almost identical fifty's style red brick semi-detached houses with two story bay windows. Tracy's house was at the bottom of the cul-de-sac and her driveway led out into a turning circle.

Emma stopped at the edge of the driveway for fear of not being able to reverse out, and after hugging Emma, Tracy climbed out of the car.

Emma wound down her window and shouted,

"See you Friday Trace, eight p.m., make sure you're ready!"

Tracy chuckled to herself as she waved her off.

The next two days, Thursday and Friday dragged for Tracy. She had agreed to work both days in the café, now regretting that decision due to the continued heat wave. The small narrow twelve tabled café was stifling. Other than the café's entrance door and fire exit off the kitchen, there were no other windows or doors that could be opened. The café felt like a sauna. The fans on the ceilings were on full, but it hardly made a difference and only served to circulate stale warm air.

The café was almost empty on both days. However, Tracy and Debbie were exceptionally busy preparing takeouts for the locals, to be enjoyed down by the river, which was only a hundred yards away.

Other than the café, a small corner shop, a few pubs and a fish and chip shop further up the road, there weren't any other places to get food in the village. So, the café was always popular, especially during the summer.

Debbie was the owner of the café and had worked there for as long as Tracy could remember. She worked all hours, with only help from students and school mums who could offer a few hours here and there.

Debbie was vast approaching retirement but didn't show any signs of slowing down. She was a short plump lady with wiry grey hair and only ever wore floral aprons. She was a good boss and looked after her staff well. She had never married nor had children of her own and looked at her workers as extended family.

As Tracy wiped down tables, she couldn't help but watch people as they walked past the window. Everyone seemed so jolly and were dressed ready to enjoy a day of embracing the sun. Tracy glumly thought that knowing her luck, the forecasted rain would come on her days off.

Friday afternoon eventually came and at five thirty Tracy locked the front door and flipped the open sign to closed.

"Can I get off as soon as I've swept the floor Debs?" Tracy shouted to Debbie, who was in the kitchen washing up.

"Yes, love you can." Debbie shouted back. "Thanks for today, it's been another busy one."

Tracy quickly swept the floor, removed her apron, and left the café. She took a brisk walk home, appreciating what was left of the late afternoon sun as she watched shapes form in the light fluffy clouds which adorned the sky.

As Tracy opened the front door, her mother Jean shouted from the kitchen.

"Tracy, is that you?"

Jean Hopkins, a middle-aged housewife, had worked in the village shop until Tracy was born. Giving it up in favour of being a stay-at-home mum to her two daughters; Tracy and Angela. Jean supported Tracy's father, her husband Peter, by allowing him to build his career, whilst she looked after the children. She always dressed smartly and wore just the right amount of makeup to shave off a few years from her aging face.

"Yes mum." Tracy shouted back.

"Do you want some dinner dishing out, I'm making spag bol?" Jean continued.

"No thanks mum, I need to get ready and anyway I ate some leftovers in the café."

Jean tutted, "That's not proper food you know, don't make a habit of missing meals."

"No mum." Tracy replied, as she was halfway up the stairs.

Despite being seventeen, she still felt that her parents treated her as a child at times.

Tracy turned onto the landing and could see her sister Angela sat on her bed painting her nails black. Three years her junior, Angela was going through a goth stage and was taking advantage of the holidays to embrace the radical style. Today's outfit of choice appeared to be a long black long sleave dress, a studded choker and heavy black makeup.

"Hey sis." Angela said loudly as she looked up at Tracy.

Barely audible music that mainly consisted of angry shouting thumped out of Angela's stereo making any kind of conversation difficult.

"Can you colour my hair tonight?" Angela pleaded, grinning her teeth. "Mum said I could as it's the holidays and I want purple hair."

"No sorry Angela. I'm out tonight and turn that god awful music down."

Angela replied by sticking up a newly painted middle finger but said nothing.

Tracy headed straight for the bathroom to take a shower and stood under the warm running water for several minutes longer than she usually did. Making sure to wash away the café's fried food aroma that lingered in her pours.

A short while later Tracy was in her bedroom, wearing a towel wrapped around her body and second towel around her head.

She closed her bedroom door and pressed play on the stereo that sat on top of her chest of drawers. Turning up the volume and hoping that Blur would drown out Angela's music, booming from the room next door.

Tracy was very different to her sister. She was more of a girly girl. Her wallpapered walls with little red hearts against a white backdrop provided a suitable background to her carefully displayed posters, taken from her weekly Smash Hit's magazine. And her pink curtains matched her pink bedspread. In contrast, Angela's bedroom was dark, and she couldn't remember what her wallpaper was like, as it was hidden under wall to ceiling posters of scary looking men and women, wearing lots of black.

Tracy's bedroom was small, although larger than her sisters and as well as her single bed, wardrobe and chest of drawers that doubled up as a bed side table. She had room for her make up stained dressing table which was cluttered full of various make-up and sprays.

Tracy set to work choosing her outfit for the evening, looking for something which would complement her five-foot curvy frame. Emma was a good six inches taller than her and was generally more popular with the boys. Tracy hadn't had many boyfriends, and neither was she actively looking for one. She felt that the boys at college were too immature and

10

the thought of dating someone from within the village felt incestuous. She was happy to just hang out with her friends and enjoy a good time.

Tracy continued to look through her brightly coloured wardrobe and knew that whatever she ended up wearing, she would definitely be wearing her favourite shoes. A pair of platforms that added a further three inches to her height. She eventually opted for a strappy light blue mid-length dress and accessorised it by adding an open white buttoned shirt over the top, tying the bottom around her waist.

And once dressed, she went about applying her makeup and styling her hair. Her permed blonde hair was easy to style, providing she had plenty of moose, and hairspray and used the diffuser setting on her hairdryer.

By five to eight, Tracy was ready to go and finished off her look by spraying herself liberally with her favourite CK One perfume. A gift that Emma had bought her for Christmas and was warn only on special occasions.

Tracy heard a beep and peered out of the landing window to see the now familiar site of the white roof on Emma's Mini waiting in the cul-de-sac.

She ran down the stairs and noticing her father was home from work, popped her head into the living room to greet him. Peter sat in his red leather armchair, where no doubt he would remain for much of the evening. He worked as a regional sales manager for a firm of convenience stores. He hated having to wear a suit for work as they never fitted well over his bulky frame. He had gained weight over the years and put it down to spending most of his days behind the wheel, as he drove from store to store, snacking on subsidised meal deals. His shirt buttons strained over his stomach and there was stubble on his face. Tracy thought he looked tired.

Her parents were both engrossed in the television. So, after a quick goodbye, she left.

CHAPTER 2

Tracy was the second of the girls to be picked up. Simone was sitting beside Emma in the front passenger's seat and jumped out of the car when she spotted Tracy walking up her driveway.

Simone was the only one of the girls to have a serious boyfriend, Paul, who would be joining them at the club. They had been seeing each other for nearly a year having met at college. Simone was dressed in low waist jeans and a pink crop top, showing off her flat stomach and large breasts. She wore an almost transparent cardigan over the top, and although looked fab, it did nothing to hide her midriff. Tracy was more than slightly jealous of Simone's gorgeous tall curvy figure and long naturally wavey blonde hair.

Simone pulled her seat forward, to allow Tracy to climb in and once they had taken their seats, Emma wearing baggy khaki cargo trousers and a white cropped top drove around the village to pick up Jo and Francis.

Jo, having recently split up with her boyfriend Lee, was determined to look for an immediate replacement. Lee was a year older than Jo and finished their relationship of six months, as he didn't want to start university with the tie of a girlfriend. Jo was devastated and would talk endlessly about how much she missed him.

Emma pulled up outside Jo's house, repeating the same ritual. She beeped and Simone got out of the car to allow Jo to climb in. Jo promptly left her house and walked up to the car looking dressed to impress.

"How short's your dress Jo?" Simone joked,

as Jo climbed into the back, practically revealing her bum in the process. The skimpy purple boob tube dress did not give much to the imagination.

Jo was equally short like Tracy. And Tracy thought that if Simone or Emma had worn that dress, with their height, the outfit would have been obscene.

Jo smiled and replied, "Well if Lee is there, I want him to see what he's missing and if he's not, well..."and winked as she trailed off.

Francis was last to be picked up. She was always late and somehow took the longest to get ready. Even though she wore a more natural look to her hair and makeup. It had become a standing joke and true to form, she kept the girls waiting for a good five minutes after Emma first honked her horn. Resulting in several more honks and a twitch in the curtain from one of her neighbours.

Francis eventually emerged, sporting a slightly grunge edge to her look. She wore a puff sleeve mesh green and black mini dress with black boots. Tracy had to admit she pulled it off well and it certainly complimented her five feet three-inch height and cropped black hair.

The drive was full of chatter, laughter and singing along to the Spice Girls that played out over the car's stereo. Emma paid less attention to the excitement in the car. Concentrating as she drove along the country roads that separated Toddington and Portsmouth.

The evening was walm and light, although a few grey clouds had started to appear in the distance. The car's windows were open slightly. Not enough to ruin any of the girl's hairstyles, but just open enough to allow for a cool breeze to flow through the still humid air.

The back seats where Tracy, Jo and Francis sat was a squeeze, but that seemed to add to the fun of the drive.

Emma parked her Mini in the open-air carpark around the

corner from the club and was pleased to see that parking was free after six p.m.

The girls walked around to the club and joined the queue of clubbers eagerly waiting to gain entry. Although still being sober, the girls were giggly and the short wait to get into the club went unnoticed.

After the girls passed the bouncers, paid the entrance fee, and got their hands stamped in the shape of a snake, they made their way up three flights of stairs. The faint pumping beat of the music got louder with every step they climbed. As soon as they opened the double doors to the club room, they were instantly met with a musty smell. A foggy atmosphere filled the room, a result of cigarette smoke combined with light penetrating through from the DJ booth. A thumping yet enchanting beat of dance music bounced off the walls. And the vibrant energy in the room meant the dancefloor was already starting to fill up, despite it still being reasonably early into the evening.

The girls headed straight to the bar. Passing a number of purple plush booths which had already been seized by earlier arrivals. Clearly eager to bag a base for the evening.

As Emma was designated driver, the girls had agreed to buy her drinks for the evening. Tracy went first to get a round in and joined the row of others also trying to be served. After patiently waiting a few minutes whilst others pushed and shoved around her, it was finally her turn to be served.

Tracy shouted across the bar, "Four pineapple Bacardy Breezers and a coke please?"

She handed the bar man a £10 note and pocketed the change, before handing out the drinks to her friends.

The girls with drinks in hand, walked in the direction of dancefloor. Simone spotted her boyfriend Paul and his friends heading in their direction. Paul with his signature blond curtains was wearing a horizontal multi-coloured stripy shirt and a pair of jeans. Jo had been frantically looking around to see if she could spot Lee within the ever-growing crowd.

Instead, she spotted a lad amongst Paul's friends who she hadn't seen before and instantly felt flushed. Even though the weather was hot, Paul's friend was wearing a zipped-up bomber jacket over baggy jeans and had chin length messy brown hair. With a look of ruggedness that Jo was attracted to. Paul introduced him as Tom, and Jo enthusiastically reached out her hand. Tracy caught Emma smirking and returned the gesture.

After a casual few minutes of chatting over the music, they made their way to the dance floor. And apart from occasional trips to the bar and breaks to freshen up, they all spent the next few hours dancing.

At around eleven thirty, Francis who had been unusually quiet all evening, suddenly leaned into Emma and shouted into her ear.

"I'm going to go home. I'm not feeling too well."

"You sure?" Emma replied. "Can't handle your drink?" smiling sarcastically.

"It's not from drink," Francis was quick to explain. "I feel weak and achy, as though I'm coming down with something."

Emma being the sober sister, took Francis to the payphone in the lobby where she called her mum, then waited with her to be picked up. While the rest of the group remained on the dancefloor.

Forty minutes later Emma reappeared at the side of the dance floor waving. She had a drink in her hand and a boy by her side that Tracy vaguely recognised from college. They slowly made their way through the crowd of dancers to re-join the group.

"Everything ok with Fran?" Tracy shouted over the music.

"Yeah, her mum picked her up. And as we were waiting, Jonny from college came in with a few of his football mates."

"Hi Jonny." Tracy gestured, at the tall good looking chiselled boy. Wearing a tight white understated t-shirt, which gave the impression he too was dressed to impress. The others were oblivious that Emma had returned with Jonny in tow.

The next few hours went by with bouts of dancing, drinking, and sitting in a booth which Simone had commandeered when it had become vacant. And it wasn't long before Jo and Tom started snogging, engrossed in each other and ignoring all others around them.

Tracy saw this as an opportunity to dance without fear of losing the booth, so grabbed Simone and Emma, and they made their way back to the dance floor.

Emma frequently disappeared with Jonny to the bar. It was clear to Tracy that Emma had taken a fancy to him, and nearly always reappeared minutes later with a full glass of coke in hand.

At two a.m., the club was thriving as it entered its final hour before closing. The drinks were still flowing, and the group had become increasingly livelier. On several occasions Emma was asked to stop dancing on their table by one of the bouncers, which she had found hilarious. It seemed Emma really was embracing the night, regardless of being the sober one.

Half an hour later, Jo was still embroiled with Tom. And at the other end of the booth, Simone and Paul had also begun to kiss furiously, with hands rubbing all over one another. Not knowing where to divert her attention, Tracy looked at Emma cringing and pointed to the dance floor. Emma nodded appreciatively, and they headed off to dance for the final few minutes of the night.

Although Tracy was quite drunk, she watched Emma become increasingly sloppy, spilling her drink, and bumping into others whilst dancing.

"Are you ok, Em?" Tracy asked.

"Yeah, I'm fine" Emma slurred.

Tracy knew Emma was sensible and tried to dismiss her doubts, convincing herself that Emma was simply enjoying herself and the atmosphere of the club.

Simone appeared on the dancefloor and shouted. "Hey, Jo and I are going to go back with Tom and Paul. We won't all fit in your car Em, so Tom is going to pay for a taxi."

"Jesus!" Tracy exclaimed. "That's not going to be cheap, he's obviously desperate to shag Jo." and laughed.

Emma simply said "yeah, whatever." And carried on dancing.

Jo and Simone left, and Tracy realised that Jonny too, who had been hanging around Emma for the past few hours, had also disappeared.

It wasn't long before the lights came on, blinding those that remained in the club.

The DJ stopped playing music and over the microphone said. "That's all folks, please make your way out, and enjoy the rest of your night."

Tracy was buzzing. She had finally stayed out late enough to see the end, and the night did not disappoint.

A few minutes later, the girls arm in arm, staggered down the stairs and out into the night. A refreshingly cool breeze offered them comfort in contrast to the heat and stuffiness of the club.

As the girls walked back to the car, they could now talk without having to shout over music.

Tracy asked Emma in a slightly croaky voice, "What happened to Jonny?"

"Jonny was trying to get into my knickers and then admitted he had a girlfriend. So, when I told him to fuck off, he did." She slurred, before laughing.

It was then that Tracy realised Emma was indeed drunk, very drunk, more so than she was. *Had Jonny been adding something to the many cokes he'd bought her, to get her to comply? Shit!* She thought.

As Tracy continued to walk back to the car park, Emma was becoming increasingly less mobile with every step she attempted. The fresh air seemingly accelerating her drunkenness.

Tracy spotted a phone box and deposited Emma on a nearby bench so that Tracy could call her parents, to ask them to come and pick them up. She knew this wouldn't go down well with their parents but was left with no choice. Tracy opened the door to the phone box. Whilst trying not to breathe in the heavy smell of stale urine. Fished a ten pence coin out her pocket, before looking up to see that the handset was missing.

"Fuck!" Tracy shouted out loud as she slapped what was left of the phone.

She left the phone box and looked over to where Emma was sat and saw she was being sick over the bench.

"What the fuck am I going to do now?" Tracy said to herself and found that she was suddenly sobering up. She looked to see if Simone and Jo were still around, but they had long gone. In fact, much to her surprise, everyone had disappeared quickly. Tracy could see in the distance that the club's doors were bolted shut. They were alone.

Light rain had started to fall. Tracy scooped Emma up as best she could, and half dragged her back to the car.

When they arrived at the car, Tracy noticed that the car park was deserted. *Clearly designated drivers opted for an early finish,* she thought to herself. The rain had now started to come down heavier and Tracy shivered. Emma, who was now virtually unconscious and simply mumbling nonsense, hadn't noticed the rain. She also hadn't noticed that Tracy was feeling deep into the pockets of her cargo trousers for her car key. After retrieving the key, Tracy fumbled to get the key into the lock of the passenger's door, whilst also trying to hold Emma upright.

As soon as the door was open, Tracy put Emma into the passenger seat, closed her door and ran around to open the driver's door. Once inside, Tracy sat staring out at the rain and listening to the pitter-patter of raindrops as they hit the windscreen. Her mind was a haze and she panicked for not knowing how they were going to get home.

CHAPTER 3

Several minutes passed, with each minute feeling more like an hour. Tracy looked over at Emma. She was passed out with her mouth wide open.

Tracy hoped desperately for a sign, for some inspiration of what to do. Her breathing had quickened, and she wasn't sure if she could hear the rain intensifying or if it was the sound of her heart hammering. Whatever it was, it was palpable. She was sure if Emma was awake, she'd be able to hear it too.

Tracy knew she had only two options. Sleep in the car until the morning, when Emma was awake and sober enough to drive them home or drive the car herself. Tracy also knew that if she didn't return home without informing her parents, she'd be in trouble. She would be forced to spend the remainder of the summer holidays in their custody, confined to home.

Tracy looked down at her watch. She realised that her window of opportunity to get home before her parents suspected a problem, was closing in on her. She had forty-five minutes at most, before their panic would set in. She could not risk letting her parents down, they'd only just started allowing her to go out in the city at night. She was not prepared to lose their trust, or her freedom.

She had no choice. She had to drive them both home and so quickly thought of a plan. Deciding that parking the car around the corner from her house, making sure to park it out of sight was the best option. Emma could stay with her, pretending to their parents that they had gotten a lift home from one of their college friends. Emma would hopefully be awake and sober enough to ring her mum when they got home, so that she wouldn't worry.

Further doubts crossed her mind. What if the police caught her? She didn't know what she would do in that case but decided to stick to as many country roads as possible. Believing she'd be less likely to pass a police car.

Tracy, although clearly over the limit herself, and having not passed her driving test, understood the basics of driving from the few lessons she'd had.

She sat for a few more moments convincing herself this was the best and only option, whilst secretly cursing Emma for being so naive.

With shaky hands, she reached over to fasten Emma's seatbelt before clipping in her own and then put the key into the ignition.

She slowly pulled out the choke as she started the engine and was relieved that it started first time. Then she immediately felt stumped. She hadn't driven in rain before, or at night for that matter and didn't know how to switch on the windscreen wipers. After a few seconds of fumbling and trying different levers, she eventually managed to turn on the lights and wipers. She put the hand break down, checked her surroundings, and slowly drove out of the car park.

Tracy was on high alert and her heart continued to hammer furiously as she navigated them both through the city. After a careful ten minutes, with barely any other cars on the road, she made her way onto country roads.

She let out a brief sigh of relief for having made it this far and drove cautiously as the rain pelted with greater force, bouncing off the windscreen in huge droplets. The wipers worked on full speed and Tracy thought she had the lights on full beam. But couldn't be sure as visibility was impaired by the rain and she was surrounded by darkness.

After several more miles and having only passed a couple of other cars travelling in the opposite direction, Tracy began to relax. She was now halfway home and a surge of relief flowed through her body. Within half an hour they would both be safely indoors.

The rain that had been holding off for days, was now making up for it. Its now torrential intensity was making visibility almost non-existent and the noise from the rain was deafening.

Until now, Tracy had wanted to drive without music, but needed to drown out the sound of the rain. She glanced at the stereo and pressed play on the Spice Girls tape they had been listening to earlier in the evening. Looking back up at the road, she realised she was approaching a sharp bend. She hadn't noticed it until it was too late. She cursed herself, slammed on the breaks and sharply turned the wheel away from the bend. Before she was able to correct the turn, the tyres screeched as the car lost control, and the car span before skidding several yards up the road.

Tracy screamed and everything appeared to happen in slow motion. Gripping the steering wheel, she glanced at Emma who had suddenly jolted awake and with wide startled eyes was staring at her. Tracy turned her attention back to the road, just in time to see the car plough into a tree.

Tracy woke and for a slight second, couldn't remember what had happened. She was quickly brought back to reality after taking in her surroundings and was overcome by a sudden and overwhelming sense of nausea, gnawing away in the pit of her stomach.

Dawn was starting to break. Giving way to the darkness, allowing the slightest amount of light to creep through and the rain had started to ease. Tracy hadn't known how long she had been out for, or what injuries she and Emma had sustained.

She unclipped her seatbelt and leaned over to shake Emma awake. But Emma didn't respond. Tracy shook Emma even harder and shouted at her to wake up, but there was still no response. It was only then that Tracy realised the car was filling with smoke.

"Emma." Tracy shouted, "We need to get out of here."

After a few attempts and little force, Tracy managed to open the driver's door of the Mini. She swung her legs around and out onto the muddy ground below. With her head pounding and stomach churning, she pushed herself into a standing position. A sharp pain immediately ran up her left leg as she fell to the ground. Although she couldn't see that well, she could make out what looked like blood on her leg and guessed, that along with the pain, it was broken.

She tried to stand a second time, using the open door as support, and only putting weight on her right leg. Using the car as leverage, she managed to get around the back of the Mini and over to the passenger's side.

Tracy pulled open Emma's door. It opened first time and she tried again to rouse Emma, but still no response. She saw that the smoke was getting thicker and leaned over and hurried to unclip Emma's seatbelt. Then whilst standing on her one good leg, she took a deep breath and pulled Emma out of the car. Once again Tracy fell to the ground with greater force and this time with Emma's lifeless body landing on top of her, and she screamed out in agony. Tracy composed herself and with each deep breath and through the excruciating pain, she dragged them both away from the car, moving a foot or two at a time. The rain had dampened the soil beneath her making it slippery and difficult to get any traction. But somehow, after several minutes, she had managed to get them both far enough away that they didn't feel any impact from the car, when it burst into flames.

Rain had stopped falling and dawn had now fully broken. Tracy sat on the cool wet ground surrounded by trees. Not paying any attention to the chirping birds attempting to make their early presence known.

She held Emma tightly whilst continued attempts to wake her failed. She looked down at her friend, who looked perfect as she slept. Tracy couldn't see any obvious injuries on Emma, other than a small amount of blood trickling from her right ear. Through sobs, she continued her desperate pleas to wake Emma and begged her to open her eyes.

In the distance, she heard the faint rumble of a car.

"Hang in there Em, help is on its way." She whispered. The rumble of the engine became louder until a dark blue Rover came into view. It slowed as it neared the flames of the Mini, crawling past and stopping in front of the girls.

A middle-aged man wearing a smart pin stripped suit jumped out of the car and with a panicked look on his face stuttered. "I have a mobile phone; I'll go call for help."

He ran back to the car and Tracy could just about hear the man speaking to an operator, asking for an ambulance and fire engine, as there had been a car accident involving two young ladies.

"Not long now Em." Tracy pleaded with Emma who continued to lay motionless in her arms.

A few minutes later, the man reappeared with a blanket "I guess you might need this" he said, as he laid it over them.

"Help is on its way."

Tracy opened her mouth but could only manage a raspy "Thanks."

The man in the suit paced back and forth, nervously looking into the distance in both directions, hoping to spot a sign of the emergency services being nearby.

A new feeling began to overtake Tracy as the reality of the events played out in her head. She knew she was in serious trouble and facing jail for what had happened. An overpowering sense of panic set in and with no warning she vomited on the ground next to her.

Several minutes later, Tracy could hear sirens in the distance. They were becoming louder by the second. She felt a shortened sense of relief. Immediately followed by a surge of anxiety that gripped her chest, making it difficult for her to control her breathing.

An ambulance arrived parking behind the Rover. And seconds later, a short man with a reassuring smile and kind eyes jumped out of the passenger's side, holding a bag. Directly followed by a taller, leaner man with a shaved head and beard from the driver's side.

Before Tracy could say anything, the man in the suit advised the ambulance crew that he was just passing by on his way to work, spotted the car in flames and girls sat on the verge.

The paramedic with the kind eyes knelt next to Tracy and with a thick Geordy accent said, "It's ok, we're here now. What's your name pet?"

Tracy tried to speak; she opened her mouth, but no words came out.

"It's ok," he said gently as he removed the blanket from Emma and placed it over Tracy's shoulders. "I'm going to assess your friend first, given that she is unconscious, ok?"

Tracy nodded.

The shaven headed paramedic positioned himself to Tracy's other side.

"On the count of three, we'll pick her up." He said as he put his hand beneath Emma in anticipation. The other paramedic doing the same.

"One, Two, Three," they heaved, gently picking Emma up and moving her onto the ground. Making sure to give enough distance so that they could work on her.

Further sirens could be heard in the distance, and it was only a matter of seconds before a fire engine and police car came into sight.

"A police car?" Tracy quietly managed to rasp.

"It's standard procedure in serious road collision accidents." Said the shaven headed paramedic, who momentarily looked up at Tracy.

The fire engine stopped in front of the flaming Mini. Four firefighters jumped out, immediately unravelled a hose, and set to put the fire out.

Whilst the police car stopped further away, parking before the Mini. Moments later a young-looking male police officer appeared. Tracy couldn't see if he was alone or if there was another officer present. He stayed back assessing the Mini from a far. Tracy could see him talking into his radio, although she couldn't make out what was being said. Before approaching Tracy, Emma, the paramedics, and man in the suit, who by now had retreated back to his car. The police officer began by taping off the perimeter.

Tracy turned back to look at the two paramedics who were still frantically trying to revive Emma. She caught them looking at each other and the one with the kind eyes shook his head at his colleague who nodded in agreement.

Tracy managed to splutter, "What's happening?"

"I'm sorry," the bold paramedic said turning to her. "Your friend didn't make it. I think she would have died on impact. There was nothing we could do."

The words seemed to echo in Tracy's head as it span. Her throat was dry, she opened her mouth to speak but no words came out. Inside she was screaming as fresh tears ran down her cheeks.

The police officer appeared by her side, taking note of his surroundings, and realising what had been said.

He lent down to Tracy, placed an empathetic hand on her back and with a calm deep voice asked. "Can you tell me what happened?"

Tracy's head now span faster, feeling out of control. A further bout of nausea rushed through her, and her heart raced so fast and hard she thought it was going to explode out of her chest.

After a several second pause she managed to compose herself enough to quietly utter the words. "On our way home. It was raining. We hit a tree."

"Ok," said the officer. "And who was driving the vehicle?"

Tracy hesitated for a few more seconds before mumbling, "Emma."

And that was all she remembered before blacking out.

CHAPTER 4

Tracy hadn't remembered the journey to the hospital or the various tests that followed, and the next few days went by in a blur.

Tracy laid in her hospital bed feeling as though she was stuck in some sort of trance, whilst the world continued around her. She was oblivious to her surroundings and to her parents who were offering solace by her bedside. Oblivious to the sounds of machines beeping and humming in the distance, hushed tones of the medics and lights that never seemed to dim.

An overwhelming torment plagued Tracy's insides. Horrendous sensations, caused by a mixture of grief, pain, various medications and most of all relentless guilt.

In addition to suffering from sever shock, Tracy had been lucky to have only sustained a minor fracture in her left leg and mild concussion.

When Tracy was deemed well enough and more alert, two female police detectives arrived at her bedside. Drawing the curtain closed behind them as they entered her cubical.

This was the moment she had been dreading the most and it happened to coincide with when her parents had gone home for a break.

Tracy doubted her ability to stick to her fabricated story when under pressure. She was sure she would blurt out that it was her who was driving, in a bid to relieve her of the burden. She also expected that even without a confession, the police would somehow have known the truth. Convinced they would question her, with some sort of twisted strategy to see how far she was willing to take her lie. Either way, Tracy was sure the truth would come out and she'd be forced to face her retribution.

"Tracy." Said a detective with an immaculate brown bob and wearing a sharp trouser suit.

Tracy, snapped out of her daze and eyed the detective.

"I am Detective Sargent Cook and this is Detective Constable Jamison." Cook said, as she pointed over to her colleague. Jamison looked a lot less confident than her superior colleague. She wore her hair in a plat and small round glasses perched on the end of her nose, which looked too small for her round face. She tightly clutched a notepad to her chest and took a seat in the green high-backed chair next to the bed. Cook opting to stay standing, proceeded to say.

"I am sorry, for what you have been through." She paused a moment, attempting a sympathetic smile. "We need to go over some of the events from the night of the accident. Starting from the beginning, can you tell me what happened?"

Tracy, despite her doubts, was able to retell her version of the story. And her extremely nervous state and tearfulness could easily be dismissed by having to relive the experience.

"And Emma, appeared to be sober, when you left?" Cook interrupted when Tracy arrived at the point when they left the club.

"Yes." Tracy replied. "I wouldn't have got in the car with her if I had any doubt."

"Very well." said Cook.

"We are waiting for the toxicology report which would confirm if Emma had any alcohol in her system. In the meantime, can you tell me who bought Emma's drinks throughout the evening?"

"We all were." Tracy said. "I mean myself, Francis, until she went home, Simone and Jo. Whenever we bought a round, we'd buy Emma a coke. It was the agreement for Emma being the driver."

Tracy hesitated for a second before adding. "Well, there was one other person."

"Go on." Cook asked, with a slight impatient tone.

"Emma met up with one of her friends from college. I only vaguely know of him; his name is Jonny."

Tracy stopped to take a breath before continuing. "He arrived around eleven thirty and bought Emma quite a few cokes. She always seemed to have a refill. I think he planned to try it on with her but disappeared before the end of the night. I guess she must have told him that she wasn't interested."

"Thank you, Tracy." Cook said with a softened tone. "I know this is exceptionally difficult for you. If you think of anything further, can you please let me know."

Tracy nodded and Cook handed her a business card.
Jamison, who had been capturing the conversation in her notebook, stood up to join her colleague.
They both said their goodbyes and left Tracy's cubicle, drawing open her curtains as the went.

Much to Tracy's surprise. The questions that were presented to her from Detective Cook, were far less challenging than she had expected. Far less than she had deserved.

The police seemed satisfied with Tracy's version of events, including Tracy's theory of Jonny spiking Emma's drinks and didn't question the matter any further.

Following a five-night stay in hospital, Tracy was discharged. She was prescribed various medications and a follow up appointment was arranged for her to return to the hospital to see a psychologist.

But, once back home, Tracy struggled to function. She barely ate, because of the constant crushing wave of nausea that consumed her. She desperately wanted to sleep, she wanted to feel oblivion. Instead, she would either lay awake continuously playing out the events of that night. A torment she felt she deserved. Or, with encouragement from her parents, would take a mild sedative to help induce sleep. But that only ever gave Tracy a short amount of respite and she was nearly always woken by a night terror. Nightmares where Emma returned and took her revenge in various graphic and excruciating ways.

Whenever Tracy woke to the sound of her screams. Her mother or father or both would rush to her bedside to comfort her, regardless of the day or night. Tracy had nearly confessed to them on many of these occasions and had even considered handing herself in to the police. Preferring to face the consequences to atone and rid her guilt.

Simone, Jo, and Francis would often visit Tracy. Sometimes on their own and sometimes together as a threesome. But no matter how hard they tried; Tracy struggled to interact. Withdrawing herself and barely acknowledging their presence.

They didn't give up on Tracy. They continued to visit trying repeatedly to encourage her to socialise. Making careful suggestions to tempt her out the house, such as join them for a walk along the river or go to the café for a milkshake. Hoping that familiarity might help.

Although dealing with their own grief of losing a dear friend, the girls tried to enjoy what they could of the summer. Be it a lot more sombre.

During their visits to see Tracy, they kept her updated on what they had each been up to. Snippets from their mundane holiday jobs, gossip, moaning about parents and siblings. Anything they could think of to avoid the awkward silence. But nothing appeared to make a difference.

The day of Emma's funeral soon arrived, and Tracy woke after yet another restless night. She had intended to go and with help from her mother had gotten ready. But, in the end, she couldn't face going. The reality was that she couldn't face seeing Emma's parents or two younger brothers. And was relieved that since Emma's death, they had not been in contact.

Her parents decided not to push the matter and attended the funeral alone. Asking Angela to stay at home and watch over her elder sister.

Several weeks later, Emma's post-mortem confirmed cause of death to be the result of a sudden bleed to her brain. Caused by the impact of the car hitting the tree and that she would have died instantly, not feeling any pain. Emma was also found to have a high degree of alcohol in her blood stream and therefore her death was recorded as death by drunk driving.

Peter returned to work and the family got into a routine of sorts. Jean would start each morning by opening Tracy's curtains and leaving a small window open to allow for air to circulate. Before encouraging her to get up and dressed.

Each day bought different challenges to Tracy. She had started to feel calmer on days when there were clear skies with no chance of rain. She would sometimes sit on her bed and look out of her bedroom window, seemingly staring into the abyss. Whenever dark clouds appeared threatening rain, her anxiety would spike. And as soon as rain fell it would trigger a chest pain so intense it left her struggling to breathe. Jean tried to avoid these panic attacks by closing windows and curtains, but it seldom made a difference.

Tracy was taken to numerous appointments with various professionals, which meant she had to travel by car, driven by her father. This too resulted in anguishing panic attacks that would occur in the hours leading up to the car journey, making her parents question if therapy was actually helping her recovery.

As the summer holidays ended, marking nearly four months since the night of the accident. Tracy's parents were hoping she would return to college. She had recovered from her physical injuries, her mental state, however, would take much longer. Tracy was adamant that she would not continue with her education or part time job at the café. She was not yet ready to face the world and doubted she ever would be.

Six months after the accident. The guilt continued to taunt Tracy, and she still relied on medication to calm her and help her sleep. Whilst still facing many challenges, she had started to interact more with her family and friends. This encouraging transformation gave her parents hope that she was finally on the road to recovery.

Tracy had also began sitting in the garden during dry days, regardless of the temperature. Preferring the garden over sitting on her bed staring out of the window. Angela would sometimes join her, and they would either chat or play cards. A site their mother loved to see.

Tracy also began tendering to their long narrow unkempt garden. Neither of her parents were particularly green fingered and the garden was in much need of some attention.

But despite the transformation, Tracy had become recluse. She became anxious if the doorbell rang and always refused to answer the telephone. And panic attacks would still occur if it rained, or she was forced to leave the house.

Christmas came and went and was a sober affair, with conservative festivities and only modest decorations to mark the occasion. Tracy tried to join in, more for the sake of her family, but it was difficult.

In the New Year, Tracy's parents had an idea to further support Tracy's recovery. They decided to invest in their garden. Thinking it would be good to give Tracy a project to focus her attention.

Once the seasonal coldness had started to wane and signs of early spring began to emerge. Hinting that warmer weather was on its way. Tracy's parents made the decision to employ a landscape gardener to overhaul the garden.

Several gardeners provided designs and quotes and each with a unique style in mind. With Tracy's input, the family decided to opt for a more conservative style. One that included a paved patio, a new lawn with bordered edges and a designated vegetable patch at the bottom of the garden.

The job was given to a man called Tony Wright, a local landscape gardener and work was to commence early March.

CHAPTER 5

March 1995

Tony Wright was a jolly middle-aged man who looked as though life was serving him well, despite being windowed in his mid-thirties. He had a broad frame, from years of heavy grafting, with a slight paunch that confessed he enjoyed overindulging.

Tony pulled up to the house in a white pickup truck that had Wright's Landscapers written in black lettering across the side. He gathered various tools and a wheelbarrow from the back of the truck's bed and set to work.

Jean ensured that Tony was well looked after by frequently taking him cups of sweet tea and as twelve o'clock approached shouted out into the garden.

"Tony, would you like a bacon sandwich?"

"Do you have any brown sauce?" He asked, with a grin on his face.

"I do indeed, I'll let you know when it's ready." Jean replied.

Tracy had been watching Tony work from the comfort of her bedroom, sitting close to her window. She overheard the conversation and chuckled to herself at her mother's attentive approach. She made a mental note to ridicule her later for flirting.

Tony worked the first couple of days on his own. And on the morning of the third day, arrived with a younger man by his side. It was another dry, but chilly day and Tracy positioned herself in her usual spot, ready to watch from her bedroom window. Being careful not to be seen, she listened intently to the conversation taking place below her window.

"This is my son David." Tony said, introducing the younger man to Jean.

It was hard to get a good look at David from Tracy's position. All she could see was that he was wearing a baseball cap and scruffy gardening clothes.

"David works at Monty's, but the factory is on its annual Easter shut down. He helps me out occasionally during the holidays but he's not working with me for free though unfortunately." Tony continued, whilst rolling his eyes.

Monty's was a well known and established manufacturing company, making furniture for a chain of department stores. It was a major employer within Portsmouth and its surrounding suburbs.

"Nice to meet you, David." Jean said, in her usually friendly nature, chuckling slightly at David's comment. "I have a daughter who's not much younger than you."

Tracy pulled a face at her mother's comment.

Tony and David began working on the bottom of the garden, where Tracy had a clear view of them both. Although she couldn't hear what they were saying to each other. She enjoyed watching the progress. It was the first time in a long time, that she had felt a sense of purpose.

At lunchtime and as Tracy had predicted. Jean appeared mid-way in the garden and shouted towards Tony and David.

"Do you both want a sandwich? I can do cheese and pickle or ham?"

Both men looked up in unison, thanked Jean and placed their orders for cheese and pickle. As David turned to look at Jean, he glanced up at the window and spotted Tracy. It was the first time Tracy had seen his face, be it slightly covered by the peak of his cap. David briefly smiled at her, his soft comforting eyes gave her a sense of ease and he raised a hand as if to say *hello.* Tracy suddenly felt her face flush with embarrassment and quickly withdrew from the window.

She secretly continued to observe David working on the garden for the next couple of days. Ensuring to be much more careful, so not to be seen.

On Friday, the morning of the fifth day. Tony and David arrived and began working on the patio. As the patio was closer to the house, Tracy wasn't able to see much of them from her window and she felt disappointed. She was enjoying David's distant company and had started to wonder what his hair looked like underneath the hat he wore and how he smelt.

She hadn't intended to be so obvious when she made regular trips downstairs, hoping to catch a glimpse of David. She made various excuses to her mother for these frequent visits. Such as needing food, drinks, and replacement batteries for her remote control. These frequent, seemingly random visits did not go unnoticed by Jean, nor David so it seemed.

As the afternoon came to an end, with Tracy back by her window, she could hear a conversation taking place between Tony and Jean.

"We are done for today; we'll return again on Monday." Tony advised Jean. "Please avoid walking over the patio until at least Sunday."

"Will do." Jean replied.

Tony continued. "We're making good progress and if the weather holds, we're on track to finish mid-afternoon on Monday."

The words echoed and Tracy felt her pulse quicken. She couldn't understand why she was experiencing these feelings. All she knew was that she liked them, it was a refreshing change from the anxiety she had become accustomed to.

Tracy grew inpatient as the weekend seemed to go on forever. She felt a mixture of emotions which she couldn't explain. A nervous energy, excitement almost. But that would quickly succumb and be replaced with feelings of guilt. As thoughts of Emma crept into her mind. Then back to excitement, in a continual loop.

Eventually, Monday morning came. Knowing it would be the last time she would see David; Tracy decided to try and pluck up the courage to speak to him.

She woke early. Grateful for another dry day, after a few drizzles over the weekend had set her back from her unusually positive mood. She was no longer used to making an effort with her appearance and didn't very often wash her hair. And whenever she did wash it, she'd usually not take any pride and let it dry naturally, causing it to frizz.

Tracy decided to wash her hair today and dry it using the hairdryer to style what was left of her perm. She dressed in a simple pair of low-cut jeans and short stripy top which sat just above her belly button. This was the best she could muster as clothes now sat baggy on her slowly diminishing frame. She decided against putting any make up on, she didn't want it to appear obvious that she'd made an effort.

Tracy waited eagerly by her window. Listening to the men complete the finishing touches to the garden and getting the occasional glimpse of David, depending on where in the garden he worked.

At two p.m. Tracy heard David calling out to Jean.

"Jean, we've finished. Do you want to come and take a look?"

"Coming." Jean replied.

Tracy knew this was her opportunity to speak to David and she had genuine reason to. Of course, she would want to inspect the garden, it was her project.

She spent several seconds mustering up the courage and convincing herself that she should venture into the garden. She took a few deep breaths, walked out onto the landing, and began slowly walking down the stairs. As she reached the halfway point, she heard laughter coming from the garden. Then out of nowhere, her breathing suddenly quickened, her heart raced, she felt her face glow and hands dampened. She froze, rooted to the spot, unable to take another step forward, as the familiar charge of anxiety washed over her.

She turned and ran back to her bedroom, slamming the door shut behind her. She flung herself onto her bed and wept into her pillow, sobbing tears of frustration.

"Tracy." Jean shouted from the bottom of the stairs a few minutes later. "Do you want to come down and take a look at the garden before Tony and David leave?"

Tracy ignored her mum. She wasn't up to a conversation and continued to sob for a while longer, wondering to herself. *Was this a form of punishment from Emma? Stopping any chance of her being normal or happy.*

Tracy overheard her mother say goodbye and the sound of Tony's pickup truck driving away. She spent the rest of the day confined to her bedroom, wanting to be left alone to wallow in self pity.

The set back, caused Tracy to become more withdrawn and retreating to those earlier days after the accident. Jean had noticed it and had her suspicions for what had caused it, but she dared say. She simply tried to encourage Tracy.

"Tracy love. Why don't you come and take a look around the garden? It's looking lovely and it's only the two of us at home." Jean repeated the same urging question several times and it took Tracy a couple of days before she eventually made it down and into the garden.

She had to admit the garden did indeed look lovely. The lawn fresh, the patio sparkled, and boarders had been created just as she had wanted. All that was needed now was colourful plants to transform the area into a focal point.

"I've got a surprise for you." Jean said with a smile. Tracy's face started to redden; she didn't like surprises.

"Nothing to worry about." Jean quickly added, realising the panic that had set on Tracy's face.

"I've been to the garden centre and have bought these." She said, pointing to trays of colourful spring bedding plants consisting of lilies, pansies, and petunias.

"Why don't we spend the afternoon planting them?"

Tracy nodded and went to the shed to fetch some trowels.

As the hours passed, Tracy and Jean were happily gardening whilst the radio played in the background through the open kitchen window. It was a warm day with a gentle breeze, and as the days were now starting to get longer, they were grateful to have a few extra hours of daylight, before the sun would begin to set, forcing them to stop for the day.

They were both oblivious to the fact that they had a visitor, neither had heard the front door knocking. The first they knew was when.

"Hello." Could be heard from the other side of the garden gate.

"Oh, Coming." Jean said as she walked over to unlatch it.

"Hello," David said, feeling slightly awkward. "My dad asked me to pop over your invoice and also to give you this." He handed Jean an envelope and a beautiful potted blue hydrangea.

"Aww, thank you, David. That's so kind of you." Said Jean as she took both from David. I have just the spot where this can go, gesturing to the plant, and walking over to where Tracy was digging. Or at least pretending to dig whilst observing the interaction from a far, without making it look obvious. David followed Jean until the three of them were standing together.

"Hi, I'm David." He said, reaching out a hand to Tracy.
She reached out a muddied hand in return and quietly muttered.

"Hi, I'm Tracy."
David looked different. He had lost the baseball cap in favour of brown curtains which sat perfectly over his ears, and he wore smarter clothes. Tracy wished she too had made an effort, instead of wearing old gardening clothes with her hair scrapped back into a messy ponytail.

Jean broke the silence by announcing "I'm going to stick

the kettle on, do stay for a cuppa David, milk one sugar!" In a
tone that told him, a refusal was not an option.

"Great thanks." he replied with a nervous smile.
Once Jean had disappeared into the kitchen. David turned to
Tracy and asked, "How do you like the garden?"

CHAPTER 6

David became a regular visitor at the Hopkins residence. Depending on his shift pattern, he would often pop over to see Tracy after he had finished work, operating machinery on one of the factory's production lines. And at twenty-six years old, he was eight years older than Tracy.

They would spend hours working on the garden together, tending to the vegetable patch or deadheading plants now out in full bloom. The once neglected garden, overgrown and lacking charm, was now an attractive mixture of vibrant colours and varied textures.

They would make light conversation as they worked side by side listening to soft rock music on David's portable CD player.

Tracy looked forward to David's visits, she enjoyed his company. And as their friendship grew, she began to feel more comfortable in his presence. One afternoon as Tracy watered the plants she turned to David and nervously asked.

"Do you want to stay for dinner?" Before stuttering "I'd have to check with mum, but I'm sure it won't be a problem."

"I'd love to." He said with a warm smile that lit up his eyes.

Tracy rushed into the kitchen and asked her mum if there was enough Dinner for David.

"Of course, there is." Jean said happily. "I'm making a curry and there's plenty to go around."

Jean was pleased that Tracy had found a friend in David. He seemed like a nice boy, and she could see that he was making a positive influence with Tracy's rehabilitation.

They sat at the patio table in the garden whilst dinner was cooking. They usually only spoke about gardening or growing vegetables, and Tracy suddenly found herself with nothing to say. David, also feeling the awkwardness of the silence, decided to take charge and start a conversation.

"Other that gardening, what do you like to do?" He asked.

"Nothing really." Tracy said shyly.

"There must be something?" He pressed. "Where do you like to hang out with your friends?"

She tensed, not knowing how much she should share for fear of scaring him off. But eventually replied with "I don't really go out much anymore."

"I'd like to take you out." David said, with a look of eagerness that spread over his face.

"I don't think I can." Tracy said tentatively with a sigh.

David was unable to hide the look of disappointment and Tracy felt she needed to justify her refusal, or she really would loose him. She paused for a few seconds whilst considering what to say.

"Almost a year ago, I was involved in a car crash with my best friend Emma, and she died." She paused again, took another breath, and continued. "Ever since that night I have found life to be, um, somewhat difficult." It was said, with a degree of hesitancy. "I find it difficult to leave the house or garden," waving her hand around gesticulating the point. "In fact, it's something I dread."

"I see." David said as he reached across the table to take hold of Emma's hands, relieved her refusal was not because of him. "I won't push you. If it means spending more time here at your house, than so be it."

Tracy felt a surge of relief. She hadn't gone into detail but had told him enough for now and it hadn't seemed to faze him.

"I don't go out much either these days." David said. "My mum died when I was a child."

"Oh, my goodness, I'm so sorry." said Tracy as she squeezed

one of the hands she was still holding. She had sensed something in David that suggested he too was troubled but hadn't felt able to ask him about it.

"She died of cancer when I was twelve. She was a wonderful woman and ever since, it's been just me and dad."

Tracy listened, saying nothing.

"I don't get much time for friends. I help dad as much as I can around the house and at work, whenever I'm not at work myself."

They both sat for a few moments, saying nothing but still holding hands until Tracy broke the silence by asking. "And you still live at home with your dad?"

"I didn't want to leave dad, especially in those earlier years. That's why I never went to university. I will move out of course one day, but for now, I'm happy supporting him wherever I can. He would have had me working for him on a permanent basis if he could." David said, rolling his eyes slightly.

"It can't be that bad working for your dad," said Tracy. "You two seem to get on well?"

"Yeah, we do and I'm lucky to have the opportunity of working with him. And if it wasn't for gardening, I would never have been able to buy and run my first car." He said proudly.

At the mention of David's car, a flash back to when Emma first passed her driving test, and they took her Mini out for a drive came to her. They were both so excited for the freedom it gave them. Her shoulders sagged and her stomach started to churn again. David sensing a change in her deminer, steered the conversation back to Tracy.

"What are your plans for the future?"
Before Tracy could answer, she was interrupted by Jean calling to tell them dinner was ready.

The next three days went by, and David didn't come over to the house. Tracy started to regret telling him about her problems and worried if she had scared him off. It didn't help when her mother noticed and commented.

"No David again today. I, see?"

"No mum, I guess he's busy." She snapped back.

Tracy knew she had to make sacrifices and overcome some of her fears to keep David interested. If she didn't, he would eventually get board of sitting in her garden, anybody would. The thought of it all filled her with apprehension. She knew if she ever saw David again, she couldn't be so dismissive to his suggestion of going out.

On the afternoon of the fourth day David returned. He knew that gardening was off as it had rained on and off for most of the day. He felt that their friendship had developed and that he could now pop by without needing to use the garden as an excuse.

"Hi David," Jean said with a smile as she answered the front door. "Come on in. Tracy is in her room, you can go on up, hers is the second on the left."

"Thank you" David said as he climbed the stairs.

Tracy was surprised to see David standing at her bedroom door. He hadn't been in her room before and as it had rained today; she hadn't expected to see him. She was having a difficult day. The frequent rain combined with anxiety over David's absence had put her on edge.

"Are you ok?" David asked sensing that Tracy wasn't her usual self.

She thought how best to reply to his question. The fact that he had returned meant she hadn't scared him off and she felt it best not to hide her phobias from him. For if he was to be a good friend, he needed to understand her.

"I'm ok, it's just been a bad day." She said with a forced smile.

"I'm sorry I've not been over for a few days. I've been helping dad, he wanted to get ahead before the rain came and it's also been busy at work."

Tracy's felt relieved and decided to tell him more details

about the accident. The version that she had told everyone since that night. She explained that certain things triggered her anxieties and affected her mood. The various medications she was taking to help her function and control those feelings and of the horrific nightmares she suffered. She tried to make a light joke of it by telling David that she was a bit mental, but he said nothing. He continued to listen intently to her every word, with a harden look on his face. It didn't even soften when she attempted to be light-hearted. She suddenly felt uncomfortable and started rambling.

"And that is the reason why I stopped going to college and packed in my job."

David, still saying nothing suddenly leaned forward and hugged Tracy tightly. Whispering, "You poor thing." into her ear. "Thank you, for being honest with me, it means a lot."

She sank into his embrace, inhaling deeply, he smelt amazing. She wasn't sure if the scent was deodorant, aftershave, fabric softener or a combination of all three.

The following evening Simone, Francis and Jo came over to visit. They usually came by at least once a fortnight and Tracy was looking forward to seeing her friends. For once she finally had something to talk about instead of listening as they attempted an awkward, one-way conversation. David had already said he wouldn't be over, so it gave the girls plenty of opportunity to chat.

They sat in Tracy's bedroom sipping cokes whilst Oasis played in the background. It was immediately obvious to the girls that Tracy was different some how, she seemed more like her old self.

Tracy sat on her bed with her legs curdled underneath her. Simone sat beside her, and Jo and Francis sat on cushions on the floor. Tracy sat patiently listening to the girls talk about themselves, until Francis couldn't take anymore and blurted out.

"Enough everyone. Trace are you going to tell us what's put

that smile on your face" Tracy picked up the cushion that had been beside her and playfully threw it at Frances.

"I've met someone?" she said, not being able to hide her smile.

"What? Where? Who?" Simone interjected with a puzzled expression. "You don't even leave the house."

Tracy tilted her head to give Simone a look that said ouch, before saying. "You know we had the garden done recently?"

"Yes" the girls all said in unison.

"The man who did it, had his son come help and we got talking. He's been over a few times since and we've become friends."

"Tell us more?" Jo asked leaning forward.

Followed immediately with Francis asking, "What's he look like?"

"His name is David. He's twenty-six, he works at Monty's and lives with his dad. He's good looking, a bit rugged, has a lovely soft smile and smells incredible." Tracy stopped talking and realising she had closed her eyes, opened them to see her friends all staring at her.

"David, also knows about my problems and is understanding and supportive."

"He sounds perfect." Said Jo.

"When can we meet him?" Asked Simone.

"He is and not yet." Tracy was quick to reply. "I don't want to scare him off." She laughed.

The girls continued to talk about their weeks for the next hour before embracing Tracy and saying their goodbyes.

Tracy went to bed that night feeling content and managed to sleep the entire night without any nightmares.

David and Tracy grew close, and David had started to drop by almost every day. On the days where he couldn't come by for what ever reason, he would call and speak to her over the phone. She would still not answer the phone if it rang but was happy to intercept once someone else had picked up, providing it was David on the other end.

Tracy felt lucky to have David in her life. Supporting her and he was a great listener, she felt she could tell him almost anything. He didn't talk too much about his own life though and Tracy assumed that was because he found it too difficult to talk about his own grief. And she thought it best not to press him too much.

The one-year anniversary of the accident arrived and as expected, it was a difficult day for Tracy. Her friends had suggested coming over to spend the day with her. Keen to do something to remember their lost friend. However, she didn't want to spend it with anyone, preferring to spend it quietly on her own, in her room. David had also offered to come over and spend the evening with her, but she too had asked him to stay away.

She was thankful the day was dry, but it did little to stop the remorse she felt. She longed for things to be different. For Emma to still be with her, and for them to be planning their future adventures together. They had always planned to take a girl's holiday when college ended and she imagined them both laying on a beach, basking in the sun and sipping cocktails.

David ignored Tracy's ask to stay away and turned up early evening with a bunch of roses, insisting that she shouldn't be alone. That was the moment she realised she had fallen in love with him.

He held her as they sat on her bed and said, "I have something to ask you."

"What's that?" Tracy said slightly pulling away from David's embrace so that she could face him.

"I want to take you out somewhere."

"No. No." She stammered.

"Hear me out." He interrupted. "We will do it on your terms and any time you want to come home, we will. We'll take baby steps." He said encouragingly.

Tracy said nothing and continued to look at David.

"I'd like to take you to the coast. It's thirty minutes away. I'll make sure to arrange it for a dry day when there is no rain forecast and will ensure you are home before it gets dark. What do you say?"

Tracy thought for a moment. She trusted David. He had been very patient with her, but she knew the relationship couldn't remain just one way. She remembered the promise she had made to herself, to face her fears to maintain a relationship with him.

Tracy nodded slowly and said. "Ok."

CHAPTER 7

June 1995

David arrived at Tracy's house early afternoon and knocked on her front door. To his surprise she answered, and he could see she'd made an effort. She had tied her hair up and was wearing a summer dress which her mother had bought her, especially for the occasion.

"Are you ready?" He said with a reassuring look.

"I think so." She replied with a slight element of apprehension to her voice.

Jean appeared and hugged Tracy before letting go and leaning her head towards Tracy's.

"You will be fine; it will be good for you." She said.

Tracy nodded.

Five minutes later they were walking up the driveway holding hands. David let go of Tracy's hand, opened the passenger door to his red Fiesta and helped her to climb in. Before closing the door and raising a hand to Jean as she watched from the living room bay window.

David reversed out of the drive and gently pulled away.

"Do you want to listen to music?" He asked.

"Um, can we not, I'd rather we didn't." said Tracy, who was squeezing her hands by her sides in anguish.

"Fair enough." Said David, and for a while they sat in companionable silence.

Tracy stared out of the passenger door window. Doing all she could to hold her nerves at bay and looking up at the few white fluffy clouds that had gathered in the sky.

David was first to break the silence. "We should be there in about fifteen minutes; it might be busy with it being such a nice day."

"I guessed it would be." Tracy said in return. Offering little in the way of conversation and not diverting her eyes away from the window as she spoke.

David could feel irritation set in. He had expected Tracy to be more talkative and better company, or at least allow him to have the radio on to break the monotony of the drive.

A short while later they had arrived, and David parked the car in an open aired carpark within walking distance from the beach.

"Stay put, I'll go and get a ticket." He said as he climbed out of the car and walked over to the ticket machine. He returned minutes later with a ticket in his hand and stuck it to the inside of his window as Tracy got out the car.

"You did it." he said, pulling her close. "I'm so proud of you. Your first time in a car with me." He spoke loudly and Tracy was convinced anyone passing by would have heard. She broke away, looked up at David and managed an embarrassed half-hearted smile, whilst her insides tensed.

As David had predicted, the warm day had brought people out in droves. Tracy clung to him as they took a slow walk up the promenade, navigating the crowds. They stopped every few minutes to appreciate the view or to look at one of the many ships heading for the harbour.

They eventually headed to the beach. And as they approached the sand, Tracy removed her trainers and socks. David was more hesitant to do the same but after considering the uncomfortable drive home with sand in his shoes, quickly removed his too.

They walked onto the beach, feeling the moist cool sand between their toes. David found a quiet spot for them, and they sat down directly onto the sand. Tracy was starting to feel more relaxed and was glad she had agreed to come. David had been the best thing for her, and she cared for him deeply.

David sat down and put an arm around her, she nuzzled into him putting her head against his chest.

"I think I'm in love with you." He said. Tracy wasn't expecting to hear that and immediately withdrew, looking up at him. "I love you." He repeated.

"I love you too." She said, and their lips met.

They sat for a while, embraced in each others' arms, lost in the moment, and forgetting they were surrounded by others. Tracy wanted to capture the moment. She listened to the squawks of the distant seagulls and the hypnotic sound of gentle waves crashing. She breathed in the sea air and for a brief time was able to forget her troubles.

David eventually pulled away, looked at his watch and said. "It's teatime, we should think about getting you home soon. How about some fish and chips before we leave?"

"That sounds perfect," She said with a smile. David pulled himself up to standing and Tracy went to do the same.

"What are you doing?" He asked.

"I'm going with you to get fish and chips" She said with hesitation.

"No, you stay here, I am a gentleman and so I will go get them." He said almost sarcastically.

"I'd rather come with you." She pleaded.

"You'll be fine, stay here and enjoy the scenery. I'll be back in a couple of minutes."

With that David walked off in search of the chip shop carrying his socks and shoes in his hand. When David stepped back onto concrete, he dusted the sand from his feet and looked back at Tracy as he pulled his socks and shoes back on. He could see she was hugging herself and obviously feeling apprehensive at having been left alone. David dismissed the feeling and walked off in the direction of the vinegar smell wafting over.

A few minutes later he located the chip shop and as he

predicted it too was busy. He joined the long queue and waited his turn.

Tracy felt panicked. David had been gone ages. When she had agreed to come, she hadn't considered being on her own at all. The sounds that she had enjoyed only a few minutes earlier, now seemed threatening. The once calm waves now appeared rough as they crashed onto the sand with greater velocity. And she was sure the tide was coming in. *What if something had happened to David?* She thought as she frantically took in her surroundings to see if she could see anything that suggested danger or that something had happened. Remembering what she had been told in one of her many therapy sessions, she tried to convince herself that she was being irrational. That there would be a perfectly reasonable explanation as to why David had been gone so long. She looked at her watch, he'd been gone twenty minutes. She could no longer control her emotions as the tears ran down her face.

Fifteen minutes later, David walked out of the shop cradling his bundles of fish and chips. He walked back towards the beach and when Tracy came back into view, he noticed she was anxiously looking around. Even with the distance between them he could see she was terrified. David stopped and watched with growing interest. *What a performance,* he thought to himself. A few moments later, realising that the fish and chips would start to get cold, he took a slow walk back to the beach. Stopping to remove his shoes and socks once more before stepping onto the sand.

When David reached Tracy, he could see she had been crying and looked petrified.

Still standing, he looked down at Tracy and said, "What on earth's the matter?" With forced empathy in his voice.

"You were gone for so long." She murmured.

"There was a queue." He said with a sigh. "Seems everyone here had the same idea for dinner."

He sat down on the sand next to Tracy and handed her one of the fish and chip bundles. They both ate in silence and as David ate, he watched the nearby seagulls searching for their own fish and chip dinners, as they circled the beach.

He realised that Tracy's vulnerabilities meant she really was dependent on him, and he liked the idea of that.

CHAPTER 8

July 1995

Tracy woke to see her mother standing over her.

"Hi mum. What time is it?" She asked with a sleepy voice.

"Your nan's had a fall." Jean quickly interjected without replying to her question.

Tracy's nan lived in Eastbourne, which was a two-hour drive away and the family tried to visit at least once a month.

Tracy hadn't seen her nan for over a year due to her phobia of travelling and her nan was now too frail to travel to her.

"We need to go and be with her, check she is ok." Jean continued.

"Of course." Tracy said pulling herself into a sitting position.

"We might be gone for a day or two."

"I can't…." Tracy started to say before Jean interrupted.

"It's ok, I'm not expecting you to come. I don't feel comfortable letting Angela stay at home, so she's going to come with us. Why don't you ask David to stay over whilst we're gone, to give you support?"

"Ok." Tracy said cautiously. The conversation of David staying over had never been discussed before.

"We'll be leaving as soon as your dad get's home. I've called him and he's on his way back from work. He'll probably be an hour or so."

Tracy glanced at her bedside alarm clock and saw the time was already eight fifteen.

She got up and dressed while Jean and Angela packed. They we're both ready with overnight bags in the hallway when Peter pulled onto the drive.

"Are you sure you are going to be, ok?" Jean said to Tracy as they prepared to leave.

"I'll be fine, don't worry. I'll call David when he gets home from work."

"Ok, call your dad's mobile phone if you need us for anything. I'll call you later to check in."

"Ok mum, I will, and give my love to nan." Said Tracy as she hugged her mother goodbye.

Knowing roughly what time David would get home from work, she called and was glad when he picked up.

An hour later he was standing on her doorstep holding an overnight bag in one hand, and a Chinese takeaway in the other.

Tracy got two plates out of the cupboard and went about dishing out heaps of egg fried rice, noodles, and sweet and sour chicken.

David pulled a bottle of wine out of his overnight bag and asked. "Where do you keep your wine glasses?"

She hadn't expected wine. She hadn't touched a drop of alcohol since the night of the accident and suddenly felt anxious.

"They are in the cupboard on the left, top shelf." She replied pointing to the cupboard, trying not to show any unease.

David took two glasses and the wine bottle over to the kitchen table and poured them both a glass. Tracy followed with the plates of food and cutlery. She felt it more appropriate to eat at the small kitchen table rather than the more formal setting of the dining room. The round oak table sat four oak chairs and was tucked against the wall to the right side of the kitchen. The kitchen cabinets wrapped around the seating area, on opposite walls. The kitchen was slightly dated. The burgundy Linoleum floor and white spotlights still sported an 80s style.

They sat to eat, and Tracy slowly drank her wine, taking only the smallest of sips at a time. David having finished his glass topped it up and went to top up Tracy's, noticing that she had hardly touched hers.

"What's wrong?" He said curtly. "We're meant to be celebrating."

"Celebrating?" said Tracy with a perplexed look. "My nan's in hospital."

"I don't mean because of that. I mean, it's our first night together." And reached over to touch her hand.

She took a purposeful sip of wine with her free hand and said. "Sorry, I'm just not that much of a drinker."

David tilted his glass forward and said "Cheers."

Tracy did the same with a smile that didn't quite meet her eyes.

David finished off the bottle of wine. And after they'd finished eating, and plates had been washed up, they sat on the red leather sofa in the living room and watched television. The living room was modern in contrast to the kitchen. Black ash furniture adorned the walls opposite the sofa. In the middle was the television perched on top of a black metal stand with castors on wheels. The dark blue patterned carpet complimented the light patterned wallpaper and curtains.

As ten thirty approached, Tracy got up off the sofa.

"I'm going to go and get the bed ready." She said.

David smiled.

"Are you ok sleeping on the sofa. You can sleep in Angela's bed if you prefer?"

"I was expecting to sleep in your bed." he said flatly. "With you."

Tracy stood, not knowing what to say and suddenly feeling awkward.

"That is why you asked me to stay isn't it? To take advantage of your folks being away?" A sinister grin appearing on his face.

"No, no that's not it at all. I was worried about staying alone, so mum suggested I ask you to stay."

"What? I don't get it; we've been seeing each other now for what, three months. I've been nothing but patient and understanding towards your problems." He said making a circle gesture with a finger pointing towards her. "We have the opportunity to spend the night together alone, and uninterrupted and you turn frigid on me." He huffed.

"No, David, that's not fair." She pleaded, as her eyes welled up and wondered if that was the wine talking.

"What's not fair is turning down other girls to be with someone who clearly doesn't love me."

"I do love you."

"Really," he paused. "Then show me!"

They had never discussed taking their relationship to the next level and she didn't yet feel ready to either. She hoped that he would understand and that he hadn't got the wrong impression. She loved David, there was no question about that, but she was nervous.

"Actually, I think it's best I leave." And with that he stood up and walked out of the living room, into the hallway and picked up his bag.

"No wait." Tracy said. "Please don't leave."

He stood still and stared at her for a few seconds. "Fine," he eventually said. "I will stay but only because. I've been drinking and shouldn't really drive. I don't want to crash my car." speaking slowly, to emphasise the final point.

She took his hand and guided him up to her room, whilst still fighting back the tears.

"I'm sorry." She said apologetically as she closed her bedroom door.

David said nothing and started to remove his clothes, until his was left only wearing a pair of boxer shorts.

Tracy walked over to her bedside lamp, switched it on and then nervously began to take off her own clothes, climbing into bed besides him wearing only her bra and knickers.

She hadn't expected her first time to be like that. She had expected romance, with lots of caressing and for things to have progressed slowly. Just like she had read in books and seen in the movies. Instead, it was quick, and he seemed devoid of any emotion. He was distant towards her, his eyes never meeting hers and as soon as he was satisfied, it was over. He didn't say anything afterwards. Not even to ask if she was ok or to say I love you. He simply turned his back on her and went to sleep.

Squeezed by his side in her single bed, she laid awake for hours, confused by the whole experience and his icy manner. She assumed he was still mad at her. She should have managed his expectations and been clearer on the arrangements when she had inviting him to stay. She was annoyed with herself and made a promise to make it up to him tomorrow.

CHAPTER 9

David woke up early the next morning. Tracy left him getting showered and ready for work and headed downstairs to make him a cup of tea and a lunchbox.

A short while later he joined her in the kitchen.

"Do you want some breakfast?" She asked as she passed him his tea.

"No thanks, I'd better get going in a sec, I don't want to be late." And took a big gulp from his mug.

"I made you some lunch." She said, with a slight eagerness to please in her voice. And handed David a plastic tub container containing sandwiches and crisps.

"Thank you," he said and leant over to kiss her lightly on the side of her cheek. "I'll come back after work."

Tracy nodded appreciatively as David drank the last of his tea before hurrying out of the door.

After David had gone Tracy ran herself a bath, hoping it would help her to feel better after such a restless night. She poured bubble bath into the running water that smelt of lavender and promised to relieve tired and aching muscles, and climbed in. Although David had been pleasant enough in the short time, they had spent together that morning. She felt there was still tension between them. Her eyes welled again as she remembered how last night had ended and this time, she allowed the tears to flow. She sat in the warm bath, surrounded by bubbles, hugging her legs in close to her breasts and wept.

She didn't know how long she had sat there, but it was long enough for the bubbles to disappear and water to turn cold.

When she eventually climbed out of the bath and reached for a towel, she noticed that the skin on her hands and feet were wrinkled from the prolonged soak.

Tracy slowly got dressed into a casual T-shirt and jeans, and as she ran a brush through hair, heard the telephone ring. She was expecting her mother to call with an update, but even so she felt her heart rate quicken at the sound of the ring. She rushed down the stairs to where the phone was located on the wall in the hallway, and taking in a deep breath, picked up the receiver and nervously answered with a quiet "Hello."

"Hi love, just checking to see how you are and to tell you the latest on nan."

Tracy was relieved to hear it was Jean's voice on the other end of the phone. "I'm ok." She said, choosing not to elaborate any further. "How's nan?"

"I'm glad you are. We are going to be staying for another couple of nights. Your nan is back home but it's going to take a few days before she's well enough to be left alone."

"Ok," Tracy said. "I'm glad nans on the mend."

"Are you sure you're ok Tracy?" Jean asked, detecting that something wasn't quite right.

"Sorry mum, I'm fine, honestly. Please give my love to nan."

"Ok and make sure you call me if you need anything or if you......" Jean couldn't think of the right words to say, "Or you, just want to talk."

"Ok mum, speak later."

"Bye love." Jean said before ending the call.

Knowing she had a couple more days without her parents, Tracy felt even more determined to make it up to David. And she would start by cooking them both a romantic meal.

In search of inspiration, she looked through the fridge and cupboards. Both were almost empty. She couldn't expect them to live off takeaways for the next few days. Neither could she expect David to go to the supermarket after finishing a long day at work.

She pondered for a moment before realising that she had no choice other than to visit the shops herself. Maybe not to the supermarket but to the village corner shop which was branded as a micro supermarket.

Tracy opened the canned foods cupboard and took from the back an old biscuit tin where Jean kept her weekly housekeeping money. She removed two ten-pound notes and stuffed them into the back pocket of her jeans.

Five minutes later she sat on the bottom step of the stairs, tying up the laces to her trainers when she was suddenly overcome with a sense of foreboding. Lots of what ifs suddenly swam around her head. *What if she saw someone she knew, and they asked how she was? or mention that they hadn't seen her out in a while.* "Stop it." She told herself. *This is ridiculous, I can do this. I have come so far over the last few months.*

Tracy opened her front door slightly and peeked around to see if any of her neighbours were out in their front gardens or on the street. When she was sure she was alone, she walked out and closed the door behind her.

It was a dull but warm day and Tracy marched quickly to the shop, thinking that the quicker she got it over and done with the quicker she would be back home and in her safe space.

The brisk walk had left Tracy sweating slightly as she approached the door. She walked into the brightly lit shop playing quiet background music, which she couldn't place and picked up a shopping basket from a small stack, just inside the door. She kept her head down for fear of being recognised, looking up only for the occasional glance at a product and headed straight to the fridge section. She decided on two prepacked sirloin steaks, placed them in her basket and walked off in search of potatoes. Tracy continued to walk around the shop in a no-nonsense manner also picking up mushrooms, a frozen black forest gateau, fresh cream, and a cheap bottle of white wine. When Tracy was satisfied that she had everything she needed, she headed to the till. The nerves she had been keeping at bay started to creep their way back in. Underneath her T-shirt she felt a bead of sweat roll down her back and her legs felt like they were made from jelly. She took in a breath and started to unload her shopping basket. She looked up at the shop assistant behind the counter and was relieved to see she didn't recognise him. He looked as though he should have retired a long time ago and his attempt at a comb over to hide his baldness had failed him. The shop assistance eyed her, and she felt her face redden.

"Do you have any ID?" He asked with a slight nasally voice.

"Oh um, I actually don't." replied a flustered Tracy.

Even though she was now 18, she had left the house with only the cash in her back pocket and hadn't bought her purse with her provisional driving licence inside.

"I can't sell you that wine, without ID." He continued.

"No problem." Said Tracy, as she handed the wine back to the man. She didn't want it anyway and certainly didn't want to draw attention to herself by causing a scene. Tracy could see a queue had started to form in her periphery, without turning to properly look.

After Tracy paid, she hurriedly put her shopping into a plastic carrier bag and left the shop without making further eye contact with anyone else.

Once back in the safety of her home, she took a few moments to compose herself and allow her racing heartbeat to slow to its normal pace. The visit to the shops had been frightening, but a sense of satisfaction took over and she silently praised herself on her achievement.

Tracy spent the next couple of hours getting ready for David's arrival. She set the table so that it resembled a romantic restaurant and hunted through the kitchen 'odds and sods' drawer to find a couple of candles and a box of matches. *Perfect*. She thought to herself as she placed the candles in their holders and admired the setting. Putting the box of matches on the table in readiness for lighting later.

She prepared dinner and then moved on to preparing herself. She wanted to look extra nice and dressed seductively in a short sleeve, red knee length dress and styled her hair and make up. She picked up her bottle of CK One perfume and was about to spray herself, when Emma came into her mind. Determined not to allow negative thoughts to ruin her evening, she put down the perfume bottle and instead sprayed herself with her go to her Charlie Red aerosol.

As the steaks and chips sizzled in their respective frying pans, Tracy heard a knock at the front door. She quickly lit the candles and hurried to let David inside. She opened the door and was welcomed by a man who's head had been replaced with an enormous bouquet of flowers. Whilst inhaling a magnificent floral scent, Tracy could make out carnations, roses, and lilies amongst the arrangement. In various shades of reds, pinks and white. David passed the flowers to Tracy, revealing that it was indeed him hiding behind the bouquet.

"Thank you." Said Tracy as she took the flowers from him.

"These are because I love you." He said and leaned forward to kiss her.

She beckoned him inside. "I have a surprise for you too." And led him into the kitchen.

"Wow, you've made dinner and you look amazing." He said, pulling her in for a tight hug.

"Come on, dinner's almost ready. Take a seat and I'll go and put these," nodding at the flowers, "in water before dishing up."

Dinner was a success. The steak was cooked to perfection and much to Tracy's surprise, her attempt at making home made chips had tasted better than frozen ones.

As they ate, Tracy revealed that she had gone to the shop to buy the ingredients, reinforcing the amount of effort she had gone to. David placed a hand on her thigh and rubbed it in appreciation as he thanked her. Once they had finished eating, David leant back in his chair and patted his full belly.

"That was amazing babe, you'll make a good wife one day." And winked as he smiled.

"Why don't you go and get comfortable in the living room, and I'll tidy up in here."

David not needing to be told twice, promptly got up and left the kitchen.

Twenty minutes later, Tracy joined him in the living room. Feeling pleased that her evening was going well, and any tension left over from the previous night had long since gone.

They cuddled on the sofa and watched mundane television about police chases. And after a while, David bent his head down to kiss her. His kiss was long and slow, and he took his time to gently massage his tongue around hers. Tracy felt lost in the moment, her body responding as it yearned for more. Following a few minutes of kissing, David got up off the sofa, took Tracy's hand and led her to her bedroom.

This time, it was different. David caressed Tracy as he undressed her slowly. Taking his time to build up the intensity, before entering her. Tracy relaxed and allowed David to take the lead. He made eye contact with her throughout and the entire experience was polar opposite to that of the previous evening. She was immersed in new sensations that overwhelmed and took control of her body. It didn't take long before her endorphins peaked, and she climaxed. And once over, he smiled and kissed her gently before moving to lay on his back. She laid her head against his chest, listening to the sounds of his shallow breathing, as he drifted off to sleep. Unable to fight sleep herself she too drifted off, feeling euphoric for winning the affection of the man she loved so dearly.

CHAPTER 10

Despite being a Saturday David had to work, and he left taking with him another pack lunch courtesy of Tracy. After waving him off she turned on the small radio that sat on top on the kitchen windowsill and danced around the kitchen in her dressing gown and pyjamas. She couldn't remember the last time she had danced, and it felt good.

Tracy was desperate to call her friends but didn't think they'd appreciate a nine-a.m. call on a weekend. So, she took a shower in a bid to waste some time. As ten a.m. approached, she couldn't wait any longer and began making her calls. She struggled to contain her giddy mood as she spoke and without giving it much thought invited them over for the evening.

As her parents were to be away for at least one more night she felt it a great opportunity for her friends and David to finally. Thankfully, none of the girls had made any concrete plans for the evening and accepted her invitation.

David arrived home from work, looking slightly deshelled and feeling exhausted. A sign that he had just worked six days straight and was in much need of a day off. Tracy put the kettle on to make them both a cup of tea when he questioned in a mocked tone.

"No romantic dinner tonight?"

"No babe, not tonight. My......"

"Do you mind if I pop upstairs for a quick shower?" He said, cutting Tracy off mid sentence. "I need to unwind."

"Yeah, sure, go ahead."

And with that David ran up the stairs before Tracy was able to tell him they had guests joining them for the evening.

Fifteen minutes later David walked into the living room where Tracy sat watching television. He wore comfortable jogging bottoms and an old, faded Star Wars t-shirt. *David was an attractive man,* Tracy thought to herself, but when he was fresh out of the shower having made no effort, she felt even more attracted to him.

"My friends are popping over shortly; they want to meet you." She said as she pointed the remote control at the television to switch it off.

"What?" David said with an air of irritation to his voice.

"I spoke to them earlier and invited them round. They're bringing pizzas and I thought it would be a great for us all to get together. My favourite people all in one room." She said with a smile, picking up her cup of tea and holding it with both hands.

"I wish you would have asked me first." He said whilst leaning against the door frame. "I'm knackered and the last thing I want to do tonight is entertain strangers."

"It'll be laid back and I'll make sure they don't stay too late, so we get some time to unwind together." She said moving off the sofa and towards David for a cuddle. He stiffened and returned a forced embrace. "I made you a cup of tea, but it might be a bit cold now."

"Don't worry, I fancy a beer." He said moving away from Tracy and heading for the kitchen in search of one. "Bingo," he said as he located four cans of Stella towards the back of the fridge and pulled one out.

"They're my dad's David."

"So, he's not here and if it's an issue, I'll replace them tomorrow." He sighed, "When are they due round?"

"In about ten minutes." Tracy said hesitantly.

David said nothing but huffed as he took his beer into the living room.

Simone, Franics, and Jo arrived together carrying pizzas and bottles of coke.

"Hello." Tracy said cheerfully as she opened the front door and indicating for them to come inside. They each attempted to hug Tracy as they walked past, although it proved difficult, given that their hands were full, and it caused them to giggle.

"Thanks for bringing the pizzas." Tracy said and led them into the dinning room. "We're not all going to fit around the kitchen table, so I suggest we eat in here tonight."

"Fine by me." Jo said as she placed a pizza box onto the dining table.

Tracy went back to the kitchen and took out five glasses from the cupboard and placed them on a tray along with the kitchen roll.

"David." She called out, as she passed the living room, poking her head around the door. "They're here and the pizza is starting to get cold. Are you joining us?"

"I guess I am." He said unenthusiastically, pulling himself off the sofa and picking up his beer before following Tracy into the dining room.

Once the pleasantries and introductions were over, involving lots of hugging, much to David's distaste. They all took their seats and began eating. They ate slice after slice of BBQ chicken and pepperoni pizza as they chatted amongst themselves. The girls, eager to know more about the man that made their friend smile again, asked David various questions. David, although not overly talkative did answer each question politely, giving off the impression that he was a bit shy. Tracy, oblivious to David's annoyance at his interrogation was in high spirits. Her friends and boyfriend had finally met and seemed to get along.

Once they'd eaten enough pizza and were fit to burst, the girls moved into the living room to make themselves more comfortable. Tracy and David collected the empty pizza boxes and took them into the kitchen, dumping them on the table to clear away in the morning. David went to the fridge to help himself to another beer and as he opened the can. Tracy touched his left shoulder and asked.

"What do you think?"

"Think of what?"

"My friends?" Tracy said with wide eyes suggesting that her question was obvious.

"They're alright, I guess." He said, shrugging his shoulders and taking a sip of his beer. "I just hope they don't stay too much longer. I fancy an early night." And winked at her, before walking off.

The five of them chatted about their week and for David's benefit, stories of when they were all at school. Emma was mentioned a few times and it made Tracy feel a little uncomfortable, which she hid well. Simone, who was still seeing Paul suggested that they double date when Tracy felt ready. David was courteous but noncommittal to the suggestion.

At nine thirty, David stood up, interrupting the conversation, and said. "Right, I'm tired and going to head to up bed." And as he did, he glared at Tracy, as if to prompt her to get rid of the others.

"Ok, nice to meet you, David." Francis said from the other end of the living room.

"Yes, it was." Jo and Simone said simultaneously.

David just smiled and said nothing.

None of the girls picked up on David's non subtle hint and continued to chat for the next couple of hours, before Jo eventually yawned and said. "We should be heading home; I hadn't realised how late it had got."

Five minutes later, the girls were hugging their goodbyes and Tracy waved them off, locking the front door behind her. She turned off the downstairs lights and went upstairs to join David, expecting to find him asleep. She crept into her dark bedroom, trying to be quiet so not to wake him. And was startled when David turned on the bedside lamp to reveal him wide awake and sitting up in bed.

"What time do you call this?" He said angrily.

"Sorry, we lost track of time, chatting." She said, trying to justify the lateness.

"You said, they wouldn't stay too late, so that we could spend some time together."

"I'm sorry," she said again. "We have tomorrow together. You're not at work and my parents won't be home until late afternoon. I haven't seen the girls for a couple of weeks and time just ran away with us."

"That's not the point." He snarled and switched the lamp off before turning his back to Tracy.

Tracy cursed herself for yet again managing to ruin an evening, she should have asked them to leave when David went up to bed. *Why are relationships so bloody complicated?* She asked herself as she climbed into bed next to him. Spooning his stoney body from behind for comfort.

Tracy's parents arrived home early evening to a quiet house. David had left early, using the excuse that he wanted to spend some time with his dad, as he hadn't seen him for a few days. But it was clear to Tracy that he was still mad at her. Having barely spoken two words to her before leaving, despite her many apologies.

CHAPTER 11

Tracy hadn't heard from David since he had left on Sunday morning and that was several days ago. She missed him. She called his house several times, either for it to ring out or for Tony to answer and take a message. But he never returned any of her calls. She had enjoyed playing house with David and longed for them to have a future together. She desperately hoped she hadn't blown it.

On Friday evening, David finally turned up at her house without warning. She felt relieved when she saw his car pull up onto the drive, and after allowing him to say a quick hello to her parents, she ushered him upstairs. Once in her bedroom she threw herself at him, smothering him, as she begged for forgiveness in between passionate kisses. David eventually drew her close, held her face, looked into her eyes and kissed her back. She was forgiven.

The next few weeks went by, and they both fell back into their usual routine. Feeling more determined than ever to lead a normal life, Tracy was starting to venture out the house more often. She allowed David to take her for the occasional drive and she even ventured out to the café she once worked, with the girls. It was lovely to see Debbie again after so long. Although, she declined Debbie's offer when she asked if she wanted her job back.

Tracy turned nineteen on the fifteenth of August and unlike last year, she was really looking forward to her birthday.

She began the day with her parents and sister, enjoying a

family breakfast together, before her dad went off to work. Her mum's infamous chocolate birthday cake and a pile of wrapped presents, that mainly included clothes she had hinted to liking in her mum's catalogue, sat waiting for her on the kitchen table.

After breakfast, she got dressed into one of her new outfits. A floral short sleeved dress that sat just above the knee. She had planned to spend the day in the garden enjoying the high summer weather, whilst she waited for David, who wasn't due to arrive until late afternoon.

Tracy's plans were waylaid when at lunchtime her friends arrived unexpectedly, having arranged a surprise birthday picnic for her by the river. Although it took some convincing to get her to agree, with help from her mum, who was in on the surprise. She went and enjoyed a lovely summer's day eating cakes and soaking up the sun.

David arrived late afternoon proudly clutching a small red glittery gift bag.

Tracy was promised that she and David could have the house to themselves for the evening as her family had agreed to making themselves scarce.

She was excited and wanted to see what was inside the gift bag, but decided to wait until they were alone before opening it.

She impatiently sat waiting with David at the kitchen table whilst her parents faffed around getting ready to leave. She told him about her day. About how lovely the picnic surprise had been, how thoughtful her friends were and how proud she was of herself for going. He sat listening to her without saying a word. His jaws clenched and brows furrowed and after an intentional pause, he reminded Tracy in a slow and quiet tone that emphasised every word.

"I. Suggested. A. Picnic. By. The. River. To. Which. You. Flatly. Refused!"

"I was ambushed." she said, in defence. "And I'm stronger

now, than I was a few months ago, it's nothing to do with you babe, I promise."

David didn't say anything in response, but she could sense his disappointment in her, and she worried she had upset him.

Jean walked into the kitchen, unaware of the tension building, to say her goodbyes and promptly left. They sat in silence, listing to the sound of the front door opening and closing, and car pull away. To avoid the uncomfortable silence, Tracy left the table to pour them both a glass of orange juice. She placed one the cold drinks in front of David and sat back down in her chair, still unsure of what to say.

"You'd better have this." David eventually said, breaking the silence.

He passed her the gift bag he'd been holding as he forced a smile, still reeling about the picnic.

Tracy beamed in anticipation as she removed a small, wrapped, rectangular shaped gift from the bag and hurried to unwrap it. Her excitement soon disappeared, and colour drained from her face. She had pulled back enough of the paper to see it was a box containing a bottle of CK One. David instantly picked up on her reaction.

"What's wrong with it?" he snapped.

"It's nothing, it's lovely thank you." She lied.

"Don't lie to me, I can tell something is wrong by the look on your face. I thought you liked this one, I've seen it in your bedroom."

"I do, or I did." she began to say, before David snatched the half unwrapped present out her hands and ripped off the remainder of the paper in anger.

Tracy suddenly felt frightened of David. And got up off the chair edging slowly backwards, until her back was touching the worktop, giving a little distance between them.

"You are so ungrateful." He spat. "That cost me a small fortune and I had to go to three different shops before I found one that had it in stock."

"I'm sorry." She pleaded, "I really do like it, and you were really thoughtful to go to so much effort for me." She took a step forward towards him, putting her hands out in front of her and said. "Can I have it please?"

"You can fucking have it, you ungrateful bitch." He shouted as he threw the perfume at her and it caught her left eye socket, before crashing to the floor.

Tracy cried out in pain as she clutched her face. She ran out of the kitchen and headed straight upstairs to the bathroom. Once there she locked the door behind her, removed her hand and looked into the mirror. Blood was dripping from a small cut along the side of her eye and red bruising was already starting to appear. She removed a few pieces of toilet paper, held it to her face and sank to the floor and cried.

David remained at the kitchen table, with his head in his hands trying to understand how things had escalated so quickly. He was frustrated but he hadn't meant to loose his temper, and he certainly hadn't meant to hurt her. He felt let down that she had chosen her friends to take her to the river, over him. And was disappointed by her reaction to the perfume he'd spent hours searching for. He had been so pleased with himself, after he finally managed to source the correct bottle.

Half an hour later, he picked up the perfume box which laid unopened on the kitchen floor, put it back in the gift bag and made his way upstairs to see Tracy. Her bedroom door was open, and he could see the room was empty, so headed to the bathroom. The door was closed, and he hesitated for a moment, wondering if he should try to open it, or knock and wait for a reply. He opted for the latter and gently knocked whilst calling her name.

"Go away." Tracy shouted.

"Tracy please." he pleaded; it was now his time to beg for forgiveness.

"Go home David."

"I'm sorry, I really didn't mean to hurt you. It was an

accident, please believe me."

Tracy sat on the other side of the door; the blood had stopped flowing but her tears hadn't.

"Tracy, please let me in." He waited. "I need to know that you are ok."

There was silence for a while, before she slowly opened the door. David felt himself staring at the floor, unable to look directly at her and see the injury he had caused.

Tracy noticed and hissed "Look at me."

He eventually looked up and met her gaze, her eyes puffy with crying and left eye red and swollen.

"I'm sorry." He said quietly and reached out to hold her. He pulled her head towards his chest and rubbed the back of her hair, as tears started to fall from his own eyes. "I'm so sorry." He repeated.

David gently guided Tracy to her room and sat her down on her bed. "Wait here." He said and went downstairs in search of something frozen and suitable to help with her swelling. A few minutes later he re-appeared holding a bag of peas, a tea towel, and a glass of water. David placed the water by her bedside and wrapped the bag of peas in the towel before handing it to Tracy. She laid down on her bed and carefully placed the towel bundle over her eye. She winced as the coldness first touched her tender flesh, but shortly after, it did offer some relief to the pain. David removed his shoes, laid down next to her on his side and gently played with her hair. Exhaustion set in and it wasn't long until they had both fallen asleep, and they didn't even wake to the sound of Tracy's family arriving home some time later.

The next morning, Tracy woke first. As soon as she opened her eyes, she immediately felt the throb. A stark reminder of the previous evening. Her birthday. With David still sleeping, she got up off the bed and made her way to her dressing table, to look into the mirror and see how bad her eye looked. Last night's red bruising had now turned an ugly dark purple, but the swelling had reduced. She was unsure how long she had sat and stared at herself in the mirror before David appeared behind her. He leant down to hug her from behind and kissed the back of her head.

"How are you?" He asked.

"I'm not sure, if I'm honest." Tracy didn't know how best to explain her injury to her parents. She didn't think make up would cover it and she also didn't relish the thought of applying anything over the tender skin. And she could hardly wear sunglasses indoors for the next few days. She had no choice other than to embrace her black eye and think of an elaborate excuse for it's cause.

David moved back to the bed, sitting on the edge with his feet on the floor. He was fully dressed, as was Tracy after they had both fallen asleep unexpectedly. She stood up and walked over to her chest of drawers, took out a clean pair of leggings and a t-shirt and changed out of the clothes she was wearing.

"I'm going to go downstairs; I can't avoid them all day." She said, referring to her family. "I'm also not sure how happy they will be that you stayed over. But I guess I'll find out. You stay up here for now."

He nodded.

Tracy coyly walked down the stairs and could hear her mum in the kitchen loading up the washing machine.

"Morning." Jean said without looking up. "I see David stayed over, last night."

"Yeah, about that, sorry mum, we both, er, fell asleep."

"Umm." said Jean as she stood upright and turned to face Tracy, almost dropping the box of washing powder in her hand as she spotted her face.

"What, on earth, happened to you?" Jean said fretfully.

"I'm fine, it looks worse that it is. I was looking through the cupboard last night to find something to cook and a tin of baked beans fell from the top shelf and smacked me in the eye."

Jean didn't say anything immediately and continued to stare at her.

"Are you sure you are, ok? I am sorry love, I have been meaning to have a tidy up of that cupboard for a while now, I've had a few near misses myself of late."

Tracy was relieved that her mum had bought her excuse.

"It's not too bad now. But it did hurt a lot of last night and that's why David stayed over, to comfort me."

Jean smiled "I understand, he's a good lad that David, I'm so glad you have him looking out for you."

Tracy attempted to smile at her mum's comment, through gritted teeth.

Later, Tracy explained the real reason behind her upset to David's birthday gift. He said he understood and agreed to exchange it for a different brand which he did along with a new handbag and a pair of trainers.

CHAPTER 12

December 1995

The next few months went by with no major dramas. David spoiled Tracy, often buying her flowers, chocolates and sometimes even clothes, that he had carefully selected. And if he was a bit low on cash, he'd write her childish love letters, she loved to receive those the most.

Jo had gone off to university in October. And due to the distance, with it being in Sheffield, Tracy wouldn't see her again until Christmas. She spoke to her often over the phone and kept in close contact with Francis and Simone. They had both gotten full time jobs, favouring earning money over an education. Francis took a job in a bank as a cashier, working a steady nine to five in Portsmouth and Simone in a department store on the edge of the city.

Tracy, although still hesitant about leaving the house, was now going out much more frequently with David, and occasionally with Simone and Francis. Simone was now driving, although had to share a car with her mum.

Tracy and David had by now been seeing each other for seven months, and in all that time she had never been to his house in Portsmouth. He always came to hers. Tracy often wondered what his house was like and how tidy it would be, given that two men occupied it. David had always said that as Tracy was much more comfortable in her own home and as he drove, it made more sense for him to travel to her. Whenever she asked him about his house or mention spending any time there, he always made an excuse, preferring the company at the Hopkins household.

Tracy was not expecting so was surprised when David invited her to stay for the weekend, as Tony was away on a Christmas trip with his darts team.

She was looking forward to it. She packed a small holdall with enough clothes and toiletries to last a couple of nights and on Friday David picked her up on his way home from work.

The Wright household was a twenty-five-minute drive away, in a housing estate situated in a relatively nice part of the city.

"Welcome to the Wright residence." David said as he pulled up onto the drive of a small, detached house with an integral garage. Double glazed windows and doors gave the house a modern look and as expected, the small front garden looked impeccable, even for the time of year.

They made their way inside and into a bright spacious hallway. Along the wall opposite the front door, a lamp sat on top of a credenza unit. Its warm light gave an instant homely feel as you walked in.

David gave a brief tour of the house. The large modern kitchen dinner had a small island in the middle, dividing the kitchen from the dining area. Lots of appliances were integrated into cupboards and patio doors led out into the garden. It was too dark to see the garden, but she imagined that too would be tidy.

The living room bore cream painted walls on the top half and stripped navy and cream wallpaper on the bottom, separated by a dado rail, which seemed to feature in many of the rooms. Photos hung in gold frames on the walls and Tracy spotted one of a lady who looked to be in her thirty's, with blond curly hair, much like her own. She could see a resemblance to David and assumed it to be his mum. A fabric floral sofa sat opposite a gas fireplace and second pair of patio doors led out into a conservatory, which remained in darkness. She was struck by how tidy and clean the house was. There was no clutter, not a thing out of place and not a spec of dust anywhere. She had expected to see some disarray, but it was the total opposite, putting her own house to shame.

"Your house is so clean. Does your dad hire a cleaner?" She couldn't stop herself from asking.

"No, me and Dad do the cleaning."

"Did you make a special effort in readiness for my arrival?" Tracy mocked and gently poked David on the arm.

He looked a little bemused. "No, we always keep the house tidy. It's easy if you keep on top of it."

She wasn't sure if there was a slight insult within his reply, implying that her mum didn't keep on top of their own housework.

Once David had shown her around downstairs, he took her hand and led her up the stairs and joked that he was saving the best to last. Once inside David's bedroom he turned on the lights and Tracy began to nosily poke around as he watched. The walls were a mid shade of blue, painted over the top of wood chip wallpaper, and a few posters of Oasis and ladies in bikinis, were sporadically blue tacked against them.

"Really." Tracy said as she pointed at one of the posters.

"I'm only human." He blushed.

A single bed with a white iron headboard sat against the middle of the back wall, taking up centre stage in the room. Wall shelves that contained various bottles of deodorant and a picture in a frame, hung above a chest of drawers, to one side of the bed. And a small bedside table with an alarm clock that had a built-in lamp stood to the other.

Tracy walked over to take a closer look at the photo and picked it up. In the photo she recognised Tony, looking younger and slimmer, a boy who she assumed was David and the same lady as in the photo in the Living room.

"That was taken during our last holiday together before she died." David said walking over to stand beside her, she put the photo back and turned to give him a light squeeze.   On the opposite side of the room stood a slightly battered looking wardrobe with various remains of old stickers attached to the front and a stand which had a stereo on the bottom and television on the top.

Much like the rest of the house, his room too was spotless. It also smelt fresh, and she recognised it to be David's scent. A mixture of deodorant, after shave and fabric softer. She loved that smell. For some reason Tracy had expected his bedroom to smell like that of a typical teenage boy's bedroom - sweat and old socks.

"There's one final bit of the tour that I want to show you."

"What's that?" Tracy said inquisitively.

"Inside my bed." he said as he pulled back his duvet.

They enjoyed another weekend alone playing house. David preferred it when it was just the two of them as he didn't need to share her with anyone. She was a home bird, preferring to stay in over going out and socialising. He knew it was because of the trauma she'd suffered but he liked it. He never needed to worry about where she was or who she was with, and that suited him.

On Saturday evening, they were loading the dishwasher and clearing up from dinner when out of nowhere David asked.

"Why don't we get our own place?" Tracy wasn't expecting the question and it took her by surprise. "We don't get to be alone very often and when we do, you have to admit, it's so nice. I'm working full time and think we could just about afford something small on my wage. What to you say?"

Tracy smiled. "I think it would be great, let's look into it."

CHAPTER 13

Tracy hadn't mentioned the prospect of moving out to anyone. Besides, she didn't yet feel the need to as they hadn't discussed the matter since that night at David's house. She also assumed that with Christmas vast approaching, all planning would be on hold until the New Year.

David spent Christmas morning with his dad, and Tracy with her family. They'd arranged for David to come over late afternoon, once dinners had been eaten, presents unwrapped and Queen's speech watched on the television.

Tracy's gift to David was her favourite photo of the two of them, placed in a beautiful chunky blue and silver frame she had bought. She wrapped it in red metallic wrapping paper and placed a large red bow on the top.

David arrived empty handed, which Tracy thought to be a bit odd, but chose not to say anything. Once alone in her bedroom, they sat on her bed, and she handed him his present. He slowly opened it and brimmed with delight when he saw what it was.

"Thank you, that's really thoughtful." He said and reached over to give her a kiss. "I have got you a present, but unfortunately I couldn't wrap it."

"Ok." she said, feeling a little confused.

"I will have to take you to it." With that he got up off her bed and reached out his hand to gesture Tracy to do the same.

"Where are we going?"

"You'll soon see." He smiled. "You'll need to pack an overnight bag."

Tracy felt suddenly unnerved. "David, please tell me where we are going? You know how I feel about leaving the house, I need to know where we are going."

"All I am going to say, is that it's a surprise. And I need you to just trust me. Ok?"

Tracy began nervously packing an overnight bag and when she was ready to leave, headed into the living room to say goodbye to her parents. They were sat on the sofa, semi comatose from a day of overindulging, and immersed in the television, whilst stuffing chocolates into their mouths.

"Mum, Dad. David has a surprise for me. He's taking me somewhere and it involves staying overnight. I don't know where we are going, but I'll see you tomorrow."

Jean looked up. "Well as long as you are with David, I know you'll be safe, enjoy whatever he has planned."

Tracy leant in to kiss her parents' goodbye and said, "See you tomorrow." before leaving.

Once in David's car she tried again to get David to reveal his plans but all he would say was. "You will soon see."

They headed towards the direction of Portsmouth and Tracy wondered if they were going back to his house. But as they got closer, he purposely missed the turning that would have sent them towards his estate, and instead pulled onto the city's ring road. *So, we must be spending the night in one of the city's many hotels.* She thought to herself, feeling excited by the possibility.

Five minutes later, he was pulling off the ring road and driving through a quiet housing estate, situated on the further side of the city centre. She couldn't recall any hotels out this far and started to feel anxious. Whatever he had planned, it had pushed her to her limit, and she could feel the start of a panic attack brewing.

David eventually pulled into the parking area of a complex. She could see several identical blocks of what looked like three story flats.

"We're here." He said excitedly as he stopped the engine and climbed out of the car before reaching into the back seat to retrieve Tracy's bag. She climbed out of the car feeling even more anxious and confused about what was happening. "Come on then," he gestured as he reached out his hand for her to take. They walked through a communal looking garden which had several rotary clothes lines dotted around and faintly lit by a streetlight in the parking bay.

Tracy followed David up a path, into one of the buildings and up two flights of stairs. When they'd reached the top, she saw two identical brown front doors side by side, each with a privacy window panel at eyeline level. David took out a key and opened the door to the left.

"Ladies first." He said as he put out an arm to gesture her inside.

Tracy slowly walked into a dark and narrow corridor as David flicked on the light. There were no windows only four doors and despite the magnolia walls and beige carpet, the corridor felt dark and eery.

"I don't understand." She stuttered.

"It's our new home." David proclaimed as he guided her towards the furthest door which led into a living room. Décor matched that of the hallway and the room was empty apart from a bean bag and in the corner stood a small television on a stand that she recognised to be from David's bedroom. A light bulb hung from the ceiling with no lamp shade and yellow stained net curtains hung from a large window. The room smelt of stale smoke and was in much need of a refresh. She was stunned and didn't know what to say.

"We obviously need to get some furniture." He said enthusiastically. "That'll be the fun bit, you know, making it our own. Oh, the kitchen is through here." and gestured her towards a door at the end of the living room. "It's small but does come with a cooker and fridge freezer. So that's two things we can tick off the list straight away."

Tracy was in shock. She couldn't find the right words and could only nod. David showed her around the rest of the flat. The other doors off the hallway led to a small bathroom, a cupboard, and a bedroom that he had prepared by placing a duvet on top of a double air mattress.

"Ta Da." He said as he opened the door to the bedroom. Feeling awkward by her silence he turned to Tracy "Say something?"

"I don't know what to say. I'm in shock, I wasn't expecting this. I thought we were going to look together; I didn't think you would go ahead and find somewhere without my......" She trailed off, remembering her birthday and decided to change tact. "I love it, thank you. Sorry for my reaction. I am just in total shock that you have done this for us. It's wonderful." And threw her arms around him, fighting the urge to cry.

"It might not be much, but this is our first home and the start of our future together."

She nodded and forced a smile.

"I've stocked up the fridge ready to celebrate." He said as he moved back to the kitchen and opened the fridge to reveal a pizza and a bottle of champagne.

Tracy spent the next few minutes trying to figure out how to work the ancient looking oven and put the pizza in to cook. David opened one of the wall cupboards and took out the two plates and two mugs that he'd placed in there earlier. Popped open the champaign and poured some into each mug.

"Just a small amount for me." She reminded as he poured.

Once the pizza was cooked, they huddled together on the beanbag, sharing the pizza and sipping champagne, as they attempted to watch a grainy picture on the television.

"First thing I'll do next week is organise cable TV." David said as took a bite of Pizza.

And buy curtains. Tracy thought to herself. Curtains

provided a safe haven as she could close out darkness and most of all rain.

Tracy barely touched her pizza. She had no appetite and when David quizzed her on it, she blamed it on her earlier Christmas dinner, which he accepted.

They continued to attempt to watch the television whilst David drained off the remainder of the bottle of champagne.

"Let's go to bed," he eventually slurred and pulled himself up and off the beanbag. She followed him into the bedroom and began to get undressed for bed. David got straight into bed, whilst Tracy took her wash bag into the bathroom. When she reappeared a few minutes later she was relieved to see that he was already asleep. She couldn't face having sex with him tonight, for fear of breaking down. She switched off the light and as there was no bedside lamp was forced to navigate the room in the dark.

Tracy laid besides David, but sleep did not come. Her mind raced as she tried to process the enormity of the situation.

Yes, she had agreed to move in with him but hadn't expected it to be so soon. She wasn't ready to leave home and when the time came that she did feel ready, she wanted to live somewhere that was close to home. David had gone ahead and not involved her with the flat hunting and the all-important decision making in where they lived.

This flat was at least a thirty-minute drive from her parents and the thought of that terrified her.

She considered several ways to tell him how she really felt, rehearsing each one over and over, as she listened to him breathing beside her. But she knew that it would mean the end if she didn't agree to move in with him. She thought about how happy he had made her and how much more confident she had become as a result. Then she thought about the times he'd been mad at her and had lost his temper. But that was in the past, it had been months since she'd last upset him. She knew him better now and knew how to avoid those triggers.

By the time the sun had started to rise, and a faint amount of light crept into the bare windowed room, Tracy had convinced herself to give living together a go. She couldn't rely on her parents forever and she loved David. She couldn't image a life without him by her side.

She watched him as he slept. His floppy hair wild from sleep sat across his forehead. She snuggled into his warm body and relaxed. He stirred and pulled her closer. They began to kiss and made love, and then she fell into a deep sleep.

CHAPTER 14

Tracy's parents took the news of her leaving home better than she had expected. They saw it as progress for Tracy, for she had overcome the crippling phobias that had kept her from leaving the house for all those months. And besides, there would always be a room waiting for her if she ever needed it.

Tracy and David made the most out of Monty's Christmas shut down and spent the week after Christmas turning the flat into a home.

Donations of excess items from the Wright and Hopkins household meant they had sufficient cookware, cutlery, towels curtains, lamp shades and bedding. And each item was gratefully received. They hung pictures on the walls and once the lampshades and curtains were up, it already felt homely.

They visited a second-hand furniture shop and with help from Tony and his pickup, they soon had a bed, small table and chairs and a sofa. The flat with a miss mash of colour schemes, a wooden armed sofa with pink floral cushions clashed with the plaid red curtains, but it didn't matter.

They each took some of their bedroom furniture and suddenly the flat was furnished. The only thing missing was a washing machine. The money David had saved to pay the deposit and first month's rent along with the items they had bought, meant that there wasn't enough to stretch that far, but they could live without one to begin with.

They spent their days getting organised and evenings snuggling up on the uncomfortable sofa watching the newly installed cable television. She was glad she'd agreed to move in with David, it was the right decision, she was happy.

David returned to work at the beginning of January. And on his first morning back, Tracy handed him a lunchbox which she had lovingly made, kissed him goodbye and waved him off from the bedroom window as he walked across the path towards the car.

She spent the day cleaning and hand washing clothes and enjoyed cooking dinner in readiness for when David returned home from work. He arrived home at teatime and was greeted by a strong floral scent of fabric softener as clothes hung from every radiator and a cottage pie in the oven waiting for him.

"You spoil me." David said as he reached over to Tracy and kissed her.

"Anything for my hard-working man." She chuckled, feeling suddenly very adult.

A few weeks after David returned to work, the novelty was starting to ware off. There was only so much housework that needed to be done in their little flat and Tracy was starting to feel lonely.

A phone had recently been installed, so Tracy was now able to call her mum and she did often, sometimes several times a day when David was at work, for all manner of random reasons. The reality was, she missed her. It was difficult for them to see each other due to their locations and as neither of them drove, they relied on Peter or David.

Now that Tracy was settled, she decided it was a good time to finally invite her friends over. They paid her a visit one Friday afternoon after they had finished work, baring a beautiful purple orchid as a housewarming gift.

"It's beautiful, thank you." Tracy said as she hugged them both. I have just the place for it and put it on the kitchen windowsill, where it would get the most amount of sunlight.

Tracy gave them a tour of the flat which took all of two minutes before making tea. She hadn't seen her friends since before Christmas and missed seeing Jo when she was home from university. They had lots to catch up on and hadn't realised how late it had got until David appeared in the living room doorway.

"Hi." Said Simone, who was the first to notice. "Nice place you have."

"I didn't realise we were expecting guests?" David said, ignoring Simone and staring directly at Tracy.

"We've stayed too long." Francis said and stood holding her empty mug.

"The girls came around to see the flat. We had so much to catch up on, I don't know where the time went." Tracy said, feeling slightly embarrassed by David's rudeness.

Tracy saw Francis and Simone to the door and hugged them goodbye. Shutting the front door behind them, she leaned against it, considering what to say to David. She felt so angry.

When Tracy walked back into the living room David was stood with his arms crossed as if waiting for their altercation.

"What the hell is wrong with you?" Tracy yelled.

"What's wrong with me? What's wrong is, I've been at work all bloody day. I come home looking forward to seeing my girlfriend and enjoying a nice quiet dinner, to find a house full and no fucking dinner." He paused, took a breath, and then continued "Some warning would have been nice, or better still they've gone before I get home and even better than that, they don't come at all!" And with that he stormed passed her and left the flat slamming the front door behind him.

Tracy burst into tears. What had she done wrong. She hardly saw her friends these days and David had only seen them a few times, although each time had resulted in an argument. She didn't understand the issue, other than she hadn't gotten around to making dinner and perhaps she should have mentioned they were coming over. But she had avoided mentioning it, encase it had led to an argument. Maybe she was wrong to do that and should have forewarned him that they were coming, and at the very least she should have prepared him a cooked meal.

She started preparing dinner, thinking that David would soon come home once he had cooled off. She made a chicken curry using a jar of korma and kept it warm whilst she waited. It was now seven p.m. and her stomach rumbled.

Whilst waiting she sat on the sofa and switched on the television, flicking through channels but not actually paying any attention to what was on. At nine p.m. she walked over to the bedroom and looked out of the window, she was surprised to see David's car in the parking bay, yet there was no sign of him. And it was too dark to make out if he was in the car or not. She assumed he must have just parked up and would walk through the door any second and went into the kitchen to begin dishing out dinner.

But twenty minutes later there was still no sign of him.

It was a further hour before she eventually heard David crashing through the front door. She walked into the hallway and could see him holding what was left of a bag of chips, he staggered towards her pointing to the bag.

"I got my own fugging dinner." He slurred and staggered into the living room, collapsing onto the sofa, still holding his chips.

She followed him. She wanted to tell him that she was sorry for earlier and also to tell him how unreasonable he had been. But it was no use, she would not get a conversation out of him in that state.

Tracy went into the kitchen and scraped both plates of curry into the bin as angry tears flowed. Deciding on an early night, the washing-up could wait until the morning. She walked past David on her way to the bedroom, he was on the sofa snoring loudly and still holding the bag of chips to his chest.

CHAPTER 15

Tracy sat in the passenger seat staring out at the dark road ahead. Trees danced on both sides of the road to a storm that played out around them, causing the car to swerve as they leapt out in front, waving their branches in a wild frenzy.

Fierce rain lashed down onto the car, until it was no longer possible to see the road.

Tracy turned to look at the driver. The driver was Emma. Her signature long red hair flowed down her back. "Emma." Tracy called out, but Emma didn't respond. Instead, she tightly gripped the steering wheel in a ten to two position, fixing her attention solely on the road. "Emma." Tracy yelled again, relieved to see her friend alive. And without letting go of the steering wheel, Emma's head spun around to face Tracy. Her face was ghostly white, devoid of any colour and her emerald, green eyes had been removed and all that was left were empty eye sockets.

"It's all your fault." Emma said as they plummeted into a tree.

The impact of the crash instantly woke Tracy. It was the first nightmare she'd had in months.

Looking around at the shadows in the dark room, she tried to place herself. Her heart was pounding, and she was shaking. It took a few moments for her to remember that she was no longer in her childhood bedroom, and her parents were not coming to comfort here.

She switched on the lamp to disburse the shadows and reached out to wake David. She needed him to hold her, to comfort and reassure her. But all she felt was the empty space, remembering he had passed out on the sofa.

She thought about calling her mum, but it was the middle of the night.

A sudden sense of hopelessness hit, and she felt alone. She curled herself into the foetal position, pulled over the duvet and wept.

Tracy got out of bed just before eight. Unable to fall back to sleep after waking from her nightmare, she felt exhausted. She entered the living room to find David in the same position as when she had left him. She walked over to the window and dramatically pulled back the curtains, causing David to pull a face as daylight flooded the room.

"What time is it?" He croaked, licking his dry dehydrated lips.

"Eight o'clock." She replied, offering no further conversation, and disappeared into the kitchen to begin cleaning up.

A few minutes later, Tracy was standing at the sink washing up when she felt David's arms wrap around her waist.

"I'm sorry." He said with stale beer breath.

"What are you sorry for?" she turned, forcing David back slightly and hissed. "Sorry for being rude in front of my friends? Sorry for being angry that I invited my friends over to my own home? Sorry for walking out on me? Sorry for getting drunk? Or sorry for wasting the meal that I cooked you?"

"I'm sorry for last night. I was angry and needed to let off some steam. I walked to the Dog, the local pub up the road, got chatting to some of the regulars and had a few too many. I lost track of time; you know that feeling."

She leaned back against the sink and after listening to his excuse, said calmly. "Ok. I should have told you the girls were coming over. You seem to get arsey whenever I see them, so I purposely didn't mention it. I thought they would be long gone before you got home, but they weren't. And at the very least, I should have made dinner for when you got home."

David held his silence for a moment. "I get arsey because I don't like your friends. I don't want them here."

"What are you saying? They are my friends; you can't dictate who I have come and visit me."

"It's my flat!" He said, with a raised voice.

"It's mine too!" She stopped to take a breath whilst trying hard not to let anger get the better of her. "I am stuck here all day, ever day, when you go off to work. I'm far from home and find it difficult to venture out alone. As you well know. I get lonely at times. My friends wanted to see me, it's no big deal."

"They aren't your friends." He said slowly, through gritted teeth.

"Don't be so bloody stupid, of course they're my friends, we've been friends for years. You must still be drunk."

"I am not drunk. I heard them talking about you. I'm trying to protect you."

"What? What did you hear? And when?" she said shaking her head in disbelief.

"When they came to see you. That time when I stayed over for the weekend....... I need a drink." David stopped talking and reached into a top cupboard for a glass, filled it with water from the tap and downed the entire glass in one. Tracy said nothing but fixed him with her stare.

He continued. "You went to the toilet, and I went into the kitchen to grab another beer. On my way back to the living room, I overheard them talking so I stayed behind the door in the hallway listening to them."

"And." she said impatiently without taking her eyes off him.

"I couldn't work out who was saying what, but they were basically saying that you were to blame for Emma's death. They said you should never have let her drive that night."

"Your lying." she yelled, her voice wavering.

"I'm not babe, I promise. I've been trying to find the right way to tell you for months. When I saw those two-faced bitches yesterday, laughing and pretending to be nice to you,

I just saw red." He moved closer and reached out his arms to wrap around her, but she wriggled in protest and bowed her head, refusing to look at him.

"I am sorry for wasting dinner. I'll make it up to you and promise to cook something nice for us both tonight. But first, I really need to go to bed for a few hours. I feel shit."

Tracy lifted her head to meet his sorrowful gaze. "We're supposed to be having lunch with my parents don't forget. I've not seen them since last weekend?"

"Babe, I'm hungover and in no fit state to drive anywhere today. We'll just have to go next weekend instead." And with that he refilled his glass of water and walked off in the direction of the bedroom.

Tracy called her mum. She pretended everything was okay and said that David was coming down with the flu, as an excuse to cancel their lunch plans.

She hung up the phone, sat on the sofa and spent the next few hours alone with her thoughts. She tucked her legs in and rubbed her forehead, stunned at David's revelation. He had never lied to her before, so she had no reason to doubt him. But none of it made any sense. She had talked at length in the early days after the accident with her friends, and they all said she was blameless. Doubting who she could trust, tiredness took hold, and she drifted off to sleep.

CHAPTER 16

March 1996

"Wake up." David said, shaking Tracy. She'd been panting, waving her arms around and shouting words that made no sense.

"You've had another nightmare babe." He said, once she had come round. She was drenched in sweat, and it took her a few seconds to realise she was now awake.

"Was it another bad one?" David asked as he reached over to switch the bedside lamp on.

Tracy nodded. Unable to speak.

David pulled her into him and held her whilst rubbing her back until she finally fell back to sleep.

It had been six weeks since Tracy last spoke to her friends. They called, but she would hang up the phone upon hearing their voices. She needed more time to think things through. To find a logical explanation for what David had heard or maybe had misheard, but so far, she hadn't come up with anything. She missed them but couldn't afford to risk a confrontation. She worried that emotions would get the better of her and she'd not be able to stop herself from telling the truth. She was getting on with her life and she didn't want to drag it all up again, risking everything.

Emma was always in her mind, subconsciously tormenting her, ensuring that she would never forget her unspeakable deceit. She had learnt to live with the suffering guilt had inflicted, but it never went away. Emma even followed Tracy as she slept, entering her dreams, and turning them into nightmares.

Tracy had been devastated to learn of her friend's betrayal. But thankfully David stepped up, filling the gap that her friends once filled, he had been her rock. He comforted her when she felt down and spoilt her with random acts of kindness to make her smile. And, as he had done since the start of their relationship, would still occasionally come home from work baring small gifts to show his love and appreciation for her.

Tracy cleaned up after dinner whilst David ran her a bath. He changed out of his work clothes into a pair of blue shorts and a white t-shirt, having suggested a bath to help her to relax. She appreciated the gesture, but knew he usually only did this when there was something that he had wanted to watch on television. But she didn't mind.

She laid in the bath, relaxing, as the hot water sloshed over her, and foamy bubbles covered her entire body. The bathroom light was off, and the room lit by candlelight. The latest gift from David. She allowed her body to sink further into the water, until only her face was exposed, and she closed her eyes. Her ears were under the water, so she didn't hear the phone when it rang.

David sat watching television within reaching distance of the ringing phone. He turned down the volume on the television and picked it up.

"Hello."

"Hey David, it's Simone. Can I speak to Tracy please? I'm a little worried about her, she's not taking mine, Francis or Jo's calls."

David exhaled and quietened his voice. "Simone. Listen. Tracy's not in a good place at the moment." He looked nervously towards the living room door before continuing, conscious that Tracy could walk in at any moment. "She's struggling and I'm afraid you girls aren't helping with that."

"In what way?" Simone asked, slightly dumfounded by the comment.

"It's nothing personal or really anything you have done per say. You know how Tracy finds things challenging."

"That doesn't make any sense, she's been getting better, much better in fact." Simone disputed.

"She's taken a set back. She's struggling to leave the flat and her nightmares have returned. She's trying to put the past behind her and move on, but unfortunately, you and Fran and Jo reminder her too much of it. I've tried to reason with her and tell her that's irrational, but she won't have it. I think the best thing to do is to give her space and not call again, until she's ready to talk to you. In the meantime, I'll keep working on her."

"Ok." Simone said, whilst trying to think of what else to say. But before she had the chance to say anything else David said.

"Goodbye." And then the line when dead.

Tracy climbed out of the bath, wrapped herself in one of the slightly frayed, faded pastel stripped towels that her parents had donated and blew out the candle.

Dressed in her favourite cotton pink pyjamas with a small teddy bare pattern on the trousers, she joined David on the sofa. He was sat back in his usual position arms stretched wide and one bare leg folded over the other, giving the impression that he had not moved in the time she'd been gone.

"Nice bath." He said as she snuggled into one of his outstretched arms that folded around her.

"Yep," she said, sounding relaxed.

David and Tracy quickly fell into a routine. Visiting the supermarket each week to stock up on groceries, after David had finished work and picking up a fish and chip shop supper on their way home, as a treat.

Money was tight, and with input from David, she planned

meals to ensure they kept within their strict budget. A habit she had inherited from her mum.

Tracy looked forward to these shopping trips, despite having to overcome the initial anxiety, it broke the monotony of her week, of being stuck alone in the flat.

She had thought about attempting shopping alone whilst David was at work. It would be difficult without the use of the car, but it would give her something to do and by taking baby steps, she was certain she'd be confident enough to face it. She made a mental note to mention it to him.

Although they shopped on a budget, David had a penchant for luxury branded labels and would not compromise to supermarket own brands, even though they costed significantly less. She tried and failed each week to convince him that it all tasted the same. She'd teased him and called him a snob, and he would laugh it off and argue that it tasted better, and that he was entitled to a few little luxuries.

David had come to expect his dinner ready and waiting for him when he returned home from work and unless it was a pre-arranged grocery shopping night, Tracy happily obliged.

And today, as per the meal plan, they'd prepared, David would return home expecting sausage and mash for dinner.

In the kitchen and ready to start cooking, Tracy rummaged through the cupboard and realised she had run out of potatoes. She wasn't fazed and considered it to be a good opportunity to venture out to the nearby convenience shop, for the first time. It wasn't dark for another hour, and it wasn't raining so if she hurried, she would make it back before darkness and in time to still make dinner before David returned home.

Butterflies fluttered in the pit of her stomach at the thought of leaving the flat alone, but she had wanted to go out and this was as good a time as any.

She pulled on her trainers and coat, picked up her key and made her way to the front door. She was just about to open the door when she remembered she didn't have any money. She'd not had reason to have money, not since they'd moved in together.

David came home from work to a bowl of spaghetti meatballs and hadn't release the menu change until he was halfway through eating.

"I thought we we're having sausages tonight?" He said, looking over at Tracy.

"Yeah, we were, but we ran out of potatoes. I obviously underestimated how many we'd get through this week."

"Oh, ok, never mind." He said and looked back at his plate to load up another forkful of spaghetti.

"I tried to buy more potatoes, or at least I planned to. I've not yet been to the shop up the road, so thought I'd be brave and go." David put down the fork he'd been holding and fixed his attention to Tracy. "I wanted to make you proud. But I didn't have any money. I think it would be a good idea to, maybe...." She hesitated, feeling slightly uncomfortable by David's stare. "Maybe leave some housekeeping money so that I can nip out and buy emergency supplies or top up the electricity metre, when you're at work." There was a tense pause.

"I don't think so."

"Why not?" She said feeling confused, she thought he'd be pleased and encourage her bravery, as he had done so many times before.

"I want to look after and protect you. What if you went out and something were to happen to you when I'm at work? You aren't in familiar surroundings around here. I don't want to be at work worrying about you. I can't afford to loose concentration in my job, it could be dangerous."

"Yeah, I suppose." She conceded.

"I'm glad you understand." His face softening. "When we go shopping next, we'll buy some pot noodles, and a few extra tins of beans encase of emergency." And with that the conversation was over.

CHAPTER 17

April 1996

It was a tradition for Jean to cook a family roast to celebrate Easter Sunday. They weren't particularly a religious family but always made use of the long bank holiday weekend for family time and indulgences.

This year, Jean invited Tony to join them. It would be the first time they'd met as an extended family and since he'd landscaped their garden the previous year.

They had been blessed with a warm spring day, most unusual for an English bank holiday, when it usually rained. Peter had wanted to mark the occasion with the first BBQ of the year. An accomplishment usually reserved until late May. But Jean was having none of it, so a roast it was to be.

Jean looked forward to Tracy's visits, they'd always had a close relationship and she found it hard adjusting to not seeing her daughter every day. Angela wouldn't admit it, but she too missed her big sister.

The dynamics were different between Jean and Tracy with David being there. Not a bad one, but she felt she couldn't fully relax and be herself. Unfortunately, due to the distance and with David and Peter's work patterns, it meant David was always with Tracy. The only way for Jean to see Tracy alone, would be to visit her at the flat during the week. But that would require several busses and Jean wasn't that confident herself when it came to travelling.

Tracy stepped out of the shower, wrapped herself in a towel and went in search of something summery to wear for the occasion. She deliberated for a few minutes then decided it was warm enough for shorts and settled on a pair of denim shorts and a green t-shirt. She pulled her hair into a ponytail and put on some light make up. And once ready, she joined David in the living room. He was sat at the table drinking a cup of tea and reading the newspaper.

"I'm ready babe."

David stopped reading the paper and looked her up and down, a frown appearing on his face as he did so.

"Are you going wearing that?" He said, disapprovingly.

"Well yeah, I was planning to. Why?"

"It's just, I don't think it looks good on you. It makes your legs look fat. Haven't you got anything more appropriate to wear?"

Tracy was stunned, she had a curvy frame, but never considered herself fat and had worn these shorts many times before.

"I suppose I do." She said, without knowing what else to say.

"Why don't you wear that dress I bought you a while back, the one with the blue dots on, that looks nice on you and hides your thighs."

She felt her face flush, from a mixture of shock and embarrassment and hurried back into the bedroom to change. His choice of words had upset her. *Is that how he saw her?*

It was late morning when Tracy and David arrived at the Hopkins house and was shortly followed by Tony's arrival. Peter showed Tony around the garden, in a similar way those renovation programmes on the television finish with a 'twelve months later' clip. Tracy and David trailed behind them and listened to Peter proudly show off the further enhancements they'd done since Tony's last visit. Peter's contribution being painting the fence. Tracy ensured to correct Peter and took the credit for the plants that introduced colour and character.

Tony offered advice on how best to keep the patio looking clean and Tracy yawned playfully as she and David walked away, back in the direction of the house.

When it was near time to dish out lunch, Jean called Tracy and Peter to help. Asking Tracy to lay the table in the dining room, and for Peter to cut the Pork, which was resting under a large piece of tin foil. Tracy was under strict instructions to use the best silverware from the drawer in the dresser. And under no circumstances, was she to use the everyday cutlery in the kitchen drawer. It was as if royalty were joining them for lunch. *Somethings never change.* Tracy thought to herself and wondered if she too would be the same one day.

Dinner was served into dishes that allowed everyone to help themselves. Another sign that Jean was trying to impress. She usually just slopped a bit of everything onto everyone's plate, whether you liked it or not. Dishes were laid out containing roast potatoes, honey roasted parsnips, cauliflower cheese, carrots, peas, and pork. And a gravy boat was full to the brim. Tracy's stomach grumbled and she was glad she had skipped breakfast.

"For desert we have sticky toffee pudding." Jean said proudly, before anyone had even loaded their plates. "Dig in everyone, don't be shy."

For the next five minutes, everyone eagerly loaded their plates and clattering sounds filled the room as they dished out. Alongside the occasional politeness of "oh no, you go first," if two people reached for the same dish.

Tracy looked around the table. She couldn't remember the last time six people sat around it. She was pleased that Tony got on well with the family, she supposed they were now one big family, in a kind of way.

Tracy ate most of her dinner and was just about to reach for more when she remembered what David had said about her having fat legs. So, decided not to get a second helping and placed her knife and fork next to each on the plate.

The table soon resembled a post apocalyptic state with leftovers on plates and crumbs strewn over the tablecloth. Blobs of gravy sat in random places, and everything now looked out of place. A complete contrast to how it had looked just forty minutes before.

Tracy stood up and began to collect plates.

"Leave it." Jean ordered. "Me and your dad will sort it later."

"Will we?" Peter joked.

Jean gently hit Peter's arm mockingly. "Why don't you all go into the living room, and I'll make us some tea."

Jean headed for the kitchen whilst everyone else made themself comfortable in the living room. Tracy sat on the floor, positioned in-between David's legs. Angela sat on the sofa, reserving the vacant space for her mum. Peter in the armchair that no one else ever dared to sit in and Tony in an identical chair at the opposite side of the room, reserved only for guests. The room felt a little cramped.

Jean joined them a short while later carefully balancing a tray of cups and saucers, a tea pot, milk jug and sugar bowl. *Another sign that royalty had joined them,* Tracy thought to herself. Peter, reading Tracy's expression as she stifled a laugh, gave her a look of contempt that signalled she should be more respectful.

Jean placed the tray onto the coffee table, and it wasn't long before they all cradled cups of tea. They chatted freely for a while and the conversation often referenced Tracy and David and about how well they had settled in together, as though they weren't in the room.

Out of nowhere, David interrupted the conversation and suddenly all eyes where on him.

"On the subject of how well we have settled in together. I just want to say something." He inhaled deeply. "I agree, we have settled in well, we make a great team and I love Tracy dearly."

There was a simultaneous "aww," from the room. Apart

from Angela who gestured with her fingers in her mouth, mimicking being sick. David pulled back to free himself from Tracy, got off the floor and turned to her. He pulled a small box from his pocket and got down on one knee.

"Tracy, I know I'm a little older than you, but when you meet the one you are supposed to spend the rest of your life with, you just know. I can't imagine life without you and one thing I've learnt, is that life is too short. What I'm trying to say is.... Tracy, will you marry me?"

There was a stunned silence, indicating that no-one was expecting the proposal and five pairs of eyes now fixed on Tracy.

"Yes." Tracy said, as she got up to hug David.

Everyone erupted with congratulations as they got up off their chairs, taking it in turns to hug the newly engaged pair and to marvel at the small diamond solitaire ring that David had chosen.

August 1996

Tracy's questionable logic determined that the wedding should be in August, as summer would bring the least chance of rain. A phobia that she still grappled with. Fortunately, the weather gods were looking down on Tracy and it was a glorious day.

The wedding was a small affair and held at the local registry office. Neither had large families and the guest list comprised of immediate families, Tracy's aunt and uncle and David's grandfather. David wasn't bothered about inviting friends, his only friends being work colleagues and a few people he had sort of got to know, down the Dog, their local pub.

She considered inviting her friends. She would have loved for them to help share her special day. But they had stopped calling and too much time had passed since they last spoke. Furthermore, she still wasn't sure how she felt about them after the realisation that they'd blamed her.

They followed tradition of not seeing each other before the ceremony. Tracy spent the night before the wedding at her parent's house and David with his dad.

Also, following tradition Tracy and her small entourage, consisting of her dad and sister were last to arrive at the registry office. Tracy wore a long satin ivory gown with puffed sleeves and a square neckline. She wore her hair up and a long organza veil with laced edging rested just below her shoulders. In her left hand, she held a modest bouquet of pink artificial roses and in the other linked her arm around her dad's.

"You look beautiful." Peter whispered into her ear. She smiled, feeling like a princess.

She was full of both excitement and nerves. Those feelings intensified as butterflies turned into bats when the double doors leading into the ceremony room began to open.

She could see the backs of David and his father standing at the end of the isle and staring at the registrar. Tracy and Peter began the slow walk down the isle, as panpipes played out of the sound system. Angela was her bridesmaid and followed behind wearing a simple long sleeveless pink satin gown which matched her pink hair, much to Jean's distaste. Tracy didn't mind. She liked the fact that her sister chose not to conform and felt confident enough to do so.

Her eyes darted around as she passed rows of empty seats, until she approached the front where the few family members sat. David turned and locked eyes on her, he smiled, and she smiled back. His double-breasted navy-blue suit and white shirt matched Tony's. Both hired from a nearby suit shop. A small pink rose pinned to their breast pockets matched their pink ties and Tracy's chosen colour scheme.

Half an hour later Mr & Mrs Wright walked out of the registry office smiling and holding hands.

The reception was held in a small Italian restaurant, and only a short walk away from the registry office. An area of the restaurant had been sectioned off for them, and on arrival they were greeted with love heart shaped helium balloons floating in the corner and a banner with congratulations written in gold lettering pinned to the wall.

A large round table had been laid to accommodate the wedding party. In the middle of the table stood a centrepiece of three large candles in a glass bowl surrounded by pink and white roses, hydrangeas, carnations, and green fern. And pink confetti were scattered over the table against a white linen tablecloth. It looked stunning, and unbeknown to Tracy, Jean had nipped out earlier in the day to set up the arrangement.

A few hours later they were back in their flat and high on euphoria and each other. It wasn't the big white church wedding she had dreamed of as a girl. But it had been the perfect day and Tracy looked forward to their future together, as husband and wife.

CHAPTER 18

September 1996

Their honeymoon consisted of a couple of nights in a bed and breakfast on the nearby island, The Isle of White. Known for its sandy beaches and clear sea. And they travelled by ferry, having boarded at the city's doc, a short distance from where they lived. The newlyweds spent their time relaxing on one of the island's beautiful beaches and walking along coastal paths to marvel at the chalky landscapes. It was their first holiday together and Tracy was able to truly relax for the first in a very long time.

Once back home, David returned to work and life quickly continued as it did before.

Tracy still hadn't ventured beyond the boundary of the flat alone but had become a regular within the communal garden. She had hoped it would give her an opportunity to meet some of the neighbours and perhaps make a friend or two, but most of them had full time jobs and weren't around during the day.

Her days were long and lonely, and she was desperate to seek a companion or at least find something to occupy her time.

Feeling more confident, she even discussed looking for a part time job, but David wouldn't hear of it. His old-fashioned values insisted she be a stay-at-home housewife. She missed him when he was at work, there was only so much daytime television and housework to fill her time.

Tracy had been back from honeymoon for a little over two weeks and was in the garden, hanging out washing and making the most of the late summer sun. Grateful to now owning a washing machine, thanks to her parents for having bought them one as a wedding present.

She hung a pair of David's jeans onto one of the vacant rotary lines and couldn't shake the feeling that she was being watched. She lent down to the washing basket on the grass below and picked up one of David's polo shirts, which formed part of his work uniform. And as she did, she noticed a scruffy looking cat staring at her from under a sparse section of the green Laurel hedge, that separated the washing lines from the parking bays.

She ignored the cat and continued to hang her washing. But the cat seemed to have other ideas and sauntered over and rubbed itself against her legs, as if to demand affection. So, she knelt and stroked the slightly small, dishevelled looking tortoiseshell, who purred with delight.

"You want a fuss? You're a little cutie, aren't you?" which caused the cat to meow.

The cat became a regular visitor of the garden and Tracy felt convinced it waited for her. She often found it sitting on the path leading out to the garden, then followed her around meowing as she pegged out the washing. She always made sure to stop and stroke the friendly cat once she'd finished, before going back inside.

Tracy wondered if the cat was homeless and so started to give it food and water. She made a point to spend more time in the garden, even on days when she had no washing to hang. She filled an old ice-cream container with water and left it under the hedge, refilling it daily. And took food from the fridge that she thought suitable for a cat. Ham and cheese seeming to be the favourite.

Tracy spoke about finding the cat to David, but he straight away dismissed any mention of it, stating how he hated cats.

So, she thought it best to leave out the bit about feeding it.

It was another dry and sunny afternoon, when Tracy picked up the basket of dry laundry that she had just unpegged from the washing line. She carried it along the path, heading back towards the flat's entrance door and communal staircase.

"You can't come in here." Tracy said, speaking directly to the cat as it followed and as if could understand her.

"Meow."

Tracy opened the door with one hand, whilst balancing the basket against the door frame with the other, but before she had a chance to close it behind her, the cat dashed through a small gap between her legs and followed her up the stairs to the third floor.

I have no idea how I'm going to explain this. She thought and spent the rest of the afternoon sat on the sofa with the cat affectionately curled up in her lap.

She'd grown quite fond of the cat; it had become her companion and was helping her through the lonesomeness.

"I need to give you a name." She said as the cat let out a deep throaty purr, which signalled it was asleep. "I'm not sure if you're a boy or a girl. So, you need something neutral." She thought for a moment. "I think I'll call you Comet." She had no idea what made her think of Comet, the name just came to her, and she liked it. And it seemed to suit he or she.

"I need to get up now and make dinner." Tracy said, as she prised herself off the sofa, lifting Comet and placing it carefully back in same warm spot that she had been sitting. But Comet immediately stood up and stretched before jumping of the sofa and following her into the kitchen.

Tracy was just about to slice a pizza in half, to share between two plates, already half filled with salad and potato wedges. When she heard the key turn in the front door.

"Hi." Tracy called out nervously, unsure how David would feel about the new addition.

"Hello, Mrs Wright." he said in a sing song voice. A greeting he had recently started to use, whenever he got home.

David walked into the kitchen and took one look at Comet, as it brushed against Tracy's leg.

"What the fuck is that?" He said pointing at the cat, as though it was an unidentified object.

"It's the cat I've been telling you about?"

"I can see it's a cat. But, why, is it in our flat?" He said, raising his tone.

"I've called it Comet and it doesn't have a home, David. Comet followed me in and just look at it. It's cute. And it makes me happy." She looked at David, pleading slightly.

"I don't give a shit how cute you think it is. I don't want that flea infested moggy in this flat. Do I make myself clear?"

Tracy nodded, not taking her eyes off Comet.

"Conversation over. I'm going for a shower and when I get back, I want that thing gone." And with that David stormed out the kitchen, ignoring the fact that dinner was ready.

Tears pricked the back of Tracy's eyes. She had built a bond with Comet and didn't want to see it go. But it was an argument she knew she wasn't going to win.

She lent down, scooped up the cat, held it tightly in her arms and slowly made her way out into the garden.

"I'm sorry." She said, as she carefully put Comet down on the grass. "I'm not allowed to keep you."

The cat cried in protest as if understanding her intent.

Tracy made her way back inside the flat and ate her cold dinner in silence.

Over the next few days Comet continued to find Tracy whenever she stepped into the garden. And it always tried to follow her back inside, and Tracy had to resist the urge to allow it.

It had been a week since Tracy was forced to abandon Comet. She'd hung washing out to dry in the morning but by lunchtime, dark grey clouds appeared, threatening rain.

Tracy took a moment to build up the courage to venture outside and once in the garden hurried to bring the washing in. Conscious that not only did she not want her almost dry washing to get wet again, she also didn't want to be outside when the rain started.

She made it back to the entrance door of her block, just as the first drops of rain fell. Comet sat by the door and cried, as if to say, it too didn't like rain.

Tracy didn't have the heart to leave Comet outside to get wet, so she caved and allowed the cat to follow her up to the flat. She would make sure to take it back outside before David arrived home, so that he would never know.

It soon became a regular thing and Tracy's little secret. Autumn had arrived, bringing unpredictable weather that meant she spent less time in the garden. And instead of spending her days in isolation, whenever David was at work, she allowed Comet to come up to the flat and spend the day with her. She placed a bowl of water on the kitchen floor and continued to feed it with whatever food she was able to scrabble together, ensuring any missing food would go unnoticed by David.

By mid-October, the nights were drawing in and Tracy always made sure to let Comet back outside before the light faded. She still didn't like being outside in the dark and wouldn't be able to face it alone.

She said her usual good night to the cat as she placed it down on the path outside. It meowed repeatedly, letting its disapproval for being turfed out known, which always made Tracy feel guilty.

"Hello, Mrs Wright." David said out loud when he got home and made his way into the kitchen. Tracy had her back to him as she stirred a tomato-based sauce simmering in a saucepan. He gently kissed the back of her head and as he did, noticed the small bowl of water on the floor which Tracy had forgotten to remove.

"Why is there a bowl of water on the floor?" he asked as he took a step back.

Shit. She thought and turned to look at David. "I erm...." She tried to think of a plausible explanation, other than it belonged to the cat. "I was cleaning the floor earlier and forgot to pick it up." She tutted to herself and rolled her eyes, to gesture being forgetful.

David leaned down and picked up the bowl. A small amount of brown fur was stuck to its rim and a few hairs floated in the water. An obvious sign that an animal had been drinking out of it.

"Why are you lying to me?" He shrieked, as he threw the bowl of water into the sink. Its remaining contents splashed out, covering Tracy in water.

"I'm so sorry." her words trembled. "I get lonely during the day; Comet keeps me company. And it doesn't have a home."

"I thought I made my feelings clear. That cat is not to come inside. You disobeyed me."

"Do I not get a say?" She challenged, the tremble in her voice turning to anger.

Without warning, David pulled back his hand and slapped Tracy hard across the face. She stumbled backwards, hitting her back against the cooker and knocking over the saucepan. Hot tomato sauce spilled everywhere, over the hob, the worktop, floor, and up Tracy's back. The jumper she was wearing saved her from being scalded, but she could still feel the heat of the sauce seeping through and needed to remove it quickly.

"Look what you made me do?" He sneered. "I'm going out. You can use that cat's bowl to clean this mess up." And let out a spiteful laugh, before turning around and leaving the flat.

Tracy crumbled to the floor and sobbed.

By the time David returned home a few hours later, Tracy had cleared away the mess, cleaned herself and had taken herself to bed. She couldn't face him again tonight and certainly didn't want to speak to him. So pretended to be asleep, with her back facing towards his side of the bed.

She listened to David's movements and heard footsteps as he walked down the hallway and into the bathroom. She heard the flush followed by the sound of the tap and then footsteps as he made his way into the bedroom.

She could smell the alcohol that saturated his body, as he clumsily got undressed and flopped down into the bed beside her.

"I'm sorry." He slurred. "You made me so mad. I need to be able to trust you, especially when I'm at work all day and it makes me wonder what else you have lied to me about."

Tracy ignored him, keeping her eyes firmly closed.

"Trace... Trace, wake up and listen to me." He said as he shook her shoulders then pulled her onto her back.

"I love you."

Tracy continued to say nothing and laid motionless with her eyes closed. She continued to keep them closed when David mounted her. And with no attempt of intimacy, or to gain consent, he forced his way inside her.

The next morning, Tracy didn't get up to see David off to work, nor did she make him a lunch box. Instead, she stayed in bed and only got up once she'd known for sure he'd definitely left the flat.

She walked into the bathroom and turned on the shower, desperate to freshen up and wash him away. She looked at herself in the mirror, her left cheek was red and puffy, and it was obvious she had been slapped. She certainly wouldn't be able to offer an explanation for this one, if she saw anyone.

She sat on the toilet to relieve her bladder and was forced to hold her breath, for the warm urine stung as it trickled out. She felt sore and as though her insides were bruised. And was not suppressed when she stood up and saw a small amount of blood in the toilet bowl.

Before climbing into the shower, she opened the bathroom cabinet and took out the blister packet of her antidepressants. She was surprised to see the packet was almost empty and could have sworn she had recently started a new packet. But then again, she wasn't feeling too great and may have been confused. She popped out one of the tablets and swallowed it like she did every morning, without giving it any further thought.

Tracy got out the shower wrapped in a towel and sat on the bed in a daze. She knew David had a temper but was still shocked at how badly he had reacted and for what he had done to her. Things had been great between them for so long and she thought that now they were married, things would be different. Perhaps better even.

An hour later, Tracy hunted through the fridge in search of food to take out to the garden for Comet. She couldn't risk having him in the flat anymore but was determined to continue feeding him at least.

She walked into the garden, expecting to see the cat waiting for her by the entrance door and was surprised to find that it wasn't there. She walked over towards the washing lines and called out its name as she held out a slice of ham in her hand. *That was sure to entice Comet from wherever it was hiding.* She thought to herself.

"Comet." She called again. But nothing.

Tracy walked around the garden, peering under the hedges, and looking in all the cat's regular resting places, until she spotted him asleep, a few metres away.

She walked over and bent down.

"There you are, I've been calling you." She said and expected the cat to respond to her voice and raise its head, but it didn't, the cat didn't move.

"Comet." Tracy said once more, as she reached over to stroke the cat. But its lifeless body was stiff. She lifted the cat, but it was undeniably dead.

"No." Tracy shrieked. "What happened to you?" She held the cat close to her chest whilst she considered what to do.

"I can't leave you here like this." She said and gently placed the cat back under the hedge. Tracy ran back into the flat, her breath panting by the time she reached the top of three flights of stairs and rummaged around looking for something suitable to bury Comet.

Within minutes she was back in the garden, carrying a towel, carrier bag and some large spoons to act as a shovel.

She wrapped the cat in the towel followed by the bag and spent the next couple of hours quietly sobbing as she dug a hole, large enough to conceal the cat without fear of foxes being able to get to it.

CHAPTER 19

Tracy was devastated. She curled up on top of her bed with multiple thoughts racing through her mind.

Had Comet been ill? It didn't look injured in anyway and there was no blood. Had someone done something to harm it? Had they intended to kill it? Had David done something to it last night or on his way to work that morning? He had made his feelings towards the cat known. Was he punishing her for disobeying him? How would she handle it? How would he react if she confronted him? He'd deny it of course, or would he get a sick satisfaction from it all? And there was the slap and the forced sex.

It was all too much for her to bare and she wept again. She couldn't remember how many times she had cried that day and she felt exhausted by it all.

She wanted to call her mum. She wanted to ask her to come and pick her up and take her home. Not forever, just for a few days, so she could rest without having to face David. She wasn't ready to face him just yet. But she couldn't do that. If her mum saw her face, she would know straight away that she'd been slapped, her dad would then get involved and there would be no going back. Their marriage would be over, before it even really got started. Did she want that? No. She still loved him. No, she adored him, and most of the time he was perfect.

She decided to act normal and not mention anything from the previous night. She would not give him the satisfaction that she knew Comet was dead, and that she had her suspicions to who caused its sudden death.

She scrubbed her nails to rid herself of the mud that

had accumulated under them, from digging, and thoroughly washed the utensils she had used, several times, just to be sure. She changed her clothes and splashed water over her face. Wincing slightly from the pain on her swollen cheek. And when all traces of her grave digging had been eradicated, she began peeling potatoes for dinner.

David arrived home without the usual "Hello, Mrs Wright." and found Tracy laying the table. He approached her cautiously and asked. "Have you still got the hump with me?"

"Nope. Why would I have the hump?" She casually responded, as her heart raced, and she could feel her face flush. So, she kept her head down placing knifes and forks on the table before walking back into the kitchen to fetch salt and pepper. And purposely avoiding making eye contact with him. She was determined to remain composed and not let on how she really felt. "I'm fine," she said as she walked back into the kitchen to dish out dinner.

"Have you had a good day?" Tracy asked, once they were sat at the table chewing on their pork, making small talk to break the silence and at least pretend to be pleasant.

"Not too bad, although I felt a bit ropy this morning, I won't lie." He said with a slight laugh, as if it was almost funny.

I'm sure you won't lie. Tracy thought to herself.

"What about you. How was your day?" He asked.

Well, after I cleaned myself and tendered to the external and internal injuries that you caused. I buried the cat that I'm pretty certain you murdered. So, overall, I'd say it's been a shitty kind of day. Is what she wanted to say but stopped herself and instead said. "Yeah, it was fine. I've not done too much today."

After dinner David ran her a bath as she cleared up. She knew it was the closest thing she was going to get to an apology from him, that or, he felt awkward being in her company. Either way, she didn't much feel like spending the evening with him so didn't hesitate to take herself off for a bath.

It was Friday night, so she had the entire weekend with

David and for once, she wasn't looking forward to it. She needed to think of another excuse as to why her parents couldn't visit them the following day, so that she could avoid showing them the unmistakable bruise on her face.

Tracy walked along the road with Emma by her side. Emma was wearing school uniform. Her white shirt loose over her grey skirt, rolled up to show more of her long legs and her white socks rolled at her ankles, above black shoes. The sun was beaming down on them, and the birds were tweeting loudly in surrounding trees that lined both sides of the road. Emma began to skip and held out her hand for Tracy which she took and the two of them began skipping in unison. They were both laughing.

Suddenly, the birds went quiet, and their surroundings feel deathly silent. Large grey clouds appeared in the sky, engulfing the sun, and turning day into night. Rain started pouring in sheets and Emma seemed oblivious to it, despite her wet hair clinging to her head and droplets of water dripping down her face. They continued to skip.

A car appeared in the distance heading in their direction. And as it got closer, Tracy released the car was heading straight for them. She let go of Emma's hand and shouted at her to move out of the way, but she didn't hear her. Tracy could do nothing to protect her friend, as the car ploughed straight into her. It sent her flying high into the sky and her body contorted as it hit the ground. The car stopped and Tracy recognised it to be a green mini.

"Help." Tracy shouted, but the driver ignored her. The driver turned their head and stared directly at her. She was looking at herself. For she was, the driver…

Tracy woke and sat bolt upright. Her body clammy and it took a few minutes for her breathing and heart rate to return to normal, her mouth felt dry.

"It was just a bad dream." She told herself. "No-one can hurt me now. It was just a dream."

David's back was facing her, and he continued to sleep. She was surprised she hadn't woken him; her nightmares usually did. With shaky hands she reached over and took a sip from a glass of water that sat upon her bedside table. Then glanced over at the alarm clock next to David and saw it was five a.m. She laid back down, pulled the duvet over her and tried to fall back to sleep. But sleep did not come, and she was still awake an hour later, so gave up trying and decided to get up.

Tracy made herself a cup of tea and sat on the sofa, she'd switched the television on to provide background noise but paid no attention to what was on. She thought once more about her options. *Could she leave David? Did she want to go back to her old life?* She realised there was a pattern to her nightmares. They were always worse when she felt anxious. So, she just needed to somehow find a way to avoid feeling anxious, if only it was that simple. She went to take a sip of her tea, only to realise it had gone cold. She wasn't sure how long she had been sat there, but it was long enough for her to notice daylight seeping through the closed curtains.

Tracy got up, walked into the kitchen, and poured the cold tea down the sink, she looked up at the clock on the wall, it was seven thirty.

She headed to the bathroom, brushed her teeth, and then opened the bathroom cabinet to take her morning tablet. Something in her subconsciousness told her to check the date on the side of the box. It was dated last week. She remembered now, David had picked up her prescription on his way home from work. That meant, at most, only seven pills should have been missing. She counted the broken blisters to find twelve were missing. There was no way she could have miscounted or taken too many pills. That only leaves David. He must have taken them. *But why? To poison a cat?*

Without hesitation Tracy ran into the bedroom. David was still sleeping when she jumped on the bed and began hitting him repeatedly, in a frenzied attack.

"You bastard. How could you!"

David woke suddenly feeling Tracy's fists pounding against his rib cage. He flung her off him and she landed on the floor beside the bed with a thud. She didn't feel it, she was too enraged, so immediately got back up and went for him again. But David was now awake and held her arms tightly to restrain her.

"Why?" She shouted. "Let go of my wrists, your hurting me."

"I'll let go of your wrists, when you calm down."

"How can I calm down. You're sick." She struggled in an attempt to free herself, but he was stronger, and it was no use.

"I see you figured it out then. You figured out that I killed that stupid flea bag."

"How could you?" Her anger turning into a cry.

"I needed to make sure for the last time that you wouldn't go behind my back again and bring it into our home. I couldn't trust you."

"But...To... kill an innocent harmless creature. It didn't deserve that."

"Maybe, I just don't want to share you. And, it could have been worse. At least I didn't kill a human... I didn't kill my best friend."

Tracy stared directly into David's cold dark eyes. The same eyes that she had once found attractive and comforting, suddenly repulsed her. She opened her mouth to speak but nothing came out. She was lost for words.

Sensing that Tracy was struggling with his revelation, his face softened into a sadistic smile. "You thought I didn't know. Well let me tell you. I know that Emma wasn't driving the car when it crashed. I know that it was you driving the car that night. You crashed the car that killed Emma. Only Emma isn't here to defend herself, or to clear her name and tell her side of the story. Poor innocent Emma." He slowly shook his head. "You took the cowards way out and faked it, so that your dead, no not just dead, murdered friend, would get the blame.

No wonder you can't sleep at night. It's not the trauma that's effected you all these years, its the guilt."

"H…H…How." Tracy stuttered.

"Well, this is the fun part. Did you know, you talk in your sleep? In fact, sometimes you go into great detail about what happened that night. You've even answered my questions when asked. I know everything. So don't you dare start on me for killing a fucking cat. It was a scrawny, little, abandoned cat. It's not like I killed a human."

Tracy shook her head in denial, but it was no use.

"What now? What are you going to do with this information now that you know." She whimpered.

"Nothing. I continue being your husband and you continue being my good little wifey."

"I don't understand?"

"What is there to possibly understand Tracy. I'll keep your disgusting guilty, not so little secret, as long as you remain my obedient wife."

With that he let go of Tracy's wrists, got up off the bed and walked out into the hallway.

CHAPTER 20

November 1996

Weeks had passed since David's revelation. Her insides had healed and the bruise on her face eventually disappeared. But she was forced to cancel yet another one of her parent's visits. Blaming it this time on a fictitious stomach bug, which they didn't question and wished her a speedy recovery.

Things changed. They were slow and subtle at first which Tracy barely even noticed. David stopped making an effort and the acts of kindness, such as running her a bath and buying random gifts. They were the first to go.

She became his possession. He had full control over her, and she was too frightened to object to any of his demands, or cruel remarks, regardless of how unfair they seemed.

Tracy couldn't relax. She felt constantly on edge whenever David was home and could feel the tension between them. A tension that felt so strong, it permeated the air like an invisible fog.

She also worried who else knew of her secret. *Had she blurted it out to her parents during one of her many nightmares?*

David never again mentioned her dream confession. But he didn't need to. She saw that look in his eyes, the look that told her all she needed to know.

Whatever David wanted; David got. If he wanted a cup of tea, she would make it for him. If he wanted sex, she would oblige, and the gratification would be solely his. If he wanted to watch something on the television, he would watch it. There wasn't to be any negotiation or compromise.

One night as David climbed into bed, he requested that Tracy get up first in the morning and wake him with a cup of tea. So, she set the alarm for six a.m., fifteen minutes before David would normally get up for work and did just that.

He had the upper hand and she sensed he enjoyed the power that came with it.

The following Saturday morning, David sat at the table reading the newspaper when he looked up and told Tracy that he was going to the pub that evening. It was unusual for David to give any warning, he usually only went to the pub when he had stormed out, after loosing his temper.

"Can I come with you?" Tracy asked.

"Why?" said David, wearing a confused expression.

"I thought it might be nice to go with you. I've not been before. I'd like to meet your friends and maybe make some friends of my own. Or it could be like a date night for us. Please, can I?"

"No, I don't think so. Tonight, is a lad's night and besides the Dog isn't the sort of pub that blokes take their Mrs's to."

Tracy didn't push it any further, there was no point. It would only wind him up and she would avoid that at all costs.

David left the flat early evening after shaving and changing into a shirt that was one of Tracy's favourites. Long sleeves with a blue and white chequered pattern.

"You like nice." She said.

"Thanks." He said in return and kissed the side of her face as he placed his wallet into the back of his jeans. "Don't wait up, I'm not sure what time I'll be back."

"Ok," she said. And with that the door closed and she was alone again.

It became a regular thing for David to go out on a Saturday night. And sometimes he would go on a Friday as well if money allowed.

He would never return home before last orders and was always drunk. She dreaded him getting home as she never knew what David she was going to get. Sometimes he'd be loving and soppy, and other times he'd be horrible and gunning for an argument or demanding sex. And it made no difference if she was awake or had pretended to be asleep.

Tracy always asked if she could tag along and sometimes suggested that they go out somewhere together, such as the cinema or out for dinner. David would always refuse with one excuse or another. She even suggested that David invite the lads over to the flat one night and offered to cook for them all. He laughed at the suggestion and wouldn't even entertain that idea.

Whenever Tracy asked David about his evening, or ask who was in the pub, he would get defensive and accuse her of being a nagging wife. What did it matter to her who was there, she didn't know any of them.

Tracy felt despondent. She was a prisoner inside her own home, living a life of solitary confinement. She had fort for so long to free herself from being a prisoner inside her own mind and now this was her life. It was no life. She had no friends, no independence of her own and spent most of her time alone, detained in the flat.

Conversation with David was now virtually non-existent, and her only purpose was to give him whatever he wanted.

Sure, they would go to the supermarket, and she saw her family once a week. That was of course unless David didn't want her to. And whenever she saw or spoke to her family, she was forced kept up the pretence that all was good. They thought she was happy and married to a wonderful man who had spent many months aiding her recovery. She was lucky to have a husband who provided for her, and they wouldn't hear a bad word, be said against him. And anyway, even if she did confide in her parents, she doubted they'd believe her. If only they knew how things really were.

She thought about leaving David, she often fantasied about putting on her shoes and running out of the flat or running away from him when they were at the supermarket. But he'd threatened to share her confession and it was too big a risk to take.

The following weekend Tracy thought of an idea. Maybe when David went to the pub, she could stay with her parents for the night. He'd hardly miss her as he wouldn't be at home, and she wouldn't have to deal with him drunk and in whatever unpredictable mood he'd come home in. She would have company, just like the old times. Maybe it could even become a regular thing, something for her to look forward to.

"I have an idea." She said, one evening over dinner. They were sat opposite one another, separated by plates of lamb casserole. "What if I stay with my mum and dad on Saturday night, when you go out?"

"Why?"

"So that I can have some company. It's lonely being here by myself all day when you're at work and even lonelier at weekends. You can leave me there when we visit on Saturday and my dad could bring me home on Sunday morning. What do you think?" A small smile of optimism appeared on her face.

"I think it's a bloody ridiculous idea. Married women do not spend nights away from the marital home, without their husband. If you go home, your parents will assume we are having problems. No. No, it's not happening. You'll have to find a film to watch on the television, or I could pop to blockbuster and choose you something."

Tracy knew when she was fighting a losing battle so dropped the conversation. Taking discreet deep breaths, to stop tears from forming in her eyes as she finished eating her dinner, which she no longer had an appetite for.

Saturday came and David went out that night as usual. And as promised, he did pay a visit to Blockbuster on their way back from seeing her parent's. Tracy was ordered to stay and wait in the car whilst he went into the video shop alone, choosing a film that was more to his taste, than hers.

Tracy picked up the video, which had been placed on top of the television and took one look at the cover. Two men in marital art uniforms were fighting each other with weapons. She placed the video back down and sighed.

She'd lost all hope of a compromise and couldn't see a way out of this horrible situation. She was exhausted. More tired than usual, but she was depressed and knew from experience that depression made you feel tired.

She realised she needed to see her doctor, she needed her medication to be reviewed, but she was still registered at the surgery in Toddington. As it was, her mother would call in at the doctor's surgery to collect her monthly repeat prescription for antidepressants. She'd then give it to Tracy, when they met. And once Tracy was back home, she would have to hand it over to David for him to collect, from their nearest pharmacy.

A doctor's appointment would require David taking time off work to take her. He'd refuse of course and tell her to stop being so pathetic. If her medication was to be increased, it would also be an admission that she wasn't happy, which he would take as a personal criticism, and he wouldn't allow that.

After David had taken some of her pills, she asked her mum to collect her next prescription early, making out she'd lost a few down the sink. Her mum did so without question, and she had received the new packet of antidepressants two days earlier.

Tracy felt desperate, there was no way out of this living nightmare. She concluded that the only way out, was for her to take her own life.

She opened the bathroom cabinet. A fresh pack of twenty-eight pills sat unopened plus and she counted three remaining in the open packet. *Thirty-one pills, washed down with a few of David's beers in the fridge ought to do it, she thought.*

But she couldn't leave without an explanation, she needed

to write a note before taking any pills. She needed to admit the truth and apologise to everyone she'd hurt in the process. She wouldn't blame David at all, she couldn't, he'd be the one to find the note and her. If he was blamed in any way, she knew the note wouldn't be seen by anyone else. She needed to think carefully about what to write. She would need to lie and make David out to be an exemplary husband. She felt sick at the thought. She hadn't realised but the tears that had been streaming down her face had stopped, the fog that had filled her mind cleared, and for the first time in weeks, she felt determined.

Tracy ran herself a bath. A bath was always her go to place to relax and think. She would use the time to construct the note in her head, and then, when she was out the bath, she would put pen to paper. And then take the pills.

A few minutes later, Tracy sat in the bath rubbing a bar of soap over her body as she spoke out loud to herself.

"Dear David, Mum, Dad, and Angela. No. Dear my loving family. That sounds better, more authentic." She rubbed soap over her breasts and was surprised to find they felt tender. Was her period due? She had read somewhere that breasts can feel soar before a period and also in the early stages of pregnancy. She couldn't remember when her last period was, not that it mattered now anyway.

Tracy climbed out the bath, pulled on her dressing gown and went in search for a pen so that she could write her letter.

She walked into the kitchen, remembering that she had a couple of pens in one of the drawers they classed as 'the messy drawer.' They were kept in there for easy access to the calendar which hung from a hook on the small wall behind the door. She always marked a discreet dot to signpost the first day of her period and something in the back of her mind told her to check the calendar to see if her period was due. Today was the thirtieth of November, she scanned the entire month expecting to see a dot at the start of the month, but there wasn't one. She lifted November's page to check October and found a small blue dot against the second. That was eight weeks ago, which meant her period was four weeks late. The realisation that she could well be pregnant brought a sudden gush of nausea and with little warning she threw up the contents of her dinner in the kitchen sink.

How on earth could she be pregnant? David always wore a condom; he was a stickler for remembering. Apart from that one night, that night a while back, when David had forced himself upon her. He was drunk and angry and he didn't use a condom, not that night.

Her head spun, white spots appeared in front of her, and her breathing quickened. She recognised it as being the start of a panic attack and carefully managed to make her way to the sofa without fainting.

Although she didn't know anything for certain, her periods had always been like clockwork. The stress from the last few weeks had taken its toll on her and had meant she lost track of what day it was.

After several minutes, Tracy's breathing calmed but she couldn't think straight. Could she really put an end to her suffering if it also meant the death of an innocent child? Her child. *A foetus.* She corrected herself. *Not yet a child.* Then again, maybe a child would change David's attitude. Surely, he'd be thrilled to become a father. They'd never really spoken about having children, but it was a natural progression for a husband and wife to take, wasn't it? Besides, David couldn't hurt if she was carrying his child and he would have to allow her freedom once the baby arrived. He also wouldn't be so cruel to her; he'd want to set a good example to his son or daughter.

Tracy needed to think. She decided to spend a few days thinking things through and to see if she got her period. She needed to get her head around the possibility of motherhood.

Then, if she did decide to continue living and bring a child into the world, then, when the time was right, she would need to share her suspicion with David. For he would need to buy the pregnancy test.

CHAPTER 21

Several days passed and Tracy's period still hadn't arrived. She was starting to feel nauseous all day long but wasn't sure if that was as a result of pregnancy or nerves. Based on when her last period was, she worked out that if she was pregnant, she'd be about nine weeks. She really needed to find out for sure and guessed she'd need a check up soon.

Christmas was also vast approaching and marked the one-year anniversary of them living together. *So much had happened in that year,* she thought to herself.

David came home from work that evening in an okish mood. After dinner had been cleared away and they were ready for an evening of watching television, she finally plucked up the courage to tell him.

"David. We need to talk."

"Sounds ominous." He said. Not taking his eyes away from the real crime documentary, about a serial killer, playing on the television.

"It's important David. Can you turn the television off for a minute please?"

"Can't it wait until after this has finished?"

"No, it can't. I'm pregnant!"

"What?" he turned to look at her, with indignation in his eyes.

"Well at least, I think I am. My period's late."

"I'm always careful, you can't be..." he trailed off, as he stood and began pacing around the living room. He ran his fingers through his hair, the documentary no longer seeming important.

"Who's is it?" He leant over her and demanded.

"What on earth? David, it's yours. Why would you ask that?"

"It's not mine. I already told you, I'm always careful."

She could see his rage building as he leant further forward until his face was just millimetres away from hers.

"I said, who's is it?" He hissed and she felt his breath and spittle spray onto her face. She swallowed hard, afraid of what was to come and looked down at the carpet to avoid the venom behind his eyes. He reached behind her back and grabbed a fistful of her hair. And he pulled it hard, forcing her to look at him.

"Look at me. Are you deaf as well as being a whore. Who's fucking baby, is it?" He pulled her hair again, this time even harder until her head snapped back.

"It's yours. I promise you, it's yours. There's been no-one else." But before she had a chance to explain any further, he dragged her from the sofa and onto the carpet by her hair and she screamed. "Please, no, please stop."

He let go of her hair and she felt instant relief as she laid on the carpet. But it was short lived, as a few seconds later he kicked her hard in the stomach. So hard it knocked the wind out of her, and she couldn't breathe. And it took several long seconds for her breath to return.

She curled herself into a ball, in a desperate attempt to protect her stomach and pulled her hands over her head. She closed her eyes tightly, too scared to look, too scared to see what David would do next. She could hear him pacing and muttering incoherently to himself until he finally walked out of the living room, slamming the door behind him.

She stayed curled up for some time, afraid to move and too afraid to open her eyes. The television continued to play in the background, a dull noise that she paid no attention to.

Once she had left it long enough to suspect David was asleep, she opened her eyes, straightened her stiffened body, held both hands on her stomach and sobbed silent tears.

She woke fully dressed on the living room floor, having cried herself to sleep at some point during the night. She could hear David walking around, getting ready for work. But she remained on the floor in a silent protest, until finally hearing the front door click as it was being closed.

Her entire body ached, and she was unable to get off the floor without support. Using the sofa as leverage, she braced herself for the pain and pulled herself up into a standing position. She stood for a second to straighten herself. Feeling a little lightheaded, so she waited for the blood to circulate her body, before taking a step forward. She inched forward carefully but wobbled slightly and was forced to stop and steady herself.

After a slow walk towards the bedroom. She took off her clothes and stared at herself in the full-length mirror, which hung behind the bedroom door. A large purple bruise ran from her rib cage down to her pelvis along the right side of her body. She stroked her hand along the bruise and grimaced, it hurt to touch. She cupped her hands and held them to the bottom of her stomach. "I'm so sorry." She whispered. "I will protect you; I promise."

She pulled on her knickers and t-shirt and took herself to bed where she wept some more, unsure what to do. How could she convince David that the baby was his. If she was to remind him of that night when they'd had unprotected sex, it would involve an accusation of his violation, and she knew that would not end well.

Tracy was still in bed when David arrived home from work. She hadn't realised the time, nor that it was now dark outside. David switched on the hallway light and stood in the doorway to the bedroom cradling a six pack of beer and a pregnancy test.

"Here, you'd better find out for certain." He said, and tossed the test to Tracy, before taking himself into the living room, where she heard the familiar sound of a can being opened.

She sat up, momentarily forgetting her injury, until pain coursed through her torso, causing her to grit her teeth.

She slowly got up off the bed and made her way into the bathroom, locking the door behind her. She unwrapped the pregnancy test, not bothering to read the instructions, pulled down her knickers and sat on the toilet seat. She had expected to see blood in her knickers. Evidence of a miscarriage. Adamant that a pregnancy could not survive the kick it had received. But she was shocked to see that her knickers were clean. There was no blood.

She took off the cap from the pregnancy stick, which resembled a dry highlighter pen and held the tip between her legs. She tried her hardest to relax enough to allow the urine to flow but realised she hadn't had a drink all day and was severely dehydrated. She managed a small trickle and pulled the stick out to see one line appear under the word test. She assumed the stick had captured enough and replaced the cap before setting it face down on top of the sink, so that she could resist the temptation of staring at it. She picked up the box and read the back which stated that results could be read after three minutes. She had no way of telling the time, but decided to wait until she was certain several minutes had passed.

She wiped herself dry, pulled up her knickers, flushed the toilet and washed her hands.

She perched on the side of the bath, contemplating her next step. *What would she do if the test was positive? How would David react given his outburst last night?*

Tracy couldn't wait any longer, so after a few minutes she walked over to the sink and picked up the test. She turned it over and could clearly see two blue lines. She was pregnant.

She continued to hold and stare at the test for at least a minute. Realising that she was nearer to the front door then the living room, she wondered if she should run out of the door rather than face David. But before she could make her mind up, she heard a knock on the bathroom door.

"I've made you a cup of tea." Came a gentle voice from the other side of the door.

Tracy remained silent.

"Have you done it?"

She wavered for a moment and then said "Yes." nervously.

"Open the door?

She ignored him again.

"Please Tracy, open the door and let me in."

She hesitated for a moment longer, there was no way out, she had no choice other than to face him. She slid back the lock and opened the door.

CHAPTER 22

Tracy held out a trembling hand and handed David the test. He immediately saw two lines and tears ran down his face.

"I'm so sorry Tracy." He said wrapping his arms around her. She stiffened, unsure what to say or do. David broke away from the embrace and cradling her with one arm, guided her into the living room and onto the sofa.

He sat down besides her, his face ashen and eyes red.

"I should never have doubted you. I know condoms aren't 100%, and all that. I'm sorry. I need to trust you. I mean, I do trust you. It's just after the cat incident, where you lied to me, I couldn't stop thinking about it. And then when you told me about how you deceived everyone into thinking Emma was the driver. I never thought you were capable of betrayal Tracy. But you are." David was aware he was rambling.

"David, bringing a cat into our home is slightly different to being unfaithful. I have never considered going with other men. You are my first, and my only. I love you. And as for Emma, I was wrong and I must live with that decision every day, for the rest of my life. I cannot undo what I have done."

"I know all that deep down. I get insecure, especially with you being alone all day." He tilted his head to look down at the carpet between his open legs. "My mum once cheated on my dad. I was only seven but remember it like it was only yesterday. She even left us for a while. She walked out on dad and me." He paused, Tracy took his hand, and he looked back up at her. "She came home eventually. I can't remember exactly how long she was gone for, it might have only been days, but it felt like a lifetime. From then on in, I was scared to leave her alone, even when she fell ill a few years later. I could never trust her completely."

"I'm sorry that happened to you, that's awful, but I'm not your mum. I love you, David. I want nothing more than for us to work and raise a family together. But I'm scared. I'm scared of you."

He looked back at the carpet. "I know you are I don't know what to say. I just get so angry, it's like someone else takes over."

"And the threats?" It took David a few seconds to realise what she was referring to. He held his head in his hands and cried.

Tracy suddenly felt confident and took control of the conversation. "I've always wanted children. But I will not bring up a child in a toxic home. I just won't do it."

David raised his head once more, looked at Tracy and uttered. "I understand. I will change. I promise."

Tracy didn't respond straight away and broke the silence a few moments later with a conversation change.

"We need to eat."

David nodded.

Twenty minutes later, they sat back on the sofa balancing plates of cheese on toast on their laps and watching a soap opera on the television.

"I suppose we need to look for a bigger place. One bedroom isn't going to big enough." David said, with a mouthful of toast.

"I guess not. But can we afford to move to somewhere bigger?"

"There's talk about an opportunity for promotion at work, it's something I've been considering for a while. We'll definitely be able to afford a bigger place if I get promoted."

For the first time in a while Tracy felt hopeful. It was surprising how quickly the tables could turn and maybe this really would be the best thing for them.

The next morning David went to work as usual; it was Friday and Tracy felt a little apprehensive as to what the weekend would bring, but she needn't have worried. He returned home from work with a huge bunch of flowers, a magazine on pregnancy and stayed at home that evening. Opting for a night in with his wife over a visit to the pub.

"I need to see a doctor." Tracy said, laying on the sofa with her head in David's lap. "They'll need to register me with a midwife."

"Yes of course you do. Ring up on Monday and make an appointment."

"I can't go just yet though. I'll need to wait a while."

"Why?" said David, unsure why she would want to delay things. "Isn't it better to have a check up sooner rather than later. The pregnancy magazine said we might be able to hear the heartbeat soon."

"I can't go until I'm healed, I can't show the doctor this." She sat upright and pulled her t-shirt up to reveal the large purple bruise which spanned the left side of her torso."

David stared at the results of his handy work. His face turning crimson, as the memory of what he'd done to his pregnant wife, came flooding back. Unsure what to say and feeling awkward, he simply asked. "Does it hurt?"

She nodded, pulled her top back down and said nothing further.

David needed to say something to break the awkward silence and deflect the conversation away from his act of aggression.

"Why don't we go out tomorrow and buy a Christmas tree?" he eventually said.

"Really." She replied, taken a little by surprise.

"Yeah, why not."

"Ok, that would be nice."

Tracy imagined the weekend to be how normal couples spent their weekends together.

They went out on Saturday morning and fort the crowds of Christmas shoppers who rushed about to buy their presents, despite there still being three weeks to go. Tracy felt a little nervous at being surrounded by so many people, and remained alert to the various sights and sounds, of the hustle and bustle. Yet, felt safe being with David, who never once let go of her hand.

Following visits to several different shops, they had become the proud owners of a six-foot Normandy artificial Christmas tree and enough decorations to decorate a tree at least three foot bigger.

They took a detour on their way home to visit Tracy's parents. They'd already discussed and decided not to tell them they were to become grandparents, until Tracy had at least seen a doctor. It was hard not to say anything, and she suspected their beaming smiles might have given them away. But it didn't, or if it had, they were respectful and didn't say anything.

By the end of the weekend their living room resembled Santa's grotto. Plastic chains hung from the ceiling in various shades of gold, purple and silver and the large tree stood in the corner, having moved the television over to make space. Glittery baubles hung from branches, and several strands of red tinsel wrapped its edges, alongside colourful plug-in lights that twinkled. And a gold star sat proudly on the very top.

CHAPTER 23

December 1996

Tracy monitored her bruise and watched as the purple faded to yellow before eventually disappearing. A week before Christmas, she informed David that she was now ready to see the doctor.

"Why don't you ring up in the morning and make that appointment?" He said with a smile.

"I will, but I've been thinking." She said, as she began recalling her pre rehearsed speech. "My doctor is in Toddington. Wouldn't it make more sense to move doctor's surgery to the one nearby? It would be more convenient for both of us?" She paused for a moment to let it sink in. Hopeful that he'd agree as it would give her some independence, even if only a little. "I'll be back and forth during the pregnancy and probably again once the baby's born. If you're applying for a promotion, you can't be taking too much time off work and besides you'll loose money. And we need every penny."

David's face hardened. She panicked that she had pushed him too far and watched in silence as he considered her request.

"Let me think about it."

The next morning Tracy woke first to the sound of the alarm and hurried into the kitchen to make David's morning cup of tea.

She placed the steaming mug down on his bedside table.

"Time to wake up babe." She said, with a light hand on his

shoulder.

David sat up, rubbed his eyes, and yawned as he came too, reaching for the cup. "Thanks babe."

Tracy handed David's lunchbox to him as he was getting ready to leave the house. "Thank you." He said and leant forward to kiss her. "Oh, and I've given the change of surgery some thought. I think you are right; it would make more sense to move doctor's surgery. But let's not do that just yet."

Tracy felt deflated.

"I'm just thinking, we are looking to move and there's no saying it will be in this area. You don't want to move surgeries twice. Stay at Toddington for now, until we move. Ok?"

Tracy nodded in agreement. She supposed he had a point and at least he had agreed to the move when the circumstances allowed. She considered that to be a win, be it small.

"I'll ring up this morning and make that appointment.

Two days later and three days before Christmas, David and Tracy sat in Doctor Armstrong's office.

Doctor Amstrong had been Tracy's doctor since she was a little girl. He had supported her through her ordeal and was well versed with the trauma she had suffered.

She guessed him to be in his late fifty's. His hair was grey and in need of a cut and wiry hairs sprouted out the sides of his ears, matching his unkempt grey beard. It was evident that he no longer cared about his appearance and then Tracy remembered, he'd tragically lost his wife a while back.

"So, what brings you here today, Tracy?" Doctor Armstrong asked in a friendly yet authoritative tone.

"Tracy's pregnant." David answered before Tracy could even open her mouth.

"Ok." Doctor Armstrong replied, already making his mind up that he didn't care much for Mr Wright. He ensured to direct his gaze towards Tracy, to encourage her to speak. She met his gaze and said.

"My period's late and I've done a home pregnancy test."

"And I presume the test gave a positive result?"

"Yes, it did doctor."

"Well in that case, I'm pretty confident that means you are indeed pregnant."

"Do you not need to do a test yourself to confirm?" asked David.

"It's not necessary. All I can do here is test Tracy's urine with a dip stick, which detects levels of hormones. It is virtually the same as the test you buy over the counter at the chemist. So there really is no point. And besides, your midwife will take some bloods during your first appointment to check all is well, and that too will confirm hormone levels to further validate the pregnancy, in lieu of your scan. Which you can expect to have at around twenty weeks. But first, we need to work out how far gone you are. Do you remember when the first day of your last period was?"

"It was the second of October." She said.

Doctor Armstrong picked up a round cardboard chart and played around it for several seconds.

"I make you to be eleven weeks pregnant, and your baby should be due around the ninth of July. I'll need to make an urgent referral to the midwife, as I would ideally have liked your first appointment to have been between ten and twelve weeks. Unfortunately, though, with it being Christmas your first appointment is now likely to be thirteen weeks."

"Should we be worried?" David asked.

"Not at all. I'll do some basic checks now and check Tracy's blood pressure, then I'll see if I can hear the baby's heartbeat through my stethoscope. Providing Tracy is fit and well and I believe she is, the slight extra wait won't make much difference." Doctor Armstrong looked down at his notes. "Are you still taking your antidepressants?"

"Yes, I am. Should I continue taking them?"

"Yes. I believe you should. They won't harm the baby in any way, and you want to avoid putting yourself under any unnecessary stress."

"Why would Tracy be stressed? I'm taking good care of her." David interjected.

"I'm not suggesting anything to the contrary. It's just stopping antidepressants can put your body into withdrawal which can be stressful, and we want to avoid that at all costs." Turning back to Tracy the doctor asked. "Are you still suffering from nightmares?"

"Yes, I still get them now and again."

"And you're getting out and about more these days?" He said, as more of a presumption then a question.

"She is. We go out all the time." David said, feeling his hackles rise. Doctor Armstrong's meaningful questions felt to David like a personal accusation.

"Very well. Let's take your blood pressure."

Doctor Armstong proceeded to take Tracy's blood pressure; it was normal. He then asked her to climb up onto the bed.

"Shall we see if we can hear your baby's heartbeat? But don't be alarmed if we can't hear it. It's still very early. Sometimes we can hear it and sometimes we can't, at this stage of pregnancy."

Tracy pulled up the grey jumper she was wearing and pulled down her leggings, stopping at her bikini line so that he stomach was on full show.

Doctor Armstrong placed the cold chest piece of the stethoscope onto her stomach and moved it around whilst Tracy and David waited silently. After nearly a minute Doctor Amstrong pulled the ear tips away from his ears. "Your baby has a strong heartbeat. Would you like to hear?"

Tracy nodded and Dr Armstrong passed her the headset. She listened intently to the rhythmic gallop of the heartbeat and was instantly overpowered with a feeling of pure love for her unborn child.

It's our baby!" She said, with a lump in her throat.

"It is indeed. Congratulations." Doctor Armstrong said, with a smile. Tracy passed the headset to David, and he squeezed her hand signalling that he too, could her the heart beating.

As Tracy pulled her clothes back into place and readied herself to leave. Doctor Amstrong sat back at his desk and said.

"I'd like to see you again in just over four weeks. You can either make the appointment as you leave or give us a call in the New Year. We will contact you regarding your first appointment with the midwife. Do you have any questions at this stage?"

They both shook their heads in unison.

"Very well. Take care Tracy, congratulations once again and have a wonderful Christmas."

Once they were back in David's car, he turned to Tracy. "I don't like that doctor. First thing tomorrow I'm going to call the surgery near to us and arrange for you to be transferred." Tracy felt a pang of nerves. Admittedly, it was what she had asked, but she felt it made more sense to at least now see the midwife before moving surgeries, given that things were already delayed.

"Shouldn't we wait until I've at least since the midwife and had my bloods checked?"

"We're not going back to that surgery. If we must wait, then so be it."

Tracy didn't say anymore. She knew any attempt to overrule him would be futile and she didn't want to provoke him any further. She felt saddened, this was supposed to be a happy experience. She had expected them both to shed tears of joy and excitement when they got back to the car, but instead there was tension.

CHAPTER 24

January 1997

Christmas day was spent at the Hopkins residence with Jean insisting that Tony join them.

Having had the pregnancy confirmed by the doctor and both families being together, David and Tracy took the opportunity to share their exciting news.

Everyone was thrilled to learn of the new addition. Especially Jean, she couldn't have been happier. She was excited to become a grandmother and so proud of her eldest daughter. She had overcome so much over the past few years and was now married with a baby on they way.

When David returned to work after the Christmas break, the factory advertised the vacancy for the long-anticipated supervisor's role. He'd worked at the factory for nearly eight years so felt it was now time for progression and immediately submitted his interest.

He also followed through his intention to register Tracy at their local doctor's surgery. And as she suspected, it did cause a delay in her being seen by a midwife. And it was mid-January before she was in the system and able to have an appointment. Which happened to be the day after David's interview.

David was advised to expect a wait of several days before finding out if he'd been successful or not. He didn't cope well with stress and the suspense was agitating him. Tracy too, disliked the wait. She'd noticed he'd become more anxious, short tempered and in general a lot less tolerant.

The appointment with the midwife consisted of lots of box ticking as questions about hereditary illnesses and Tracy's medical history were asked. David booked the morning off work to be there with Tracy, who by now was fifteen weeks pregnant. He attempted to ask questions, such as, how to prepare for the birth and how to spot early signs of labour. Most of his questions were dismissed, with responses from the midwife such as "All in good time and let's focus on the here and now, there's plenty of time to discuss that." And once again, David felt the appointment to be incredibly frustrating.

David went into work after the appointment. And returned home a few hours later to find Tracy finishing off dinner. She was in a great mood; her energy levels were increasing and so far, all seemed well with her pregnancy.

She immediately sensed however, that David was not in a good mood.

"Have you heard anything?" Tracy asked, wondering if perhaps he'd received bad news.

"No not yet, and I wish you would stop asking."

"Sorry." she said. "I won't ask again." Even though that was the only time she had asked. "Sit down, I'm dishing up."

A few minutes later Tracy carried their dinner plates through and placed them onto the dining table.

"What is it?" David asked quizzically.

"It's a beef stew. I've not made one before and thought I'd give it a go."

She sat down besides David, placed a forkful into her mouth and realised she wasn't keen. It wasn't often she'd cooked a bad meal but this one lacked flavour and was way too salty. She avoided asking David if his was ok and didn't want to admit that hers wasn't, so she continued to slowly eat. A few mouthfuls later, David spat his out in disgust.

"This is disgusting and tastes like shit. I can't eat that."

"I'm sorry. It was my first attempt at making stew and I agree it's not the best."

"Not the best. Not only does it look like dog food, but it also tastes like...." He stopped himself, trying to think of how to finish the sentence. "Well, it tastes too bad to feed to a fucking dog. You'd better go and find something else to cook and don't take too long, I'm starving."

Tracy felt fed up, her good mood suddenly morphed into disappointment. She collected both almost untouched plates and took them into the kitchen, then looked inside the fridge for inspiration on what else to cook. David followed her in and took advantage of the fridge being open, by reaching over her and taking a cold can of beer, to take to the living room.

They were due to go shopping the following day, so the cupboards and fridge were scarce. She found several eggs, a little bit of cheese that was drying at the ends and half a bag of frozen oven chips in the freezer.

"I can just about muster up omelette and chips, will that be, ok?" Tracy shouted from the kitchen.

"I suppose it will do." He replied.

The rest of the night was spent in companionable silence. Tracy was too frightened to say anything, for fear of antagonising David, although it was clear he wasn't in a talkative mood.

The following evening, Tracy got ready for their weekly shopping trip. Her small bump now slightly visible, hid behind a baggy jumper worn over a pair of slight thread warn leggings. This seemed to be her uniform of late. She couldn't remember the last time she'd had new clothes and knew at some point she'd need to invest in a couple of maternity outfits. When she had tried to squeeze into her old clothes, proudly showing her bump. David had ridiculed her declaring that she looked like a pig, and she was forced to change.

She sat on her bedroom floor and used the mirror that hung from behind the door to apply a little makeup. She wore blusher, mascara, and lip gloss, just enough to make her look a little less washed out. Her hair was tied in a ponytail, her perm having long since fallen out, and all that remained were natural waves. She ran a brush through the loose strands of hair and sprayed herself with impulse. "That'll do." She told herself.

She looked over at the alarm clock on David's beside table. It was four thirty, she expected David home any minute. He liked her to be ready for his arrival so that he wasn't left hanging around and would say, the quicker they left they quicker they'd return.

She got her shoes and coat out ready and sat on the sofa while she waited. Fifteen minutes passed and there was no sign of David. *Maybe he got caught up in traffic*, she thought to herself. She turned on the television, deciding to flick through the channels to kill some time. Another ten minutes passed and there was still no sign of him. If David was late home, it meant they'd be later getting back from shopping and her stomach rumbled at the thought of a late fish and chip supper.

Thirty minutes later, Tracy started to worry. *What if something had happened to him on his way home from work?* It had been a cold day and by the looks of it, the temperature had barely risen above freezing. What if there was ice on the road and he'd had an accident?

An hour later the telephone rang, Tracy answered it nervously on the first ring, fearing the worst.

"Hello." Came a merry David on the other end of the phone. She struggled to hear him, through the multiple conversations taking place in the background.

"Where are you? I've been worried sick." She said, forgoing any pleasantries.

"I thought I'd better ring to say I've stopped off at the Dog on my way home from work and will be late home."

No shit, she thought to herself. "But what about the food shopping, we were supposed to be going tonight?"

"Oh yeah." He chuckled. "We'll just have to go tomorrow night or something?"

"But we haven't got any food in, what about dinner tonight?"

"Stop nagging woman. Don't worry about my dinner, I'll sort myself out with something later. I'm sure we've enough in for my lunch tomorrow and for you tonight. Make the most of it and have an early night. I'll see you later."

Then the line went dead, and Tracy was left speechless. How could he be so selfish! Things were going great and now he was slipping back to his old ways. She walked into the dark kitchen and flicked the light switch. The strobed light blinked a few times before illuminating its surroundings. She opened the door to the cupboard that stored tins, packets, and such like, in search of something to have for dinner. It was almost bare apart from a few packets of crisps and a couple of slices of bread. She counted the slices, there were two, just enough to make David's sandwiches in the morning. She opened the fridge. It was a similar sight in there too. A small amount of milk sat in the door and a few slices of ham, and a bottle of ketchup were all that sat on empty shelves. *Fantastic,* she thought to herself and sighed, she didn't even bother to check the freezer, as she knew that was completely empty after using up the last of the chips the previous night.

She decided to make herself a cup of tea, retrieved a cup from the cupboard and slammed it down on top of the worktop in frustration as her stomach rumbled. She was eating for two and dinner was going to consist of a packet of ready salted crisps.

David came home a couple of hours later, Tracy was still awake watching television and was surprised it was so early being only nine p.m. Then again, she realised, he'd probably been in the pub since teatime. Cradling the remnants of a kebab he attempted a drunken smile that revealed a blob of mayonnaise in the corner of his mouth. He swayed in the doorway to the living room, before walking over and plonking himself down on the sofa next to Tracy. Her anger coiled in her empty stomach. How dare he buy himself a takeaway when she had gone hungry. She hated kebab ordinarily, but the smell of the cooked meat made her stomach rumble even more.

She pretended to watch television for a few minutes in an attempt to ignore David. But her irritation festered, until she couldn't stand it any longer.

"So, you didn't think to get me anything to eat then?" She snapped.

"What do you mean! I thought you'd be in bed and would have eaten hours ago."

"Well for your information, there wasn't enough food to make any kind of meal. All that was left was just enough to make your sandwiches tomorrow."

"Did you eat my bread?" He said with a mouthful of donner meat.

"No, because I know if I don't make your lunchbox in the morning, you'll get mad at me. So, I left the bread and only ate a packet of crisps."

"I hope there's still enough crisps for me to take to work?" He said, half laughing, half hiccupping.

Tracy stood up, she needed to leave the room before she really lost her temper.

"Where are you going?"

"Bed." She shouted.

The next morning Tracy woke and was surprised to see it was light outside. She'd become accustomed to waking to dark winter mornings, as first sign of light didn't appear in the sky until at least seven thirty, the time David usually left for work.

She looked over to see David's side of the bed empty and assumed he'd gotten himself up for work. Allowing her to lay in, as a way of an apology. Glancing at the clock, she saw it was twenty passed eight. A sudden twang in her stomach reminded her how hungry she was and of how much of an arse David had been.

Tracy pulled on her dressing gown and walked into the living room to find David fast asleep on the sofa with the empty kebab tray on the floor besides him. She hurried over and shook his arm.

"David, wake up."

"What." He grumbled.

"You should be at work. You're late."

David sat up, the realisation that he was undeniably late superseded the hangover that was yet to surface.

"How the fuck could you let me sleep in?" He yelled.

Resentment took over and she yelled back "It's not my fault you were too drunk to make it to bed and set your alarm."

"What did you say?" David said as he rose from the sofa and stumbled back slightly, the previous night's alcohol still not yet out of his system.

"Where shall I start? You went out last night without a care for your pregnant wife, who you left at home with no food and no means of getting any. You arrived home drunk, having sourced your own dinner without bothering to get any for me. You then fall asleep on the sofa, which is somehow my fault. You're a fucking joke."

"I'm a fucking joke, am I?" He said, as he pulled back his hand and delivered a blow to the side of Tracy's face. She fell backwards, hitting the wall so hard, the photo that hung of the two of them on their wedding day fell to the floor with a crash. She slid down the wall until her bottom reached the carpet and sat still. Too stunned to move and shocked by David's vicious retaliation, as he hurried around getting himself ready for work.

He reappeared a few minutes later and shouted "Why are you still fucking sat there? Go and make my lunch, I need to leave."

Tracy's cheek throbbed and there was a metallic taste of blood in her mouth. Shock took hold and caused a generalised numbness over the rest of her body. It lasted long enough for her to pull herself off the floor and force herself to hold it together, knowing he'd be gone within minutes.

She handed David his lunchbox as he reached for his keys.

"Bollocks." He shouted to himself, as he remembered he'd

left his car parked in the pub's car park.

Tracy said nothing and watched as he closed the front door. She listened to the sound of his heavy footsteps as he hurried down the concrete steps, taking them two at a time, and then she bolted the door.

CHAPTER 25

Dear David Wright.

Thank you for your interest in the production line supervisor role. I regret to inform you, that after careful consideration you have not been successful on this occasion. We will keep you details on file and advise if any other similar roles become available in the future.

Yours sincerely

J.L Jones
Senior Operations Manger

Tracy found the screwed-up note whilst gathering dirty laundry and emptying the pockets of David's trousers that had been left on the bedroom floor.

She thought it at least explained his change in behaviour, but it didn't excuse it.

It was just a set back, she told herself. There was still five months until the baby was due. Plenty of time to look for other opportunities, and if they weren't able to move before the baby arrived, then they would make do. For now, however, that was the least of her worries.

It was lunchtime before she could bring herself to look in the mirror and she barely recognised the person looking back at her. The entire left side of her face was bright red and swollen. Her eye socket was so swollen it was virtually closed and it was already looking a dark shade of grey. It reminded her of the time when she was little and took her mum's makeup.

She heavily applied eyeshadow on her and her sister. She must have only of been five or six at the time and her mum went mad. She'd give anything to turn back time and be that young again. When her only worry was facing her angry mum.

David's foul mood lasted a while this time and it was always Tracy's fault, if ever he lost his temper. She didn't appreciate how hard he worked. She nagged. She failed to fulfil her housewife duties, to his standard. She made no effort with her appearance. She made too much effort with her appearance. Or she provoked him. Yes, she'd admit that occasionally she would stand up for herself and challenge back, especially when he was being cruel or unfair. Yet other times, most of the time in fact, she'd simply surrender, realising it wasn't worth putting herself and their unborn child at risk.

Small slaps generally healed within a day or two, punches and kicks to her arms or legs could be hidden under clothing and hair pulling left no mark. However, the bruising and swelling along the side of her face, after David had overslept, took almost three weeks to disappear. The hurt though, that lasted much longer.

Tracy was forced to cancel her sixteen week check up with the doctor. And she blamed intense morning sickness, the type that lasts well beyond the morning, on why she wasn't able to see her family.

May 1997

Sunlight poured through the curtainless window as Tracy laid in bed, listening to the early morning bird song. Warm sunny days always gave her renewed energy, everything seemed better with a bit of sunshine.

Another anniversary had recently passed and rather than speak to David about it, like she had on previous anniversaries. She kept this one to herself and pretended like it was any other ordinary day. And so marked the day struggling in silence, and alone.

She'd had been awake for ages and often evaded sleep these days, thanks to a bout of insomnia, the latest pregnancy trait. She glanced at the bedside clock it was only five thirty, but she decided to get up. There was a lot to do, and she'd make a head start instead of laying awake and waiting for the alarm clock to sound. And besides, her full bladder was also telling her to get up and it was unlikely she'd be able to hold it in for much longer.

She tiptoed across the bedroom floor, her nightie hugging her heavily pregnant belly. She could no longer see her feet and was convinced that if the baby didn't arrive soon, she would burst.

She reached the bottom of the stairs and was immediately greeted by removal boxes, they were everywhere. She couldn't believe how much stuff they had accumulated in the short time they'd been living in the flat.

She'd been itching to make a start. Desperate to unpack and turn their new house into a home. She wanted to get everything ready and in place before the baby arrived. They call it nesting. When a mother feels the need to sanitise everything and prepare for the impending birth of her child. She could relate but wasn't sure where moving house came into it.

Tracy made herself a cup of tea and started on what was left to unpack of the kitchen.

A month after David was turned down for promotion, another opportunity for a supervisor role was advertised, in which David was automatically short listed for. This time, he had been successful, and the extra income meant they were able to buy their first home. A small two up, two down Victorian terraced house in Chesterfield Avenue, a short walk from where their flat had been.

The house needed a refresh, but she didn't care, it was theirs and best of all they had a garden. She didn't realise how much she had missed having a garden.

The galley kitchen was at the back of the house and led out into the garden via a single back door. It was furnished with white outdated cabinets that had oak trims, and cream worktops matched the splash backs.

Tracy manged to unpack two boxes before it was time to wake David for work. Clutching a mug of tea, she made her way through the house and back up the stairs to the bedroom, where she expected to find David asleep. But as she approached the bedroom door, she could hear footsteps and was surprised to see that he was already up and about.

"I couldn't sleep." He said, as she opened the door.

"Me neither. But they say it's nature's way of preparing you for when the baby's here."

"I'm going to need more of that then." He said, reaching to take the mug from Tracy.

Tracy loved setting up the house, it felt more meaningful than when they had moved into the flat. For one, she had been involved in the process. She'd been allowed to have a say and they'd chosen this house together. That meant a lot to Tracy and for the first time she felt they were equal.

David's moods were still a little temperamental, although the last couple of months had certainly been better. Tracy had learnt to do as she was told.

She spent the rest of the day unpacking downstairs. They'd decided that the room off the kitchen was to be the dinning room. There was no hallway as the front door opened directly into the living, and as the dinning room separated the kitchen from the living room, it also doubled up as a passageway. Tracy placed newly purchased medallion patterned runners between the doorways to mark the passageway and to protect the carpet, as they would have to make do with the existing carpets for some time.

The house was very plain, as almost every room had beige carpets and white walls. She supposed it allowed them to move in without having to clean up garish decorations at least and in time, they would put their own stamp on the house. For now, she thought a patterned rug would at the very least inject a bit of colour.

The dinning room was sparse, for all that was in there was the table and chairs they had taken with them. The room was light as patio doors led out into the garden that benefited from the sunlight in the morning thanks to it being North facing. Tracy opened the patio doors to allow air to circulate, it was far too nice a day to keep them closed.

The living room took longer to unpack. Tracy paused, taking a look and considering where to start. Coat hooks screwed into the wall at the bottom of the stairs, leading to the front door. A large understairs cupboard provided plenty of storage and a beautiful ornate Victorian fireplace took centre stage in the middle of two white built in bookcases. Tracy couldn't wait to furnish them with ornaments and knickknacks that she would accumulate over time. As their current furnishings were limited, she would have to make do with a minimalist look for now.

The sofa sat in front of the window, separated from the bookcase by the small end table. Tracy dragged the television and stand into position against the wall opposite the sofa and was grateful it had casters on wheels. She couldn't work out where best to put the armchair and eventually settled with opposite the fireplace, so that its back was facing the passageway and understairs cupboard.

She spent a few minutes hunting around for the telephone and located it in a box, still to be unpacked. She plugged it into the nearby phone socket and placed it on top of the table along with a lamp, which was also a new purchase. By mid afternoon, she had finished unpacking downstairs and collapsed the boxes, before collapsing herself onto the sofa for a nap.

Over the next few weeks Tracy continued to work on the

house, unpacking the last few items, hanging photos, and preparing for their new arrival. She still had a lot of baby things to get but was slowly crossing items from her list.

David was shortly due a bonus from work and had promised her he'd use the money to buy a pram and a cot. Tracy had her heart set on a pram she'd seen in a magazine. She knew their nearest baby department store, situated at the edge of the city had one in stock as she had telephoned to check.

It was Sunday and David had slept in. He'd spent the previous night down the pub and was sleeping off the effects after too many beers. Tracy had become used to this, and had plenty to occupy her these days, so the alone time didn't bother her as much as it had used to.

She sat in the garden, enjoying her morning cup of tea. The sun was shining, and it was already warm. She ran through her baby list to see what else was left to buy. David's bonus was due on Friday, and he'd promised to take her baby shopping on Saturday.

Tracy was startled when she heard "Hello." through the fence.

She looked around, unsure exactly where the voice was coming from.

"Hello." Came the voice again.

"Hi." Tracy said, feeling slightly unsure if the greeting was meant for her.

"I'm over here." Said the voice.

Tracy could see a hand waving over the fence where a broken fence panel meant it was shorter than the rest.

"I've been meaning to say hello, since you first moved in, but I didn't want to intrude. I assumed that you had a lot on your plate with the move."

Tracy stood up and walked over towards the fence. Standing on her tip toes so that she could see over the top to put a face to the voice.

"I'm Margaret, but people call me Maggie. Welcome to the

Chesterfield Avenue."

"Thank you. I'm Tracy and my husband who is inside is David."

Maggie was middle aged, and Tracy assumed her to be a few years older than her mum. She had dark shoulder length hair tied into a low ponytail and wore blue jeans with a chequered shirt and was holding a pair of secateurs.

"Do you live alone?" Tracy asked.

"Yes, I do. I got divorced about ten years ago, thank goodness. It was the best thing I've ever done." She laughed at herself, and Tracy wasn't sure if she was meant to laugh along or stay quiet.

"I live alone, although I have a grown-up son James. He's twenty-six and has long since flown the nest. He's an electrician and lives up in Manchester."

"Oh, I see. We don't yet have any children, but we will have very soon." Maggie was unable to see Tracy's bump for the fence was in the way. "I'm pregnant and due in just over four weeks."

"Oh, how wonderful. It'll be lovely to see some young'uns on the street. The rest of us are all knocking on a bit. I suppose you're on maternity leave now then?"

"Sort of, I don't work currently. David prefers me to be a stay-at-home wife and once the little one's here, I doubt I'll have time for work."

"I understand. You must come over for a cuppa soon, I work mornings at the Post Office but am home most afternoons."

"That would be lovely, thank you."

"Tracy." Came the bellow of David's voice from somewhere within the house.

"I'd better go, David's calling me. See you soon."

"Bye lovey." Waved Maggie.

"Who were you taking to?" He asked as Tracy walked into the kitchen.

"Our next-door neighbour, Maggie, she was introducing

herself."

"What did you tell her?"

"Nothing really, just our names. We were only saying hello."

"I hate nosy interfering neighbours. She better not poke her noise into our business. Put the kettle on, my mouth's as dry as the dessert."

CHAPTER 26

After what seemed like a long week, Friday finally arrived, and David came home from work in a particularly good mood. Tracy was preparing a salad to go with dinner in the kitchen and hadn't heard the front door open.

"Hello, my lovely wife." He said from the doorway of the kitchen holding a bunch of flowers in one hand and a four pack of beer in the other."

"Someone's in a good mood." Tracy said taking the flowers from David. "Are these for me?"

"There are indeed. A little token to say I love you and thank you for all the hard work you've put into the house."

"Thank you, they're lovely. I take it, you got your bonus then?"

"I certainly did." He said as he put the beers down on top of the worktop and took out an envelope from his back pocket. "Five hundred pounds, all tax free."

"That's brilliant, and more than enough to buy the last of the baby things." She said with a smile.

"Yep and a few quid for your hard-working husband to pop down the Dog tonight?"

"I suppose." She said, rolling her eyes mockingly. "Don't forget though, you promised to take me shopping tomorrow."

"Yes, I haven't forgotten. I'll take one of these into the living room." Pointing to the beers. Shout when dinner's ready."

Tracy put the remaining beers into the fridge and could hear the television being switched on followed by the familiar sound of the hiss of a can being opened.

She loved it when David was in a cheerful mood, he was kind and thoughtful and her only hope was that this time it would last.

Tracy said goodbye to David before relaxing on the sofa in her pyjamas for an evening of watching television. Sleep deprivation had caught up with her and it wasn't long before she was asleep.

She woke to the sound of the doorbell and startled, taking a moment to familiarise herself with her surroundings. She was unsure of the time. The room was dark apart from light emanating from the television and the curtains were still open. She realised she must have been asleep for a while as it didn't get dark outside until quite late.

She pulled herself from the sofa and walked over to the front door.

"Who is it?" She shouted through the door." Feeling a little nervous of who might be waiting on the other side.

"It's me, I forgot my key. Let me in."

As soon as she opened the door and guided David inside, he pulled her in close for a tight hug. He held her face and began to kiss her with a sense of urgency. She could taste the beer in his breath as she reciprocated his kiss. It had been a while since he'd shown her that kind of intimacy. A yearning for her and she'd missed it.

"I love you and I want you, right now." He whispered into her ear.

"Right now?"

"Yep." He slowly nodded. "Close the curtains."

Tracy hurried to pull the curtains closed as David rushed to pull off his clothes. He was slightly uncoordinated and stumbled when removing his jeans.

"But I don't know if I can." She said, pointing to her exceptionally large stomach."

"Oh, course you can, it all still works, we just need to be creative."

They didn't make it to the bedroom, he had her on the sofa. And he was right, it did all still work. It was just a little awkward at times.

Tracy got up and pulled on her pyjamas, she could see David was falling asleep.

"Don't fall asleep there. I want to lay beside you and cuddle."

She helped him up, collected his clothes off the floor and a few minutes later were cuddling in bed.

"I'll set the alarm for the morning; the shops open at nine. So, I'll set it for seven thirty."

"Ok." He said with a sleepy voice. "I need to go to Nigel's first thing."

"Who's Nigel and why?"

"Nigel from the pub." He yawned. "I bought his stereo and need to go and pick it up."

"What to you mean you bought his stereo? How much did you spend?" David didn't reply. "David."

But it was no use asking, he had fallen asleep.

Tracy jumped out of bed and picked up his jeans. She fished the envelope out of his back pocket, the one that only a few hours earlier had contained five hundred pounds, his entire bonus. She counted what remained. Two hundred pounds. That meant he had spent three hundred pounds on a stereo that he didn't need. Three hundred pounds was gone from the money in which he had promised to spend on their baby. Tracy was livid, she couldn't believe he'd be that selfish. Maybe she was overreacting. Perhaps there'd be an explanation for the missing money, she thought. Perhaps he hadn't actually spent three hundred pounds. He could have put it somewhere safe; it would make sense for him not to take five hundred pounds down the pub. But then, surely, he would have put it all somewhere safe.

Too angry to sleep, Tracy looked in all the logical places she could think of in search of the cash but couldn't find it anywhere. She eventually gave up looking climbed back into bed and laid awake, allowing her resentment to fester.

Having fallen asleep at some point during the middle of the night, she woke to the sound of the alarm clock. David refused to wake up when Tracy nudged him, insisting he needed another half an hour. Tracy knew it was pointless arguing with him, she would need to bide her time, until he was awake. She showered, dressed, and tried again to wake him, sitting beside him on the bed.

"David, the shops will be open soon, please wake up." David opened his eyes and sat up.

"Where's my cup of tea?" were the first words he uttered. Tracy felt her face redden, she tried to remain calm but failed.

"How about. Where's your five hundred pounds?" She didn't say anymore and watched as he suddenly sobered up.

"Yeah, that. I um, well I agreed to buy a stereo from one of the blokes in the Dog." Tracy fixed him with her stare, whilst he attempted to justify his recklessness.

"You see, Nigel is a bit down on his luck at the moment. He recently lost his job and is skint."

"Right."

"He offered me his hi-fi, it's much better than my old thing. The CD player holds three CDs, and it has a twin tape deck with surround sound speakers."

"And how much did you pay for it?"

Now it was David's time to pause. "Three hundred pounds." He finally said, sheepishly.

"Three hundred pounds. Please tell me, you are joking."

"I'm not."

"Then tell him you changed your mind."

"I can't, I already gave him the money and said I'd drive over this morning to pick the stereo up."

"David, why would you do that. You promised we'd use that money on the baby. We need that money to buy the rest of the baby things." Tracy started to cry, tears of anger.

"Well, it's my money and I wanted to treat myself. Besides, I've been thinking. We don't need to spend that much money on baby things, there's no point, they aren't in them long enough. And there's plenty of second-hand prams for sale in the paper for a fraction of the price."

Tracy got up off the bed. She knew if she sat their any longer, she'd loose control of her temper and that wouldn't end well for her.

A few hours later David pulled up outside and proudly carried his new stereo into the house. There was that much of it, it took several trips back and forth from the car, to bring it all in. Tracy watched from the bedroom window, the little glimmer of hope that he'd cancel the transaction lost.

"Tracy." She heard him shout.

She took her time and slowly walked down the stairs, exaggerating every footstep with a thump.

"I popped to the shop and bought today's newspaper for you. Why don't you pop the kettle on and then take a look."

She snatched the newspaper from his hand and promptly left the room, leaving David to set up his new toy.

CHAPTER 27

July 1997

Tracy's due date had been and gone and she was starting to wonder if she'd be pregnant forever. It was certainly no fun being heavily pregnant in the peak of summer.

The only good thing about it, apart from the excitement of seeing their new baby, was the little bit of freedom it allowed her. She was now seeing the midwife weekly, and David was unable to take the time of work, forcing Tracy to go alone.

She once dreaded leaving the house, now she longed for it. Providing the conditions were right, for she still faced some challenges.

She'd also struck up a friendship with Maggie next door and had been to her house several times since they'd first met.

She was reluctant to tell Maggie too much about herself and so kept certain topics of conversation to a minimum. But Maggie had become a friend and Tracy enjoyed her company.

David was at work when Tracy's water's broke. It was mid-afternoon, and she knew he'd be leaving work within the hour. She called her mum, who reassured her that unless she was having regular contractions of a few minutes apart, she needn't worry. And David would be home from work with plenty of time before they'd need to go to the hospital.

Tracy was packed and ready to leave for the hospital by the time David arrived home. Her occasional twinges had now progressed into regular contractions which she had timed to be six minutes apart. David who was expecting to have his dinner ready and waiting for him, was instead met with Tracy puffing and panting on the sofa.

"You're in labour then." He said casually.

Tracy nodded, unable to speak, mid-way through a contraction.

"My water's have gone, and I'm packed and ready to go." She said, once the contraction had ended.

"What about my dinner?"

"What about your dinner?"

"Well, you can't expect me to go straight up the hospital on an empty stomach after a full day's work. It'll be hours until the baby arrives, and I need to eat. Just make me something quick tonight if you like. It doesn't need to be anything special."

For a second, Tracy thought he might have been joking but quickly realised he wasn't.

"I'm struggling a little here, can't you make yourself something to eat?"

"I can but I need a shower. I can take a shower whilst it's cooking or after I've eaten. It's up to you?"

Tracy sighed and stood up to leave the room. She turned the oven on to warm up and pulled out a pizza from the freezer.

While the pizza cooked, Tracy impatiently paced the kitchen. Her stomach tightened with severe pain as she faced two further contractions, causing her to stop pacing and grip the side of the worktop. She was no longer sure how long apart they were, but they were definitely getting closer.

David appeared in the kitchen just as Tracy was removing the pizza from the oven. She transferred the pizza onto a plate and handed it to David.

"Thanks." He said as he took the plate from her and walked off into the direction of the living room.

"Where are you going?" Tracy shrieked, feeling the start of yet another contraction.

"I'm going to eat my dinner in front of the television."

"Please, please don't. Can't you please just eat it quickly. We really need to go."

"Stop being so dramatic. We've got plenty of time. First time labours always take a long time."

"Please......" But she couldn't finish the sentence. The contraction took hold, and she was suddenly unsteady on her feet. She just about managed to make it to a dinning room chair and sat herself down.

The pain was quickly intensifying and had now spread, so that it could also be felt in her back. She could no longer handle the pain and let out an unintelligible shriek that resembled a cow mooing. David had disappeared into the living room, and she was left to ride out the contraction alone.

The contractions were also now lasting longer and once finished, she could do nothing but sit motionless, catching her breath and waiting for the next one. She desperately wanted to be in hospital. Where she could be made comfortable with pain relief and kind midwifes. Instead, she was left to deal with the agony alone, whilst her husband ate his dinner in front of the television.

It was fifteen minutes before David reappeared with an empty plate in his hand, by which time Tracy could barely speak. She remained on the chair drenched in sweat and leaning into the table.

"We best get you to the hospital." He said nonchalantly, as if it was a routine appointment. He helped her off the chair and picked up the hospital bag as they made their way to the front door.

Another contraction started as she walked down the path of their front garden. She grabbed hold of David and screamed out in pain, unaware of quite how loud she was being.

"Be quiet for goodness' sake. We don't want the whole bloody street to here you."

David opened the car door and helped her into the car, he threw the hospital bag into the boot and drove in the direction of the hospital.

The drive took twenty agonising minutes as David navigated through rush hour traffic towards the outskirts of the city, and Tracy didn't think she could take any more.

Each time a contraction came, he yelled at her to be quiet and to stop overreacting.

Every traffic light seemed to turn red, and they came to a standstill several times before finally reaching the hospital grounds.

"I'll have to drop you off at the maternity unit entrance."

"What!" Tracy said, looking petrified.

"There's no where to park and I very much doubt you fancy a walk through the car park. You go on in and I'll join you in a few minutes."

Tracy reluctantly climbed out of the car whilst David remained seated with the car's engine running. The maternity unit had several "drop off" only bays directly outside the entrance, and so she only had a few yards to walk. She'd soon be inside the hospital and at the maternity booking in desk.

"Don't forget my bag." She just about managed to say, before closing the door.

She managed to get to the booking in desk, just in time, as she could feel another contraction brewing. She bent over the desk; the pain excruciating and she could no longer contain the scream that erupted from her.

A passing midwife in blue scrubs grabbed a wheelchair and helped Tracy into it before whisking her off into a side room.

"What's your name, love?" The midwife asked.

"Tracy." Tracy was in a trance; she couldn't even lift her head to make eye contact with the short plump midwife, wearing her hair in low pigtails.

"My name is Susanne and I'm going to be looking after you. Have you got your pregnancy notes with you."

"In my bag, with husband, parking car." Was all she could manage, as she was consumed by another bout of pain.

The midwife put her hand to Tracy's stomach to confirm the contraction.

"How many weeks are you?"

"Forty-one."

"You're baby's fully cooked then." Susanne said, trying to be a little light-hearted.

"I need pain relief." Tracy managed to yell as the contraction tailed off.

"Tracy, I was going to monitor you in here for a while and make you comfortable with pain relief. However, given the frequency and intensity of your contractions, I don't believe there to be time, I need to take you straight down to delivery."

"David?"

"Is that your husband?"

Tracy nodded.

"Don't worry, reception will tell him where to find you."

Susanne quickly wheeled Tracy back out of the side room and down the corridor passing several pairs of closed double doors on their way. Tracy could hear muffled howls combined with crying babies. She clearly wasn't the only one to bring new life into the world this evening.

Once they reached the end of the corridor, they turned into a bay with three identical double doors and headed for the first door marked as vacant.

"Can I get some help?" Susanne shouted as she spun around, unclipping the top of one of the doors and pushing them both open with her back as she wheeled Tracy in.

A second midwife wearing glasses and greying hair in a messy bun appeared and followed in behind them.

"Hi Janet, this is Tracy. We don't yet know much as we're waiting for Tracy's husband David to arrive, and he has her notes. All we know so far is that she is overdue and I'm going to guess she is ten centre metres or there abouts given the duration between contractions. Can you please give me a hand in helping Tracy onto the bed."

"I need pain relief." Tracy screeched.

"Ok, lovely." Janet said with a patient tone. "I'm going to hook you up with some gas and air, it will take the edge off. But I believe you are too far gone for anything more substantial. Your baby will arrive before the pain relief would have taken effect."

Janet fetched a fresh mouthpiece and began attaching it to the gas and air outlet as Susanne pulled on a pair of blue nitrile surgical gloves.

"Here, I want you to take deep breaths from this when you get your next contraction." Janet said, handing her the mouthpiece. "It might make you feel a bit funny to begin with but stick with it."

Tracy could already feel the start of another contraction. Which Susanne recognised by the way Tracy's face contorted.

"Go on." She said encouragingly gesturing to the mouthpiece with the nod of her head.

Tracy clamped her mouth around the mouthpiece and inhaled a deep breath followed by another. She instantly felt the room spin and she could no longer make out her surroundings. She saw two of everything. Two sets of large round lights directly over her, two sets of monitors to her side and four midwifes. She closed her eyes in an attempt to stop the sensation, but it was replaced with echoed sounds, where every word was repeated several times. She tried to make out what was being said in the room, but it was almost impossible. She hated this feeling. It felt like being on the waltzers at the funfair and she never did see the point of the so-called thrill. But it was taking the edge off the pain and so as instructed she stuck with it.

She thought she heard a man's voice. *Was it David?* She felt a hand grab onto her free hand.

"Tracy, I'm here." Came the voice of the man. It was David.

Once the contraction had ended, she lowered the mouthpiece and opened her eyes, allowing herself a few moments for everything to come back into focus.

"David."

"Tracy, love." Susanne interrupted. "I need to examine you and see how many centre metres dilated you are. And I need to do it quickly before your next contraction."

Tracy gently nodded, not wanting to speak anymore so to conserve what little energy she had left.

Sussane and Janet hurried to remove the bottom half of Tracy's clothing, a pair of leggings and knickers and Susanne began her examination, whilst Tracy laid her head back against the bed, making the most of the short relief.

"Tracy, you are ten centre metres, and I can see your baby crowning." Turning to Janet, she said. "Can you call for the doctor to attend."

"What's happening, what does all that mean?" David said with an air of panic.

"It means, you baby is getting ready to make their appearance and I will need Tracy to push on her next contraction. I've called the doctor in as a precaution. Because I've not had time to complete a proper examination or monitor the baby."

Tracy took a large inhale of gas and air as another contraction began to build.

"Ok Tracy, when I say, I want you to push."

She nodded, with her eyes tightly closed and mouth firmly gripped on the mouthpiece."

"Right Tracy, push."

Tracy removed the mouthpiece and pushed as David squeezed her hand.

"Come on Tracy." David said encouragingly.

"Push." Susanne continued several more times until the contraction subsided. "Ok, stop pushing now Tracy, until the next contraction comes in. You might still have the urge to push and if so, I want you to pant."

Several contractions later, with lots of pushing and no baby, Tracy was beginning to tire.

"You need to keep going Tracy." Susanne urged.

"I can't. I'm too tired." She rasped.

"You can and you must, it's really important that we get your baby out in the next couple of contractions."

Seconds later Tracy's next contraction was on its way.

"Tracy, I need you to push with everything you have so that we can avoid intervention."

Tracy did as she was told and pushed so hard, she thought she was going to pass out.

"Don't forget to breathe Tracy." Came the voice of Janet who had reappeared alongside Susanne.

"I can see the head." Susane said excitedly. "Good girl, not much further to go. Dad, do you want to come and take a look."

David looked frightened, unsure what to expect when he briefly let go of Tracy's hand to look at the top of the baby's head.

There was barely any time until the next contraction and Tracy felt a sudden rush of adrenaline and heaved once more.

"Well done, Tracy, the head is out, one more push and you will have your baby."

She pushed one final time and felt the slight pull as her baby entered the world.

"You did it." David said and kissed Tracy's wet and clammy forehead.

"Congratulations, you have a son." Said Janet.

"Do you want to cut the cord, Dad?" Susanne said, looking at David.

David shook his head, feeling a little squeamish by it all. Susanne cut the cord and rushed the baby to a table at the far end of the room, just as the doctor walked in.

"What's happening?" Tracy said.

"It's all fine, they are just checking him over. They will bring him back to you in a few minutes, in the meantime let's get you ready for round two... The placenta." Janet said reading Tracy's shocked expression.

CHAPTER 28

Daniel Lewis Wright was born on the eighteenth of July weighing seven pounds and ten ounces and he was simply perfect. After a two-night stay in hospital they were both were discharged.

Their first afternoon back home was exhausting. It was a Saturday, so no-one was working. Tracy's family came to visit, shortly followed by David's dad and they spent the entire afternoon entertaining and making cups of tea.

Tracy was grateful for their parent's support and generosity at the things they had bought, but she wanted that time alone just the three of them. In their baby honeymoon bubble, taking their time to adjust to their new life as parents.

After finally saying goodbye to their visitors and Daniel asleep in his carry cot. Tracy plopped herself down on the sofa.

"How about a fish and chip supper." David said enthusiastically.

"That sounds amazing." Tracy said with a tired smile. "I'm shattered and don't much feel like cooking."

"I didn't think you would tonight. I'll pop out in a minute then."

"It's a bit early, isn't it?" She looked at the clock it was only just after three.

"I might make a slight detour on the way to the chippy." He said with a grin. "And wet the baby's head." The look on Tracy's face must have said it all as he quickly followed that with "I promise you; I won't be home late. I'll be home by six."

It was eight before David arrived home and Tracy was

starving. He walked through the front door wearing a stupid grin on his face and clutching a carrier bag of fish and chips. The smell of alcohol came off him in waves. He swayed as he made his way from the living room to the kitchen, bouncing off the wall a few times as he went. Tracy felt her anger rise, combined with hurt. They would never get this time again, and all she wanted to do was for the three of them to spend this precious time together.

Tracy dished out their dinner and took their plates to the dining room table where David had already taken a seat next to a sleeping Daniel in his carry cot. They began to eat but after a few mouthfuls Daniel started to cry.

"What's wrong with him." David slurred.

"He's hungry David, there's nothing wrong with him."

"Well feed him then."

Tracy sighed and tried not to let her emotions get the better of her. She was tired, emotional, and hungry, and all she wanted to do was eat her dinner.

She left the room to prepare a bottle for Daniel. Returning to the table a few minutes later and sat back down to feed him. She awkwardly cradled him whilst attempting to unsuccessfully shovel the odd chip into her mouth. And watched David eat his dinner, with contempt at his ignorance towards his wife's struggles.

A few minutes later David abruptly threw down his fork.

"I don't feel very well." He said and got up to make his way to the kitchen. But he didn't make it in time and threw up over the dining room carpet.

"Are you fucking kidding me!" Tracy shouted, causing Daniel to startle and cry.

"I'm sorry babe. I think I need to go to bed. You'll need to help me."

David leant against the wall for support, she needed to sort him out quickly.

She put Daniel down in his carry cot, and he started to cry in protest at the unexpected end to his unfinished feed.

She stood up, scoped her arm under David acting as a pillar, and walked him through the house and up the stairs. Gritting her teeth as she did, at the pain caused by his weight pressing against her.

She could hear the angry cries from her new-born son, she desperately wanted to tend to his needs and not the needs of this arsehole she was holding. He didn't deserve her attention.

She helped David into bed and undressed him as best she could leaving him in his boxer shorts and socks.

He mumbled a "Thanks." Before turning his head to vomit again, this time over her side of the bed.

Hot tears stung Tracy's cheeks as she cried out in frustration. She thumped him hard on the chest unable to contain her anger any longer, but he'd passed out and didn't even flinch.

Tracy grabbed a clean nightie from the chest of drawers and headed back downstairs to be with Daniel. She couldn't bare the stench of the dining room so took him into the living room to finish his feed. She was sobbing uncontrollably by now and tears dripped onto Daniel's soft head of light blond hair.

"I'm sorry." She whimpered to her new-born son.

She binned the fish and chips, having suddenly lost her appetite and spent half an hour removing David's vomit from the dinning room carpet. She retched as she scraped up what she could and no matter how much she scrubbed the carpet, she couldn't rid the smell. It pained her to bend down, her body still recovering from childbirth.

She desperately needed the comfort of her bed but knew that was not an option tonight. So, was forced to spend a restless night on the sofa with Daniel besides her in his carry cot.

Although expended by exhaustion, she couldn't sleep. Too afraid to close her eyes encase something were to happen to Daniel. She'd heard too many horror stores of infant deaths, so laid awake watching him in the dimly lit room, observing his every fidget and stretch. He was just so precious.

She couldn't fight it any longer and eventually nodded off but was soon woken to the sound of Daniel's hungry cries. And his cries continued on and off for the remainder of the night.

Daniel seemed more settled the next morning. Tracy took advantage of this and slept for as long and as late as she could. Desperate to reclaim some of the sleep she had lost.

She managed a couple of hours before she was woken by yet more crying. She picked Daniel up and held him close to her chest, but his crying only grew louder.

She wondered if he needed a fresh nappy, so laid him on the sofa and changed him. But Daniel continued to cry; his hands balled into angry fists that thrashed around.

"You can't be hungry again?" She said as she closed the poppers on his baby grow, before placing him back in his carry cot and heading to the kitchen to prepare yet another bottle. A few minutes later Tracy was back holding a warm bottle for Daniel and found David leaning over him.

"Can't you shut him up?" He said, turning his face towards Tracy as she walked towards them both.

"He's a baby David and baby's cry."

"Yeah, well my head's pounding and I was trying to sleep."

Tracy ignored David and picked Daniel up. He was now bright red in the face and walling so loud she'd be surprised if the entire street couldn't hear him. *She must apologise to Maggie when she saw her,* she thought to herself.

Tracy sat on the sofa and got them both into position, ready to feed.

"Can you move?" David said unapologetically. "I need to lay down and can't go back to bed. Can't you go and sit on the chair."

Tracy was too tired to argue and did as she was told, remembering that at some point she'd have to strip the bed.

David laid down on the sofa and went back to sleep, where he remained for most of the day.

David went back to work the following day, putting an end to his short paternity leave. Tracy couldn't put into words how let down she felt by him. Their marriage may have been a sham, but this time together before he returned to work was supposed to be cherished, they were meant to be a team. She had been naïve to think things would be any different after Daniel arrived. She couldn't stop herself from crying and even blubbered down the phone to her mum when she called.

"Tracy, love. What on earth's the matter?"

Tracy couldn't admit the truth to her mum. She couldn't tell her how unsupported she'd felt by David. She wouldn't understand anyway and always somehow saw the good in him.

"I don't know mum. I'm just really tearful today."

"You have the baby blues. All mum's get it a few days after giving birth. I've no idea why, I think it's something to do with hormones. You'll be fine again tomorrow."

"Will I?"

"Yes, also sleep deprivation is catching up with you and that will make you feel a bit melancholy. And didn't you say David was back to work today? That's bound to be tough, flying solo and not having his support." Tracy stifled a laugh. "Make sure you sleep when the baby does. Forget about the housework for a while."

"Yes mum."

"Call me if you need anything. I'll speak to you again tomorrow."

"Ok mum, bye."

"Bye love."

Tracy did follow the advice she'd been given and tried to nap as much as she could. She'd lost track of time and wasn't even sure what day it was. She also desperately needed to wash her hair and feel slightly more human.

Tracy laid in a much-needed bath with Daniel in his bouncing rocker on the floor besides her. She was oblivious to the time and hadn't heard the front door open. The first she knew of David being home was when she heard him shout her name from the bottom of the stairs.

"I'm up here." She shouted back, startling Daniel and making him cry.

"Shit." She said to herself.

A few seconds later David appeared at the door to the bathroom.

"What are you doing?" He said.

Tracy wanted to say, "*What does it look like I'm doing.*" But felt better of it. "I'm taking a bath."

"But it's dinner time. You've had all day to take a bath."

Tracy couldn't think of an appropriate response so not to upset him, she decided to say nothing.

"Where's my dinner?"

"I, um, didn't realise the time. I'm sorry I've not yet started making it yet."

"For fuck's sake Tracy. You only have one job, and you can't even manage that. I've been slogging my guts off at work all day to provide for you and I come home to a messy house and no fucking dinner. Seriously, what have you been doing all day?"

"I'm sorry." She said as Daniel continued to cry. "I'll finish off my bath quickly and start making it. Can you please pick Dan up? I startled him when I called down to you. I think he just needs a cuddle."

"No, I can't, I'm going to get changed." And with that he left the room, leaving Tracy to quickly finish washing whilst trying to pacify her crying new-born.

After a challenging half an hour, Tracy came downstairs holding a sleeping Daniel in her arms. David was sat on the sofa, watching television, and clutching a cup of tea.

CHAPTER 29

Tracy opened the front door and was pleased to see it was Maggie standing on her doorstep. She was holding a Pyrex dish covered over with tin foil.

"I thought you could do with a night off cooking." Maggie said as she handed Tracy the dish. "It's Shepherd's pie. Oh god, you're not vegetarians, are you?"

"No, we're not." Tracy giggled. "Thank you, Maggie, that's really kind of you. Why don't you come in, I'll stick the kettle on."

"I don't want to intrude."

"You're not, besides I could do with the adult company and there is someone here who would like to meet you."

Maggie sat cradling Daniel in her arms.

"Oh, I have forgotten just how tiny newborns are." Said Maggie "It's a shame they don't stay like this for very long." She leant towards Daniel's tiny head and inhaled. "Oh, and that fresh baby smell, I wish you could bottle it. How are you keeping Tracy?"

"I'm ok, I guess. A little more sleep would be nice but that's to be expected."

"Yes, I have heard the little man cry. How many hours is he sleeping at night?"

"Oh Maggie, I'm so sorry. I'm sorry if his crying has kept you awake as well."

"Don't be silly, he hasn't at all. It's only occasionally when I'm in my living room that I can hear him. I said that purely out of concern for you my dear. And how's David? Supporting you

I hope?"

Without warning Tracy began to cry, she had no idea where the tears came from. She was so used to keeping her emotions in check and keeping up the pretence that all was great between them. It took her by surprise.

"What on earth's the matter?" Maggie said, patting the sofa next to her, to signal for Tracy to sit.

Tracy spent the next ten minutes opening up to Maggie and telling her all about David's recent behaviour.

"Oh, you poor girl. That is horrendous. Why do you put up with it? He sounds like a cunt."

Tracy burst out laughing. The shock of Maggie's use of profanities was unexpected and seemed so refreshing.

"Well, it's true." Maggie said as if to read Tracy's mind. "One thing you will learn about me, is that I don't mince my words. But in all seriousness. If you ever need to vent or escape, I'm here for you. I mean it. It's tough having a new-born and to also have an arse for a husband to content with, well, that only makes things a hundred times worse. Trust me, I've been there, it took me years to gather the strength and leave mine."

Somehow confiding in Maggie made Tracy feel a little better, she finally had an ally, someone who could relate to her problems. And the realisation that she wasn't alone.

The following day was shopping day. And it was to be their first shopping trip with Daniel in tow. Tracy ensured that Daniel was fed, changed, and sitting in his car seat ready to leave by the time David pulled up outside the house. Tracy picked up the car seat. It seemed heavy for such a small baby, and she hooked the changing bag over her other shoulder. It was the first time either of them had left the house since leaving the hospital and she was looking forward to getting out for an hour or two.

David remained in the car whilst Tracy shuffled down the path, struggling with her heavy load. And so, she didn't bother to ask for his help, as she fumbled with the seat belt, clipping Daniel's seat in place.

Tracy and David walked around the supermarket; David pushed the special baby trolley that allowed Daniel to lay in an attached reclined plastic baby seat. Having spent a frantic five minutes trying to locate that specific type of trolly.

David's patience was already wearing thin before they even made their way through the entrance to the supermarket. And they weren't even halfway around the store before Daniel started to cry. Tracy tried to pacify him by placing a dummy in his mouth, but that only seemed to aggravate him further as he spat it out and wailed.

"For fuck's sake, Tracy, can't you just shut him up." David said quietly so that only Tracy could hear and smiled for the benefit of other shoppers passing by.

"I can't David, he might want another feed."

"Let's just pay for what we have in the trolly and go then."

"We can't go yet. We only have a few items; I can't even make a meal out of this, and we've not even been to the baby isle yet."

"Well, I can't take any more of this. Here, take my wallet and I'll meet you back at the car."

He turned around and marched away before Tracy had a chance to say anything. She couldn't quite believe what he'd done. He'd left her in the middle of the supermarket with a screaming infant and she didn't know whether to join Daniel and cry at the humiliation of it all or feel overjoyed at the fact she was holding money. Actual real money. She peered into his wallet and counted seventy pounds. It had been nearly two years since she last had money in her possession.

Tracy continued to whiz around the supermarket, Daniel eventually succumbed to the dummy and the motion of the trolly meant he was soon asleep. She was in her element; it was another small step towards freedom.

Much to her surprise David got out of the car and helped

Tracy to load the shopping into the boot and even clipped Daniel back into his car seat when Tracy took the trolly back to the front of the store.

"I'm not doing that again." David said after climbing back into the car.

"Doing what?"

"Taking a bloody baby around the supermarket. I can't handle it. From now on, I'll give you a weekly allowance. You can get the shopping done when I'm at work."

It took a moment for the realisation of what David had said to sink in. He was giving her more freedom and money. Yes, it would be a pain having to lug the shopping back, but she didn't care, it was a small price to pay for the independence it would bring.

Tracy took Daniel to the park the following morning, it was to be his first outing in the pram. Daniel had given her a reason to venture outside, and she was determined to make the most of the fine summer weather.

She dressed him in her favourite outfit. A white baby grow with little blue ducks and a matching hat, and as it was warm, she wrapped him in just a cotton cellular blanket. She made sure to pack enough nappies, a spare change of clothes and a bottle, just encase. And she left the house feeling confident.

Tracy still suffered from the occasional bout of anxiety when leaving the house. She wasn't one who could just rush out the door on a whim, but she was able to go out on her own, providing the weather held.

Tracy enjoyed a lovely morning walking around the park, pushing the pram and beaming with pride. She felt the sun against her face and the smell of freshly cut grass mixed with wildflowers, it reminded her of her childhood, when she and Angela used to explore the meadows and play in the park.

She spoke to Daniel as she walked, pointing out everything that they passed. It was Tracy's first time visiting this part of town and she didn't really know what the park had to offer.

After a short walk, they reached a small lake and stopped to watch the ducks.

"Next time we come, I'll bring some bread so that we can feed them." She said to Daniel who was oblivious to it all.

The trip to the park had lifted Tracy's spirits and once back home Daniel slept for a solid three hours in his pram. The fresh air obviously doing them both some good. In the time Daniel slept, Tracy had prepared dinner, cleaned the house, and enjoyed an uninterrupted cup of tea in the garden. It was just what she'd needed to lift her from her sleep deprived haze.

Her cheerfulness soon dissipated though, when David arrived home in another fowl mood, after having a bad day at work. One of the machines on the production line had broken down, putting them behind on an order, which David was responsible for.

He reached straight for a beer in the fridge before even acknowledging his wife and child and he didn't even bother to ask how their day had been.

"I'll be in the living room, call me when dinner's ready."

Was all he could manage to say.

A short while later they were tucking into a home-made chicken curry. Although no words were exchanged, Tracy sensed the tension building and decided to steer a conversation.

"What do you fancy watching on TV tonight?"

"I dunno." He said, shrugging his shoulders.

The awkward silence was broken by Daniel, who woke with a cry. His radar had sensed it was dinner time and decided that he too, wanted his dinner.

"Not again." David huffed.

Tracy said nothing as she abandoned her dinner and left the table to make Daniel's bottle.

Although he was fed, winded, changed and cuddled, Daniel had a restless evening and despite Tracy's best efforts, she just couldn't settle him.

"Can't you take him out for a walk or something?" David said, without offering to take over from Tracy who was pacing around the living room clutching Daniel to her chest.

"It's dark David. I'm not going outside."

"He's doing my head in. I can't hear the television."

"I'm sorry, I'm trying my best."

David stood up. "Fuck this, I can't stand it any longer. I'm going out."

He retrieved his keys and wallet from the side table and left the house.

"Prick." Tracy shouted after being sure he was no longer in ear shot. She was relieved he'd gone out. He was clearly stressed, and she sensed the tension mounting once more.

Tracy and Daniel were both upstairs when David got home. She had managed to settle Daniel after a fretful couple of hours and had taken herself to bed.

However, the peace and quiet was short lived, as Daniel woke up hollering soon after David climbed into bed.

"You have got to be kidding me!" He said, throwing his arms down by his side against the mattress in temper.

"Maybe he's ill." Tracy said, as she paced around clutching Daniel to her chest once more.

"All I know is that he never stops bloody crying and I have to get up for work in the morning." David grabbed his pillow, and pulled it over his head, in a dramatic attempt to block out the sound of Daniels cries and light from Tracy's bedside lamp.

But nothing would settle Daniel, his little face red from anger as he continued to cry.

"I'm going to try him on another bottle. Can you please hold him for a minute while I go downstairs and make the feed?" She said holding Daniel and gesturing at David to take him.

David removed his head from under the pillow and reluctantly took hold of his of crying son. Tracy went to make a bottle and reappeared a few minutes later to find her husband standing by the side of the bed holding Daniel at arms length, his head was unsupported, and he was shouting at him.

"Why wont you just shut the fuck up!"

"David stop." She yelled, dropping the bottle she was holding. She reached out and snatched Daniel from David, pulling him in close and wrapping her arms around him. She knew what David was capable of when he lost his temper. And had she been gone for another couple of seconds, she couldn't be sure, what she would have been walking into.

Tracy was shaking. An overpowering need to protect her child overruled her senses and she shouted. "Don't you ever speak to my son like that again."

"Why. What will you do?" David said, inching slowly towards her. "Come on then, what exactly will you do Tracy."

She felt scared and twisted her body away from David to shield Daniel from his father's temper.

"Stop it, he's only a baby David." She shouted.

"He's a fucking inconvenience, that's what he is."

Tracy bent down, picked up the bottle and headed downstairs. And a few minutes later, David heard the click of the front door closing.

CHAPTER 30

"Thank you so much for looking after us last night Maggie, I really don't know what I would have done without you."

"I'm glad I could help. But you know, you don't have to go back to him."

"I know." Tracy said, feeling a little unsure of her next move.

"It's not just you at risk, you have your son to think about too. And you don't want Daniel growing up thinking it's okay that his dad would think nothing of hurting him or his mother. I mean, what kind of influence would that have on him."

Tracy began to cry.

"Look, why don't you go back to the house later this morning once David has gone to work and collect some things. And I'll drive you both over to your parents' house. I'm sure they would want to help, if only they knew."

Tracy nodded.

Maggie and Tracy had sat up all night talking. Neither felt like sleeping after Tracy banged on the front door in the early hours of the morning. Wearing only her pyjamas and cradling Daniel and a handful of baby things, that she had managed to grab before fleeing their home.

Tracy watched David walk up the path and get into his car from behind the net curtain of Maggie's living room.

"He's leaving now." She shouted to Maggie who was in the kitchen making tea.

"Ok. I would leave it a little while before going over, just encase. Do you or David have a mobile phone?"

Tracy shook her head. "No, neither of us do, why?"

"I just wondered, if he had the means to call you from work."

"There is a phone in the office, and I believe a pay phone in the canteen, but he's never called me from either of those before. And he doesn't seem the point in mobile phones."

An hour later, once Tracy was sure David wouldn't be returning home, she left Daniel with Maggie and went back to pack a few bags of essential items. She would come back for the rest later. She loaded Maggie's car, with her bags and the pram, and strapped Daniel's car seat into the back of Maggie's blue Vauxhall Astra.

Maggie pulled up to the cul-de-sac where Tracy once lived and stayed in the car whilst Tracy went to knock on the front door. Having decided against calling her mum in advance to forewarn of their arrival.

"Tracy, love. What are you doing here?" Jean said as she opened the door to see a tear-streaked Tracy standing in front of her.

"I've left him mum. Can I come in?"

"Oh Tracy." Jean said hugging her daughter.

"Whose car is that and where's Daniel."

"Daniel's in the car and that's my neighbour Maggie she was kind enough to drive me over."

Jean helped Tracy get Daniel and their things from Maggie's car and thanked Maggie for helping Tracy before saying their goodbyes.

"You better tell me what's been happening?" Jean said once they were safely inside.

"It's David. He got angry at Daniel for crying."

Jean let out a sigh. "Oh Tracy. It takes time for new parents to adjust and it's not uncommon to loose your temper, especially when you aren't getting much sleep. Everything always seems far worse when you're tired. I'm sure David didn't mean anything by it. He adores Daniel."

Tracy then went on to tell Jean about him walking out on them both in the supermarket.

"Your dad did that to me once. He was embarrassed when you were crying. He said people were looking and so he went and sat in the car. By the time I met up with him again both me and you were crying." She laughed as she recalled the memory. "The point I'm making is that all new parents go through a phase of difficulty, it perfectly normal. You're sleep deprived, your hormones are all over the place. It's bound to be playing havoc with your perception and it's hard for David as well you know. He's the one at work all day."

"Seriously mum, you think this is all in my head because I'm tired and just had a baby."

"I'm not saying that. I'm merely saying it takes time. Why don't you go upstairs and run yourself a nice warm bath and then take yourself off to bed for a few hours. You look shattered. I'll keep Daniel down here with me to give you a chance to rest. How does that sound?"

Tracy wasn't sure how long she'd been asleep for but was sure it was for more than just a few hours. She woke to the sound of the telephone ringing and could hear her mum speaking to someone as she descended the stairs.

"Yes, she's here. Where else would she be... Yeah, I know she is and that's what I told her... Well I did wonder that myself to be honest, maybe it wouldn't be a bad idea to make an appointment... Ahuh...Yep, ok love, see you soon."

"Was that David?" Tracy asked as soon as Jean hung up the phone.

"Yes, it was. He was calling to check you were here, he's on his way to pick you both up."

"What. No. I can't go back. I told you; I've left him."

"Tracy, listen to me. You are a grown woman. A grown married women for that matter, with a child. You need to grow up and stop acting like a spoilt child. You are not the only person to have ever had a baby and you have a husband who works hard to provide for you both. David's a good man, you need to look after him."

"But mum, you don't understand."

"No buts Tracy, you are going back home."

Tears pricked the back of her eyes as she tried to process what her mum had said. She couldn't believe that her own mother even sided with David.

"Look, I know you're struggling and that too is not uncommon, a lot of new mums suffer from their emotions and extended baby blues after having a baby. You have been through a lot over the last few years and that's bound to have an effect. We think it would be a good idea for you to see your doctor for a check up."

"We, whose we?"

"Well, David and I."

"You and David have been discussing me and you both think I'm mental?"

"No, not at all. We just think you might need a little help and David spoke to me because he's worried about you Tracy, that's all. We all are."

Tracy wouldn't speak to David on the drive home, she couldn't find the right words to say. Even though she'd had a few solid hours of sleep, she felt totally depleted of energy.

Once they were back at home David placed a sleeping Daniel in his car seat on the carpet and turned to Tracy.

"No more silly business Tracy. Remember our agreement. You don't want to me to share your secret, do you?"

She didn't say anything. She couldn't even look at him and so stared at the floor."

"Do you?" David repeated. "Look at me when I'm speaking to you." Tracy slowly raised her head and spat in David's face. He immediately slapped her with the back of his hand sending her stumbling backwards until she fell into the sofa.

"Clearly you need reminding of our agreement." He said as he leant over her and drew the curtains closed before undoing the buckle on his belt and unzipping his jeans. Tracy watched in disbelief as he tugged off her leggings.

"David no." She begged. "Not like this."

He didn't say anything, it was his turn to stay quiet.

"Please, David don't. I'm not ready, I'm not healed."

He pulled Tracy up from the sofa and twisted her around so that her back was facing him. He bent her over the sofa and spread her legs wide with his own.

"David, stop, please I'm begging you."

"Shut up your stupid bitch. You will learn to obey me." He grabbed a fistful of her hair and pushed her face into the sofa cushion. He thrust himself inside her and she tried to scream but the cushion muffled her cries. She realised the more she struggled the less she could breathe. So, she screwed her eyes closed and gave up trying to stop him, letting him finish, in the hope it wouldn't last too long.

CHAPTER 31

They sat in front Tracy's new doctor, Doctor Douglass. David having made the appointment.

"What can I do for you Tracy?" Said the doctor. Tracy had only seen him a handful of times during her pregnancy and didn't yet feel comfortable opening up to him about her feelings. Not like she had once done in front of Doctor Armstrong. She thought Doctor Douglass seemed a little young to be a general practitioner, he couldn't have been any older than thirty-five. He had light brown hair that was greying at the edges and perfect white teeth.

"Tracy." The doctor prompted, still waiting for her to answer his initial question.

"I am um." She didn't quite know what to say.

"Tracy has been struggling a little since becoming a mother, quite a lot actually." David spoke on her behalf.

"Is this true Tracy?" Doctor Douglass said, looking at Tracy who was visibly uncomfortable.

She nodded.

"She's upset a lot, hysterical even at times and she's even started to act a little paranoid. It's gotten so bad that I've started to worry about leaving her alone with Daniel."

Tracy shot David a glance.

"Right, I see. That is quiet worrying for you both no doubt."

"It is doctor, I'm worried sick about her."

"I suspect Tracy, you might be suffering from extended baby blues. It's a type of depression that can occur as a result of childbirth. Your hormones are playing havoc with your body, and it wouldn't be wrong of me to assume you're in need of more sleep? I remember those times only too well." He paused to glance at a photo on his desk of three small children, which Tracy presumed to be his. "The whole experience of having a baby can be quite frankly overwhelming for some mothers and it can lead to depression. The good news is, it won't last for ever and we can give you some medication to help settle those symptoms. Let me take a look at your current medication."

The room feel silent, whilst the doctor reviewed her notes. Tracy looked around the exceptionally neat and tidy office. Plants sat along a shelf above his desk alongside several more photos of the doctor's family and a handful of books.

"Right, I see you are already taking antidepressants, I think the first course of action would be to increase the dosage, you are currently on what we call a medium dose, and I can see you have previously been on higher, I assume you tolerated that ok?"

Tracy nodded again.

"Ok, I'm also going to prescribe some diazepam to be taken occasionally, when things are feeling particularly tough or when you are experiencing further episodes of paranoia. Would you be happy to try that?"

"Ok." Tracy said quietly.

"Also, why you are here, it might be a suitable time to talk about contraception. I'm guessing it's far too soon for you to be thinking about intercourse, but women are extremely fertile just after they have given birth so it's better to air on the side of caution. I see you have never been prescribed contraceptive medication before. I'm happy to prescribe some for you?"

"I think that would be sensible, don't you think darling?" David said, playing the doting husband.

"I guess so." Said Tracy.

"Right, you are then. I'll go ahead and write you out your prescription. I'd like to see you again in four weeks to review how you are feeling and how you are getting on with the medication. I see that will co-inside with when you are due your post partum check-up, so that all ties in nicely. If you feel you need to see me again before that appointment, don't hesitate to call and make an earlier one. One final thing before you leave. Have you considered joining any of the local baby community groups? There's a few of them that meet regularly once or twice a week. I hear they provide lots of support and useful advice to mums in those early months. It's worth popping along to one of them. Your health visitor will be able to advise when and where they meet."

"Tracy's not too confident at meeting others so I don't think that will be her thing but thank you for mentioning it." Said David, as he rose from his chair and picked up Daniel's car seat. Tracy followed, before saying her goodbye and leaving the office.

David returned to work after dropping Tracy and Daniel at home. Ten minutes later she heard a knock at the front door and was surprised to see it was Maggie.

"You have some explaining to do." Maggie said as she barged past Tracy, not waiting to be invited in. "Why are you back here?"

Tracy spent the next few minutes explaining everything that had happened since she had last seen her neighbour on the driveway of her parent's home. Maggie fell silent. She was shocked and felt so sorry for the young girl sitting in front of her.

"Tracy, he will destroy you. He's already starting to make others see you differently, your own mum for one. He won't stop until you are completely defeated, you know that don't you? I've seen it before, I've been you. You have to leave him Tracy."

"It's not that easy though. Especially without my mum and dad's support."

"Granted, its very unfortunate that the bastard has them eating out of his hands, but you can still leave him."

"There's something else." Said Tracy when she was able to get a word in.

"What else?"

"He knows something about me, something that no-one else in the world knows and if it ever got out, it would land me in a lot of trouble, prison even. He threatened to tell my secret, if I ever left him and I cannot risk that, it'll leave Dan without a mother."

Maggie didn't say anything for a few moments, whilst she thought about what Tracy had said.

"Well then, I see you are left with three choices. Number one, you stay with him, let him berate you, beat you and rape you. Let your son see you as the victim and for him to think it's okay to treat woman like shit. Number two, you kill him. That's my preferred option. Or number three, you leave him and disappear. Far away, somewhere where he won't ever find you. You change your appearance, change your name the full works. Move abroad even if you need to. But that will mean leaving your parents behind, they can't be trusted."

Tracy was stunned, lost for what to say.

"I'm sorry for being blunt. But sometimes you need to be, to get your point across. And when you get to my age and have experienced shit of your own, you learn how to become a survivor and take no prisoners."

"I appreciate the straight-talking Maggie, I really do. Thank you once again and I really am sorry for burdening myself on you the other day."

"Don't mention it and it's fine, I'm here for you, you don't need to apologise to me. But promise me you won't take those bloody pills, if you do, you'll be giving him what he wants, more power. Whatever you decide to do, take back control. Oh, but do take those contraceptive pills. I would strongly recommend taking those.

"Have you taken your tablets?" David asked once they'd finished eating.

"Not yet, I was going to take them later, before I go to bed."

"Where are they?"

"In the cupboard above the kettle, next to where we keep

the other medications and such like."

David went into the kitchen and returned with a glass of water and two tablets.

"What are you doing?"

"We don't want you forgetting, especially the contraceptive pill, take them now as we don't want any further mishaps do we? I have your antidepressants as well. I'll leave the diazepam for when you don't behave."

He handed her the tablets and the water and watched as she swallowed each pill. *What did he mean if she didn't behave? Was he planning on drugging her as way of punishment?*

Supervising her nightly pill taking became part of their daily routine. Each evening David would gather Tracy's tablets and watch as she took her medication. But she had no way to stop it and was aware that she was handing him even more control.

CHAPTER 32

October 1997

"The factory is putting on a dinner dance." Said David as he pulled off his coat. "It's for employees and their partners." Daniel was nestled in Tracy's arms; she held a bottle to his mouth and looked up at David. "You want me to go?"

"Well, that's kind of the point, you are my partner, well wife."

Tracy was surprised that David had wanted to go and was even more surprised to learn he wanted her to accompany him.

"When is it?"

"Next Saturday night, at the Riverside hotel in London."

Tracy was taken aback. She'd never met any of David's work colleagues before and she suddenly felt nervous at the thought.

"London! But what about Dan?"

"Can't you ask your mum if she would have him? I bet she'd love to have him to herself for the night."

"I suppose I can." She wondered.

"Well, we'd be staying overnight, and it would look a bit odd if I didn't take you."

So that's why he'd asked her to go. So that he wouldn't look out of place.

"What would I wear?"

"It's a formal dance so you would need to wear a dress, I'll wear the suit I wore for our wedding. Do you have anything suitable? It's a pity I didn't get advanced notice, you could have lost some more of that baby weight you've been struggling to loose."

Tracy was taken back by his comment. She thought she looked ok and had lost most of the extra pounds she'd gained through pregnancy. She put on a brave face, ignored his comment, and replied. "No, I don't think so. I'll ask my mum and see if she does. She's been to loads of functions over the years."

Jean was thrilled to be asked to have Daniel overnight and she and Tracy spent Saturday afternoon hunting through Jean's wardrobe, in search of an outfit. Luckily, they were the same dress size although Jean was almost three inches taller. Something Tracy had always envied about her mother. Tracy found and fell in love with a long black strapless organza gown, it fitted well, apart from the length, so Jean agreed to take the bottom in a few inches to make it fit.

They were not the same shoe size however, but she reckoned the silver open toe stiletto sandals that Tracy wore on her wedding day would go perfectly with the dress.

As Tracy packed for their night away, she felt a little apprehensive at the thought of the long car drive, meeting all those new people and for leaving Daniel overnight for the first time.

When it was finally time to leave, they loaded their bags into the back of the Fiesta and after dropping Daniel off with Tracy's parents, hit the road for the two-hour drive to London.

Tracy's stomach was in knots by the time they hit the motorway. She tried to curb her anxieties with thoughts of spending the night partying with her husband, a change of scenery and a lay in. The thought of a lay in, in the morning without being woken by a crying hungry child seemed amazing. And maybe some husband-and-wife time, alone without Daniel, would bring back the David she had first fell in love with? She could only hope.

David parked his car in a multistorey carpark adjacent to the Riverside hotel and as they approached the main entrance to the four-star hotel on foot, Tracy could tell it was grand before even stepping inside the building. They made their way through revolving doors that led into a huge reception area with marble floors and a faint smell of furniture polish permeated the air. They passed a large floral display which sat centre stage on top of a round accent table, before arriving at the reception desk.

Their room for the night was equally as nice. Elegant gold curtains matched a runner at the bottom of the huge bed which Tracy thought to be twice the size of theirs at home. Tracy checked out the spacious bathroom and saw a bath, a separate shower cubical and double sinks. Double sinks confused Tracy, she couldn't understand why anyone would need two sinks. She was excited to find white towelling bathrobes hanging from behind the bathroom door and complementary toiletry products such as shampoo and shower gel in little bottles, lined up on a shelf above the toilet. She re-entered the bedroom to see David had discovered the mini bar and asked. "How much did the room cost for the night? It can't have been cheap."

"I dunno, the company paid for the rooms. It's nice though, isn't it?"

"Isn't it just. I'm going to make a cup of tea and have a nice bath. What time does the dinner dance start?"

"We need to be downstairs by seven."

Tracy looked at her watch it was nearly five, two hours would give her plenty of time for a soak before getting ready.

It had been a long time since Tracy had been able to lay in the bath without feeling the pressure of a small child, a ticking time bomb that could suddenly demand her attention at any time. She savoured the moment. But it was shortly superseded by a nervous tension that began to build in the pit of her stomach at the thought of meeting David's work colleagues.

She secretly wished she could just stay and enjoy a peaceful night with room service in their hotel room.

It was nearly an hour later before she emerged from the bathroom wearing one of the hotel's fluffy bathrobes. David was led on the bed holding a small can of beer which she guessed had come from the mini bar and she took a seat at the dressing table.

"Best take these before we forget." David said as he is came out of the bathroom, freshly showered, and wearing a towel wrapped around his middle. He was holding a handful of Tracy's tablets in one hand and a bottle of the hotel's complimentary waters in the other. Tracy was mid-way through applying her make up.

"I suppose I had." She said, placing down the brush she was holding and forcing a smile.

"What's that one?" She said noticing an extra tablet.

"It's one of those diaze thingies. I knew you'd be nervous about this evening and thought it might help you to relax."

Tracy didn't question David's logic; she was indeed extremely nervous and appreciated his forward thinking.

It didn't take long for Tracy to feel the effects of the diazepam, she felt mellow and the nerves she'd been harbouring had almost disappeared. She looked at herself in the full-length mirror. Having gone on a strict diet since David mentioned her weight, she had lost almost all of the few extra pounds she'd been carrying, and she looked good. She saw David standing besides her in his suit and for a moment, had a flashback to their wedding day. Those days before things had gotten so bad between them.

"How do I look?" She asked.

David looking her up and down. "The shoes make you look like a prostitute; can you help me with my tie?"

She turned and helped him with the knot on his tie, avoiding the temptation to strangle him with it as she fort the urge to cry.

Five minutes later they walked up the corridor holding hands and to any onlookers, they looked like any other happily married couple. They arrived downstairs in the lobby to find a crowd of people dressed smartly in suits and frocks. Tracy clutched David's hand tightly, her nerves creeping back in slightly.

"You'll be ok." He said, acknowledging Tracy's hand squeeze.

"Thanks." She replied quietly.

Tracy was soon introduced to people whom she'd never met before and whose names she'd forgotten within minutes. Everyone seemed so friendly and made an effort to ask how she was.

A waiter walked past holding a tray of champagne flutes. David grabbed two glasses and passed one to Tracy who hesitated before accepting the glass.

"A couple won't hurt." He whispered into her ear. "It's sociable."

Tracy started to relax as they mingled through the crowd, passing pleasantries as they went.

"Please prepare to take your seats in the ball room." Came a loud male voice from beyond the crowd

David scanned the seating plan on an easel adjacent to the entrance of the ball room and said to Tracy. "We're on table six."

They made their way through open double doors and located their large round table which sat ten, found their placenames and took a seat.

David was sat to the left of Tracy and the vacant seat to her right had the name Sandra Jones written on a place card.

"That's my boss John's wife." David leant over and whispered to Tracy. "You better be on your best behaviour." And smirked.

Shortly after, everyone was in the ballroom and taking their seats.

"You must be Tracy. Nice to meet you, I've heard so much

about you." Said Sandra, as she took her seat.

"Yes, it's nice to meet you too." Tracy said with a blush. It occurred to Tracy that she knew nothing about David's work colleagues or their partners. He'd never spoken about any of them. Yet so far, everyone they'd met seemed to know who she was. Sandra and Tracy made awkward small talk whilst waiting for their first course to arrive.

"How are you, Tracy?" Sandra asked as she filled the empty wine glass in front of her with one of the several bottles of wine sitting on the table. "John and I have been worried about you."

"I'm good thank you." Tracy replied, slightly puzzled by the strange question.

"Would you like some of this, or would you prefer the red?" Sandra asked, pointing to the bottle of white wine in her hand.

"White's fine, thank you." And found that she needed to raise her voice for Sandra to hear above the chatter in the room.

"My sister had what you've got. It really isn't very nice."

Tracy smiled and turned to David who was engrossed in conversation with a man sitting to his left. She tried unsuccessfully to get his attention to ask what Sandra was referring to.

"I'm doing ok." She finally said.

"My sister even had psychotic episodes, she was convinced for a while that her baby had been swapped at birth and that the child, she bought home wasn't hers. It was awful. John said, David has been very worried about you."

Had he now, Tracy thought to herself. *Exactly what had he been telling people.*

The first course started to arrive by waiters and waitresses wearing white shirts. It all seemed very posh which Tracy found to be a little overwhelming. She looked down at her cutlery, there were two sets of knifes and forks and she had no idea which set she should eat her prawn cocktail with. She really couldn't understand the fascination with posh people having two of everything. So, chose to wait before eating, and follow what the others did. She placed her napkin on her lap in anticipation and looked across the table, her eyes blurred for a moment. She reached for the jug of water that sat in the centre of the table next to the wine bottles. There was a small empty glass next to her wine glass which she assumed to be intended for water. She filled it and took a large sip.

The starters began to arrive and within minutes everyone on her table had been served and were happily tucking in. She took a bite of hers.

"Oh, this is nice." She said turning to Sandra who nodded in agreement. She didn't notice when David picked up a bottle of the white wine and topped up her almost empty glass before refilling his own.

The main course was chicken wrapped in bacon with a creamy sauce alongside roasted vegetables. Tracy tried to place the ingredients in the sauce, so that she could attempt to recreate the dish back at home, when she overheard a conversation taking place between David and the man sitting to his left.

"Yeah it has been tough, I must admit, and at times I've really felt out my depth."

Tracy assumed David was discussing his recently promoted role as a supervisor, until she heard.

"Yeah, she's seen the doctor and they have prescribed medication, but it only helps to a certain extent."

What the hell was going on? She wondered. *Why was everyone talking as though she was on the verge of being sectioned?* She pulled her chair back, placed her napkin on the table and stood up.

"Where are you going?" David asked, holding Tracy's arm.

"Toilet. Is that ok?" She said curtly. Sandra pretended not to have overheard the exchange and pushed her fork around her plate daring to look up.

Tracy walked off in the direction of the double doors which

led into the hotel reception. She felt a little unsteady on her feet. But then again, she wasn't used to wearing stilettos so slowed down her walk and focused her attention on each step.

"Are you ok?" Asked a lady wearing a hotel uniform standing in front of the reception desk, as Tracy walked past looking a little confused.

"Toilet." She slurred.

"Just over there madam." The lady said pointing towards the far side of the reception.

"THANK you." Tracy said overpronouncing the word thank.

Main course plates were collected, and David decided on Tracy's behalf that she had finished with hers, despite barely touching it. She'd been gone ages.

"Before we bring out your deserts, there are a few announcements I'd like to make." Said a portly man, standing on the empty dancefloor, holding a microphone.

He continued to speak as the double doors at the back of the room were dramatically flung open making a clatter, grabbing the attention of a number of people sitting nearby.

Tracy stumbled across the room, oblivious to the man at the front talking. She felt disorientated and couldn't remember where her table was. She stumbled around several tables, drawing even more attention to herself as people whispered between themselves at the spectacle. She eventually found the correct table and clumsily sat herself back into her chair, just as everyone started around of applause. Tracy began clapping without understanding why, in a frantic motion, which didn't match the pace of those around her.

"Where's my dinner?" She asked once the clapping had stopped.

"You've been gone ages, so they took it away." David whispered angrily.

"Oh." Was all she could say. Her mouth felt dry, so she leant over to grab the jug of water to refill her glass. In doing so she knocked over a bottle of red wine which fell in Sandra's direction and spilling its contents over her dress. Sandra screeched and immediately stood up; she was horrified.

The man with the microphone stopped talking and all eyes suddenly fell on Sandra. Realising what had happened, Tracy grabbed her napkin and leant forward to pat the front of Sandra's dress. Annoyed at Tracy's carelessness, Sandra pulled away and Tracy lunged forward, falling off her chair.

"I think you had better get her out of here." Shouted John in disgust.

"Christ, it's not even nine and look at the state of her." Said the man sitting beside David.

David was mortified and wished to God he could erase the last ten minutes.

Although not fully comprehending the conversation around her, she was sure she heard another voice say.

"Maybe you were right in the first place when you said not to bring her."

She couldn't remember anything after that.

CHAPTER 33

Tracy woke alone in the enormous bed. The room was dark apart from light which spilled in from the open door of the bathroom. She wasn't sure where she was at first and it took a few seconds for her to realise she was in the hotel room.

Laying on top of the duvet with her shoes by her side, she shuffled towards the edge of the bed, reached over towards the lamp, and fumbled to locate the switch. She switched the lamp on, and the room suddenly came into view. She looked down and saw that she was fully dressed. She felt confused. She had no recollection of getting back to the room and couldn't understand why she was still dressed. She couldn't remember dancing or much of the evening for that matter. She glanced at her watch, it was blurry, but she made it out to be twelve fifteen. *Where was David?*

"David." She called. There was no answer. Her throat was dry, and she needed a drink. She sat up and the room span. She blinked her eyes a few times to let the sensation settle, swung her legs onto the floor and braced herself in preparation for standing up. She closed her eyes again for a second to steady herself then reached out to the wall for support and slowly made her way to the bathroom. She half expected to find David in there, but the room was empty. She filled the empty glass with water from one of the sinks and downed it in one. She filled it twice more before making her way back to the bed.

The dance was due to finish at twelve so she assumed David would be back any time. She tried to piece together what had happened. She remembered sitting at the table and people were talking about her, they were showing sympathy towards her and towards David, *but why?* She felt sick and her head throbbed.

It was gone two before the door to their hotel room opened and David walked into the room.

"You're alive then." He said bitterly seeing that Tracy was awake.

"What happened? I don't understand."

"What happened was you got paralytic and made a total show of yourself. You were a disgrace, a total embarrassment."

"But I couldn't of David, I barely drank a thing. You know that I really don't get it."

"You say you didn't drink much but how do I know? It was free flowing." David walked towards the bed and Tracy could hear the hatred in his voice.

"But you know I'm not much of a drinker." Tracy stood up and reached her arms around him, seeking comfort but he pulled her arms off and pushed her back onto the bed.

"You disgust me. You need help."

Tracy remembered the pity that Sandra had taken and the confusion she had felt by it, wondering what David had been telling others about her.

"Why have you told the people you work with I'm crazy?"

"I needn't say anything. You proved that only too well yourself tonight." David said and slowly clapped, sarcastically.

Tracy reached for one of her shoes and threw it at him, it caught the corner of his face causing a small amount of blood to trickle.

David stood still for a second, frozen to the spot while he contemplated his next move. Tracy suddenly felt bile rise in her throat and rushed past him to get to the bathroom and made it just in time before throwing up in the toilet.

Once Tracy was sure there was no more to come and that her stomach was empty, she flushed the toilet and pulled herself up to standing. She hadn't noticed David enter the room and could now see him in the reflection of the mirror, standing behind her and shaking his head.

He grabbed the back of Tracy's hair and pulled it down hard, forcing her back onto her knees.

"David, no, stop it." She pleaded, as he pushed her head with the hand still gripping onto her hair towards the toilet and thrust it into the toilet bowl.

"Stop." She cried. "Please."

And without letting go of her hair he flushed the toilet. Water poured over her head engulfing her face and she couldn't breathe. He pushed her head further into the bowl, and he didn't let go until the flush had finished.

"Look at the fucking state of you." He sneered as she collapsed on the bathroom floor gasping for breath.

He kicked her hard and his foot caught her backside, causing her to shunt forward at the force and banging her head on the bottom of the toilet bowl. Tracy clutched her head to protect it as he repeated the action several more times.

Then it stopped, she thought he had finished. Until she heard him unzipping his trousers. She clenched in anticipation of what was to come but it wasn't what she had expected. Instead, she felt the spray of the warm liquid as he urinated over her crumpled body.

Tracy locked the door to the bathroom, although it was pointless, she realised, as it could easily be opened from the other side if David had wanted to.

She removed her clothes and grimaced at the pain as she slipped off her knickers. She turned on the shower and set the temperature to hot, letting the water run over her naked body. It hurt as she rubbed over the soap, but she was desperate to wash away his stench. She washed her hair twice, and only when she was convinced she had removed all traces of his piss, turned off the shower and wrapped herself in a towel. She also grabbed the two remaining unused towels from the shelf on the wall, a hand towel, and another bath towel. Using the hand towel as a pillow and bath towel as a makeshift blanket, she led down in the cold dry bath and tried to make herself comfortable.

David went down to breakfast alone, leaving Tracy to sleep it off in the bath. He'd seen her in there, when he let himself in to use the toilet and brush his teeth. Tracy was aware of his presence but refused to open her eyes.

Neither spoke on the drive home and Tracy flinched when she lowered her body into the passenger's seat. Her entire body ached, and the drive back seemed to take an age.

"What have you done to yourself?" Jean said as she took one look at Tracy and saw the bruise on her forehead. She hadn't prepared an excuse and didn't know what to say.

"Don't get me started." David said, shaking his head disapprovingly. "Tracy mixed her tablets with alcohol. She had a lot to drink, and I hadn't realised until later that she'd also taken once of those diazepam's. It was embarrassing Jean; she was a right state, and she smacked her head on the side of the table during dinner."

"Tracy, how could you. David's worked hard to forge a career for himself at the factory." Jean said, berating her daughter.

"Do you not care for David's reputation?" Said Peter, joining in.

"It's going to take a lot of apologising tomorrow, that's all I know and possibly a new dress for my boss's wife. Long story." He tutted and rolled his eyes.

"Any what happened to your face?" Jean asked David pointing to the small cut below his eye.

"Tracy threw her shoe at me as I tried to undress her and help her into bed. I suppose it could have been worse; her fists were flying all over the place."

"Tracy, I'm ashamed of you." Peter said.

"Oh my god, you look worse that I feel." Angela said as she passed through, suffering after her own night out on the town.

Tracy's eyes welled. She wanted to scream the truth out

loud and defend herself. But she had no choice and was forced to take the hounding. Her dad was ashamed of her. Hearing him utter those words hurt more so than the beating she had endured.

"How's my little man been?" David said as he looked down to see Daniel laying on the living room floor, under his baby gym, whacking hanging rattles.

"He's been absolutely fine, haven't you Daniel?" Jean replied, as she reached down, scoping him up. Tracy put her arms out to take Daniel from her. All she wanted to do was hug her son and to feel his soft skin against hers.

"I think he'd better go to Daddy." Jean said ignoring Tracy. "I don't think we'd better risk you holding him for now."

Tracy wanted to scream at the humiliation of it all. David once again was the victim and all-round good guy. Why couldn't they see him for what he really was?

Tracy pounded Maggie's front door. "I'm coming, hold your horses." Came a familiar voice behind the door, as the bolt slid back, and the door opened.

"Where's the fire?" She said impatiently before taking one look at Tracy and softening her tone. "You'd better come in."

"I want option number three." Tracy said as she gingerly took a seat on Maggie's sofa holding Daniel in her arms.

"Number three?" Maggie said, not following.

"Daniel and I need to disappear."

Tracy filled Maggie in on the events of the weekend and for once Maggie was lost for words.

"Show me all your injuries." Maggie eventually asked. "I think we should photograph them all, just encase you ever need to provide evidence. And then we can start planning your escape."

CHAPTER 34

February 1998

Maggie assured Tracy that she had an idea how to help. But the first thing Tracy needed was money. Well, that was never going to be easy. She could hardly go out and get a job or take out a loan, no bank would ever lend her money if she wasn't earning.

Tracy asked Maggie not to share the plan with her until she was ready. If previous experience was anything to go by, she couldn't trust herself with a secret around David. The fact that she had made her mind up to leave and hide money from him was already taking a huge risk.

It had been six months since David had first given Tracy a weekly shopping allowance to buy their groceries.

It felt liberating pushing Daniel in his pram to the supermarket, having the freedom to make decisions and she loved the ability to pay. Her enthusiasm felt almost child like.

She was limited to how much she could buy at any one time, so went several times a week, buying small amounts each time. She planned meals meticulously, ensuring her grocery bill came in under budget each week. And with a little careful planning, had managed to syphon just over a hundred pounds, all of which she had managed to hide from David. It was a start but at the rate she was going Daniel would have grown up and moved out by the time she had saved enough to leave.

Tracy came up with an idea to swap David's preferred

premium brands with supermarket cheaper alternatives and hid them in the back of the cupboard. Accepting the risk that he wouldn't look and sometimes she even kept the labels from premium tins and jars and stuck them over the top. David never noticed the change in produce, and it was satisfying to know that she had tricked him. But who was she kidding, that only gave her a couple of extra quid here and there.

"How's things?" Maggie asked one afternoon over coffee.

"About the same, David's not really been any different."

"And how's the fund raising going?"

Tracy's looked forlorn. "I can't see I'll ever be able to leave. Raising money is impossible as David controls all the money and bills. I can hardly go out to work. I'd need to pay for childcare and David would soon find out and put a stop to it."

"But what if there was another way?" Maggie said, her face suddenly lightening.

"Like what?"

"I've been thinking. The Post Office has a community board where people leave cards advertising for sale items or services, but there is never anyone advertising ironing services. People sometimes even ask me if I know of any, like I'm some sort of yellow pages. What if you were to set up your own little business doing people's ironing from home. You could do it when David was at work, you wouldn't need childcare, and David would never need find out."

"It's a great idea but wouldn't he question why we had baskets full of other people's laundry waiting to be collected and what if someone knocked on the door when David was at home. I don't know how I'd be able to hide it from him. I just couldn't risk it."

"What about if we pretended it was my business? I could advertise my details and people could drop off and collect from me. You come to me and take a basket at a time and keep all the profits?"

Tracy thought for a moment. "Would you actually do that

for me?"

"Of course. I'd give you the money myself if I had it, so if this helps in any way, I'm all for it."

"How much do you think I could make?"

"I know a few people have said they are willing to pay eight pounds an hour, so I'd start with that. I can write out a card and place it on the board in the morning and spread the word. What do you think?"

"I'm willing to try anything. Thank you, I think it's a great idea."

Within two weeks, the word was out, and Tracy was spending several hours a week ironing. It wasn't much, but it was a start, and she was managing to iron when Daniel napped.

It wasn't long before her business had grown, and she was spending on average of three hours a day ironing. The additional hours proved a little more challenging as it meant she also needed to iron when Daniel was awake. He was a good baby and would sit happily and play with a few of his toys for a short while. But he was almost crawling, and when he was on the move Tracy had to make use of the play pen. Daniel wasn't a fan of being confined, which Tracy could relate to. He would cry and place his arms in the air demanding to be freed.

Within four months Tracy had managed to earn and save nearly fifteen hundred pounds. She felt hopeful and just needed to keep going that bit longer until she finally had enough to disappear.

"I've got lots of annual leave left so I'm taking next week off of work." David said gulping the last of his tea before heading off to work.

"That's great." Tracy lied. "Why the short notice?"

"It was only agreed yesterday. It was a case of use it or loose it."

"Do you want to do anything together as a family or go away somewhere perhaps?" She asked, the thought of having him at home for a week filled her with dread. But she needed to keep up the pretence. Tracy didn't take her eyes off Daniel, who sat in his highchair being spoon fed his porridge. She didn't want David to see her fretful expression.

"It's been full on at work over the past few months, so I just want to relax."

David kissed the top of Tracy and Daniel's heads and headed out the door.

Tracy rushed over to Maggie's as soon as she saw her car pull up.

"We've got a problem. He's taking next week off work, and I've already committed to lots of ironing jobs. What am I going to do?" She spoke quickly in a panicked tone. She was worried she'd loose clients if she let them down and the loss of earnings for a week would mean an extra week living with Him.

"Slow down Tracy. Don't panic, it's just a week. It happens. I'll just make up an excuse and contact those booked in for next week. If anyone makes a fuss, I'll do the ironing myself. Don't worry."

Tracy flung her arms around Maggie; she be lost without her.

It was no surprise to Tracy when David didn't return home after work. He didn't even bother to ring and let her know. It wasn't the first time he'd done this on a Friday night, and she knew by now that if he wasn't home by five thirty, there was only one place he'd be.

So, she didn't bother making him any dinner. The last few times he'd gone straight to the pub after work, he'd come home with a kebab and the dinner she'd cooked ended up in the bin.

She was in bed when David arrived home and was abruptly woken when she heard her name being yelled.

"Tracy."

She quickly climbed out of bed, not wanting David to shout again for fear of waking Daniel. But it was too late. Just as she stepped out onto the landing he bellowed once again from his position at the bottom of the stairs, and Tracy could hear

Daniel's cries coming from his bedroom.

"For fuck's sake David. What do you want? You've woken Daniel."

"Where's my dinner?" David shouted up the stairs.

"Dinner? I didn't make you any, you didn't bother to tell me your plans and I assumed you'd sort yourself out, again."

"We stayed in the pub for a lock in and the kebab shop was closed when we left. I'm hungry and want my dinner. Come down and make me some."

Tracy huffed. "I'll settle Daniel and be down in a minute." She went back to their bedroom to fetch her dressing gown and saw the time on the bedside clock, twelve forty-five.

"What do you want to eat. I can make you some beans on toast?"

"That's not a proper meal." David said, having made himself comfortable on the sofa. "Got any eggs?"

"Yeah."

"I fancy egg and chips."

"I bet you bloody do." She said under her breath as she headed towards the kitchen.

She lit the oven and located the bag of chips from the bottom of the freezer pouring some onto an oven tray and placing them in to cook.

Whilst she waited, she looked at the calendar, she was hoping to leave by mid-September and counted the weeks realising it would realistically be the end of September before she had saved enough.

The timer on the oven beeped, signalling that the chips was cooked, and she quickly fried two eggs in a pan. She dished out the eggs and chips onto a plate and carried it into the living room.

She found David, out cold and snoring on the sofa. Her first instinct was to force chips down his throat, but she thought better of it. Instead, she placed the plate on the table and took herself back to bed.

Daniel was the first to wake up, shortly followed by Tracy after hearing Daniel's babbled "mamma" calling from his bedroom. She was tired having not long regained her sleep following a bout of teething which had made Daniel restless for several weeks. She never complained about it though, he was a child who needed his mummy. David on the other hand, was just an arsehole.

Tracy changed Daniel's nappy and carried him downstairs as he happily babbled away. She never understood how anyone could wake up instantly cheerful and so full of life.

She placed him on the floor in the dining room surrounded by toys whilst she went to prepare his breakfast. She emerged from the kitchen a few minutes later holding a bowl of mashed Weetabix and banana to find no sign of   Daniel. She found him in the living room holding a couple of cold chips and standing up at the sofa where David still slept. Daniel poked David's face with a chip and it made his nose wrinkle. Tracy knew she really ought to stop him, but it was funny watching David being abused by a baby. "DaDa." Daniel poked again, this time putting the end of the chip up David's nose, causing him to wake with a startle.

"What the fuck is he doing?" David shouted and pushed Daniel away. He fell to the floor, landing on his bottom and started to cry.

"He's trying to say good morning to you." She said as she picked Daniel up, still holding a fistful of cold mushed chips.

"Sorry mate." David said, sitting up and reaching his arms out to Daniel for a cuddle. But Daniel turned away, burying himself deep into Tracy's arms. Tracy didn't deny the satisfaction it gave when Daniel refused David. But what did he expect, his son was scared of him.

CHAPTER 35

September 1998

Tracy sat in Maggie's living room and counted three thousand two hundred and forty-five pounds.

"I've got enough." Tracy said.

"I think you do." Maggie said with a smile.

"Ok, what next?" It was now time for Maggie to share her idea.

"Well, I've mentioned to you about my son James."

"Yes, what about him?"

"So, a few years back when he was in his late teens, he hung around with a bit of a bad crowd and went off the rails a bit, like some lads do. It didn't last long, thankfully. He saw where it was heading, distanced himself from them and went off to college and took an apprenticeship. I've got no concerns about him now; he's a good lad and is doing absolutely fine. I would never have moved down here if he wasn't."

"That's really good to hear Maggie, but I can't see what that has to do with my situation."

"Hear me out. James keeps in touch with a couple of his old friends from time to time. One of his friends, Mickey I think his name is. Well, he served a few years at her majesty's prison service for fraud. Anyway, he's out now but still dabbling with a bit of forgery now and again, as a side line. Apparently, he is great at making counterfeits. You know, driving licences, passports, and such. For five hundred pounds he's agreed to create new identities for you and Daniel."

"And you're sure about this?" Tracy asked, feeling a little uneasy.

"Yes, of course. I wouldn't have suggested it if I wasn't. James has assured me that Mickey can do it and I've told James all about your situation. He wants to help."

Tracy couldn't quite believe what she was hearing. "But how do we......"

Maggie cut her off. "So, James is long overdue a visit to see his old mum. All I need to do is arrange when and he's agreed to take you both back with him. He has a spare bedroom which you and Daniel can stay in until you get yourself sorted with your new IDs and a place of your own. You'll have plenty of money leftover to set yourself up somewhere, you don't even have to stay in Manchester, but it'll be far enough away to begin with. I take it you don't have any connections to Manchester?"

"No, I don't know anyone in Manchester, and I don't know James either."

"No, you don't, but you know me, and you trust me, don't you? It's the only way I know how to help you, Tracy. You have come so far. What have you got to lose?"

Tracy sat in silence whilst she processed everything that Maggie had said to her in the last few minutes. Daniel walked over and handed her a toy car he'd been playing with and smiled at her.

"Daniel is still incredibly young; he won't remember any of this if you leave now. He won't remember that man who calls himself his father. But if you leave it too long, he will. He's been lucky to avoid the brunt of David's temper but what's not to say that won't change? If you go to Manchester, it will at least give you some breathing space and buy you some time at least."

"Ok." Tracy nodded. "I'm ready."

Tracy had just under a week until it was time to leave. She couldn't pack until the last minute, but she could get things in order and get organised. She gave Maggie some money and asked if she could buy another car seat for Daniel, as theirs was permanently kept in David's car. Maggie was only too happy to help and kept it at her house in readiness.

Tracy called in at Maggie's house on Friday morning to go over the final plans in preparation for Monday's departure. And she was taken by surprise when a man opened the front door.

"Hi, you must be James." Tracy said holding a hand out to greet him, whilst holding Daniel against her hip.

"You must be Tracy and you must be Daniel." James said ruffling Daniel's hair. "Come on in."

"I'm sorry I didn't mean to intrude; I didn't think you were coming until this evening."

"Not at all, it's fine. I wasn't due until this evening but managed to finish a job I've been working on earlier than expected, so took advantage of having an extra day off and thought I'd surprise mum."

There was something about James that made Tracy feel safe. He was tall and slim and had cropped hair that on other men, looked thug like, but not on James. It suited him and his chiselled jawline.

Maggie appeared. "I'll leave you two to talk while I go and stick the kettle on. Daniel, do you want a biscuit?"

"Yep, bicket." He said, clapping his hands and followed Maggie into the kitchen.

"He's cute." James said.

"Yeah, he is, most of the time." She smiled and rolled her eyes jokingly.

James also smiled. His smile lit up his face and she noticed he smiled through his eyes.

"Mum's told me about some of things you've been through. It sounds like you've had it tough."

Tracy nodded, "just a bit. Do you think I'm wrong to take David's son away from him?"

James thought for a second before answering. "Well, if he'd been a good husband and father and you were simply running away, I would have said yes. But he's not and by all accounts doesn't deserve either of you."

Tracy blushed. "I was extremely vulnerable when we first met and he took advantage of it, exploiting it and using it to his own advantage." Tracy couldn't believe how much she was opening up to this complete stranger. "Have you ever helped any of you mum's previous neighbours in need?" She said trying to be a little more jovial.

"No, this is a first for me. I remember what it was like to live with my dad though, and my only wish from my childhood was that she'd left him sooner. He was a master manipulator, a monster."

So that's why he and Maggie were so keen to help. She knew she'd be in safe hands.

"I really appreciate what you have offered to do for us. I really can't thank you enough. I have some money saved so I will pay my way."

"Don't worry about any of that for now, let's just take it one step at a time. The first being to leave. I'm planning on heading back on Monday, does that work for you?" Tracy nodded. "I take it you'll need a few hours to pack and get things sorted once he's gone to work."

"Yes, I will."

"Do you need anything getting?"

"No, Maggie, your mum." Tracy corrected. "Picked up another car seat for me. That was the only thing I needed to get. I have the rest."

"Ok, I'll help you load up the car. I'll come over once he's gone to work and it's safe to do so."

The only other thing left to do was to say goodbye to her mum, dad, and sister. She'd invited them over for lunch and was dreading it. She had no idea what to say and couldn't exactly just blurt out, *goodbye we're leaving, and you won't ever see us again.*

David answered the door when they arrived at eleven

thirty, having only woken up twenty minutes earlier following another heavy night, down the Dog.

"Jean, Peter, lovely to see you. Come on in."

Tracy was in the kitchen preparing lunch and Daniel who was playing with his blocks in the living room, suddenly abandoned them to rush over and greet them.

"Nanny, Bampy." He said with a squeal.

Tracy felt a lump in her throat as she watched the interaction from a far. Jean now holding her grandson, left the men chatting in the living room and went to join Tracy in the kitchen.

"Where's Angela?" Tracy asked, noticing her sister's absence.

"She was going to come but didn't get home until the early hours and wasn't feeling it this morning. You know what she's like. She said to say hello and that she'll see you next weekend."

Tracy felt a tear run down her face.

"Are you ok?" Jean asked placing her free hand on her shoulder.

"Yeah, I'm fine, I'm just feeling a little emotional." Tracy said dismissively. "It's that time of the month and I'm being silly."

"You dafty. I thought for a minute you were upset that your sister wasn't here. It wasn't that long ago that you couldn't stand to be in the same room together." Jean let out a laugh. "Now what can I help with?"

They ate lunch like any other Saturday. Tracy had spent all morning preparing lasagne and Jean helped to finish the salad whilst she laid the table.

"Tracy, can you pass me the garlic bread please?" asked Peter.

Tracy was lost in thought and hadn't heard her father.

"Tracy." Peter said, trying to get her attention. "Are you with us?"

"Sorry Dad, I was miles away. What did you say?"

"I asked if you could pass me some garlic bread."

"Sorry, here you go." And passed the plate of sliced garlic bread to her dad.

"You've been out of sorts since we arrived. Are you sure you're, ok?" Jean asked once more.

"Daniel had me up in the night and I'm not feeling a hundred percent. That's all. Sorry if I've been a rubbish host today."

Daniel sat in his highchair covered in tomato sauce and happily tucking into his dinner.

"Someone's enjoying their dinner." Jean said, changing the subject.

David joined in. "That's my boy. He likes his food."

"Good lad." Said Peter patting his stomach with pride.

"It is possible to like food too much you know." Jean said looking at her husband disapprovingly and as he popped another slice of garlic bread into his mouth.

Tracy would miss this, the normality of her family and her patent's harmless banter. She would miss them terribly. And it was all *his* fault. He had left her with no alternative other than to leave her family behind. The family that had been there for her and had supported her when she couldn't even get out of bed in a morning.

She stood up and picked up her plate.

"Where are you going?" David asked.

"I'm suddenly not feeling very hungry." She said, a little more sharply than she had intended. Jean picked up on her tone but chose not to say anything and watched as Tracy took her plate into the kitchen.

Once out of sight Tracy held onto the worktop and took several deep breaths, determined to keep herself calm. And she began to question herself. *Could she really go through with leaving them all behind?*

CHAPTER 36

Tracy couldn't sleep. Her mind went over and over the enormity of what she was about to do. Should she leave? Should she stay? She laid awake contemplating and several times even talked herself out of leaving. She even tried to convince herself that as David hadn't hurt her in several weeks, it meant he'd changed. Then she'd berate herself, he would never change.

By four thirty, she couldn't stand laying next to him and listening to his snores any longer so decided to get up. She felt smug as she placed her feet on the carpet. This would be the last time she'd ever lay next to him; she would soon be free.

Tracy tiptoed into Daniel's room and watched as he slept soundly in his cot. Laying on his belly with his arms sprawled above his head and oblivious to it all. She could not describe the love she had for that little boy, he gave her the strength to wake up each morning and was the reason she was breaking free.

David got up and ready for work like he did every other workday.

Tracy made his packed lunch, took him up his cup of tea and woke him. All the while thinking he'd have to make his own cup of tea and packed lunch from now on. She'd no longer be forced to be his slave, or anyone's slave ever again.

Unaware that Tracy had already been up for a couple of hours, David said his goodbyes and headed out the door.

Tracy hurried Daniel to finish his breakfast. Who had he

chosen that morning to play up and mess about with it. Once he'd finished, she cleared up the mess and began washing up out of habit. But then suddenly stopped herself. Why was she bothering to wash up? She wouldn't benefit from it.

She picked Daniel up and placed him in his cot with a few toys whilst she quickly got washed and dressed. And then set to work packing. First, she dragged a suitcase down from the top of their wardrobe and inside it found a few large sports bags.

She methodically went through each cupboard and drawer, removing items that they'd need. Focusing more on Daniel's belongings than her own.

It was nearly nine thirty before she'd finished packing and once, she was done she dragged each bag and case one by one down the stairs, before going up one last time to get Daniel.

She heard a knock at the door and for a moment her heart sank.

"Tracy. It's me. James." She heard through the letterbox, so opened the door and quickly ushered him inside.

"How are you getting on?"

"I'm almost done, just the last few things from down here then we can start packing up your car."

"Good job I've got a big car." He said and his eyes glistened as he took one look at the luggage pilled in the living room, before breaking into a smile.

"Oh god, have I packed too much? I can leave some of it. I mean to be honest I questioned myself, do I really need this much." She babbled.

"Relax, it's fine. It's all going to be fine." He said and placed his hands on her shoulders in an attempt to calm her.

"Sorry, I'm a little nervous."

"I know you are, but you don't need to be sorry."

Tracy packed the last few things whilst James sat on the floor and played with Daniel, who was showing him various trains from his Thomas the Tank Engine train set. Tracy stood and watched for a few moments. *Why couldn't David had been like that?* She had never seen him sit on the floor and play with Daniel. He'd never taken him to the park or invested any of his time on him at all.

"I'm ready." She crocked, aware that she was welling up.

James stood up. "Why don't I take this little man around to mums whilst we load up the car? My car's parked a little further up the road but now David's gone I can bring it outside the house."

Tracy nodded. "Yeah ok. Daniel needs to say goodbye to Maggie."

"She's going to miss you both you know. She looks at you as a daughter." And with that Tracy began to sob.

"Hey, it's ok." He said pulling her in for a comforting hug. "You'll see mum again and you can both keep in touch." James's hug felt good, she could feel the warmth from under his soft white t-shirt and could smell the faint and not too overbearing smell of his aftershave. It was true what he'd said. Maggie would be able to know where she was and who she was.

Tracy collapsed the play pen which doubled up as travel cot and as she pulled the Velcro strap around to secure the frame in place, the telephone rang. Tracy froze for a moment. Unsure whether she should answer the phone or not, decided to ignore it. It would probably be her mum and she had already said her goodbyes, as far as she was concerned. Speaking to her again, might set her back.

It took longer than Tracy had expected to load up the car. And James was right, his four-by-four Jeep was rather large. But fitting everything inside, still felt like solving a jigsaw puzzle. At one point James tried to fit the highchair in the boot and couldn't fathom how it was going to fit.

"Give it here." Tracy said leaning forward and taking it from him. "If you move it around like this and put that bag here. It will fit." She stood back, marvelling at her car packing skills.

"How did you...?"

"What can I say, I have many skills." And broke into a smile.

"What the fuck is going on here." Came an angry voice shouting up the street as it approached.

Tracy took another step back from the open boot to see David marching towards them.

"David. What are you doing back?" She said as she stepped out in front of him.

"What am I doing back? I live here. What I want to know is who the fuck is that?" Pointing to James who remained standing by the boot. "And why does it look like he's playing happy fucking families with my wife."

"Hey mate, I'd calm down if I was you." James said edging closer until he was standing besides Tracy."

"I'm not your fucking mate." David shouted, drew back his right fist and punched James's square in the jaw. Causing James to stumble back before correcting his balance.

But he was not deterred. "Don't make me hurt you. I will if I have to." He said to David.

"David, please don't." Tracy pleaded.

"I tried to call you, but you didn't answer. You never said you were going out today and now I know why."

"But why, you never call me. How did you find out?"

"Find out what? Although looking at this." David said gesticulating to the car, Tracy, and James. "I think it's fucking obvious. You cheating little whore."

"Woo that's enough." Said Maggie who appeared in front of her gate holding Daniel.

"Give me my son?" David demanded, snatching Daniel from Maggie's arms, as he cried in protest. Unsettled from the argument and tired from missing his nap.

"Come with me Tracy. I've parked further up the street as this little twat parked in my space. We're leaving." David said.

"I'm not coming with you David. I'm finally leaving you. I should have done it a long time ago. I'm not putting up with your shit anymore."

"Oh really." He said, taking a step closer towards her,

Daniel still crying in his arms. "That would make an interesting conversation with the police. Don't you think? How my wife has abducted our child, especially when they find out the truth about her past. I give it a day, two tops, before there's a warrant out for your arrest and Daniel will soon be back in my sole custody. Well, that is if he is mine. I've always had my doubts as you know. And now. Well now I can see what you get up to as soon as my back is turned. Who knows. I might put the little bastard into care."

"Now you just wait a second." Maggie interjected. "I know what you've been up to, and I have plenty of evidence to get you locked away. I know how you charm and manipulate others into seeing the good in you, but I'm not easily fouled."

David's demeanour softened and he started to sob, clutching Daniel closer to his chest.

"Spare me the theatrics, you're pathetic." Maggie continued.

"My dad has had a heart attack; he's been taken to the hospital. That's why I rang and came home. I need you both to come with me and say goodbye, they don't think he's going to make it." David said, holding out his spare hand to Tracy.

Tracy looked behind to see Maggie shaking her head and James staring at the ground. She was torn, she had an opportunity to leave but she also felt she owed Tony the chance to say goodbye to his grandson. Tony was nothing like David, he was a good man and had been good to her and Daniel.

"I will come with you, but I'm doing it for Tony. Not for you David. We're over."

CHAPTER 37

Neither spoke on the way to the hospital and Daniel was asleep in his car seat within minutes of the car pulling away.

They arrived at Accident and Emergency and was immediately ushered into a side room where they were asked to wait for the consultant.

A male doctor wearing blue scrubs and a matching surgical cap arrived a few minutes later and gave his name and title, but Tracy hadn't listened properly to either.

"I'm afraid you father has suffered a major heart attack." The doctor paused for a moment to let the news sink in. "We are still running tests but what we know so far was that he collapsed at work this morning and was unresponsive when the paramedics arrived. They managed to revive him, but he suffered a second cardiac arrest shortly after arriving at the hospital. The cause of which was a blockage to one of his coronary arteries. We have fitted a catheter to open the artery and get the blood flowing again, but what we don't yet know is the level of damage this has caused to the heart itself. He is currently in recess, but we will soon be moving him into ICU, the intensive care unit. I need to warn you, the next few hours are critical."

"I don't understand." Said David. "He has always been so fit and well. He's never even taken a day of sick in his life."

"Unfortunately, heart attacks don't always come with a warning. Someone might appear to be slim and healthy but in actual fact suffer from high levels of cholesterol, which ultimately is what is responsible for clogging arteries. We're still waiting on the lab result for your father's bloods, which will confirm if his cholesterol levels are dangerously high. Has he recently shown any signs of being unusually tired or complaining of any chest pain?"

"No, no chest pain." David shook his head. "I did mention to him when I saw him last week that he looked tiered, but he just put it down to working hard, given the time of year. He's been flat out getting people's garden's ready before the end of the summer. Can't you operate and fix the issue."

"Surgery might be an option in the future, but for now, we have done all we can. We need to wait to see how your father's heart responds, now that we have opened the artery. And to the various medications we are giving to help thin his blood and make it easier for the heart to pump."

"Can we see him?" David asked.

"Yes, you can, but I would advise not taking the child in with you."

"You go David." Said Tracy. "I'll call mum to see if her and dad can come and pick up Daniel."

David nodded and followed the doctor out of the room.

Tracy made her way back out to the reception area, pushing Daniel who was still asleep in his stroller. She found a payphone, opened her purse in search of a ten pence coin and called her mum. She answered after several rings.

"Mum, it's Tony he's had a heart attack." Tracy sobbed down the phone, the events of the morning proving too much.

"Try to stay calm love, where are you?"

"I'm at the hospital with David and Daniel but they won't let us take Daniel in to see Tony."

"I'm not surprised, a hospital is no place for a little one. Let me call your dad and get him to come and pick Daniel up. He's working locally today so it shouldn't take him too long to get to you."

"That would be great, thanks mum."

Tracy found a second coin; her next phone call was to Maggie.

"Maggie." Tracy said as soon as it was answered.

"No, it's James. Is that you Tracy?"

"Yes, I wanted to call and explain."

"There isn't much to explain. You had the opportunity to leave with me and you chose not to." She could hear the disappointment in his voice.

"It wasn't as simple as that. He caught me and he would have told the police."

"He would have contacted the police either way Tracy. All you needed to do was hide out with me for a few days until Tracy became someone, untraceable."

James was right of course, but under the pressure she hadn't thought logically.

"I'm sorry, I appreciate everything you and your mum have done for me. I really do. How's your face? I'm sorry for what he did."

"Don't worry about me, I'm fine."

"Thank goodness."

"So, what now?" James asked.

"I honestly have no idea. I'm at the hospital and it's not looking good for David's dad."

"Is Daniel, ok?"

"Yes, he is. My dad's going to come and pick him up shortly."

"That's good. I'm going back to Manchester in a little while." Tracy fell silent, she didn't know what to say. "Take care of yourself Tracy."

Daniel woke grizzly and unsettled, Tracy checked the time and realised it was lunchtime.

"Are you hungry buddy? Let's go and find you something to eat."

Tracy went in search of something suitable to feed Daniel, but her options were limited to a vending machine selling crisps and chocolates. She usually avoided giving him foods like that, but needs must and so she purchased a bag of cheese puffs. She considered giving him the bag to feed himself, but changed her mind, preferring the puffs stayed in the bag and not be tipped all over the floor. She took a seat in the waiting room and waited for either a doctor with news of Tony, or for her dad to arrive.

It was Peter who arrived first, and Tracy immediately threw her arms around him.

"How are you bearing up sweetheart?" He said, as they hugged.

"He's in a bad way. They say the next few hours are critical."

"He's a tough one that Tony, I'm sure he'll pull through. What about this little munchkin?"

Peter looked down and saw Daniel covered in orange and clutching handfuls of congealed cheese puffs.

"Look's like someone is enjoying those."

"That's his lunch I'm afraid. There wasn't much choice."

"Not to worry, I'm sure your mum will make him something when we get him home."

"Thank you, I need to get Daniel's car seat out of the car. Can you stay with Daniel for a moment, and I'll go and fetch the keys."

Tracy went in search of recess and found David sat in a plastic chair holding his dad's hand. Tony was hooked up to all manner of beeping machines and he wore an oxygen mask over his face. David was drained of colour; she'd never seen him look that way before.

"Hey." Tracy said putting a hand on his shoulder.

"Where's Daniel?" He said quietly.

"My dad's just arrived and is going to take him home. He needs the car seat; can I please have your car keys so that I can get it for him?"

"I need some fresh air. I need to clear my head. Can you sit with Dad, and I'll go and sort the car seat?"

"Ok, if you like."

David stood up and kissed his dad before turning to walk

away and Tracy took over the vigil.

"Tony appears to be stable, that's a good sign and we are now ready to move him to ICU." Said the same doctor that had spoken to them earlier.

"That's good. David has nipped out; he'll be back shortly."

Several others arrived in the room who Tracy guessed to be nurses and a porter. She moved out of the way to give them room as they prepared to move him.

"Can I follow?" Tracy asked.

"Sure thing." Said the doctor.

They wheeled Tony and the various machines keeping him alive out of recess and along a corridor before entering a lift that took them to where the ICU ward was situated on the third floor.

The ICU ward was filled with cubicles of extremely sick looking people, surrounded by vast amounts of equipment that gave a chorus of beeps and rhythmic sounds.

Everywhere was brightly lit with artificial lighting, Tracy could see no windows.

Tony was taken to a cubical at the end of the ward, closest to the nurse's station. *Was this one reserved for the poorliest of patients?* She wondered to herself as they reversed his bed into place.

"We're going to need a few minutes to get him set up." Said a young nurse who wore a badge which read *Samantha critical care nurse.* "There's a family room just up the corridor." She said pointing beyond the nurse's station. "Why don't you pop along there and make yourself a brew. I bet you could do with one."

Tracy thanked the nurse and headed off as directed.

She found the room and made herself two cups of tea from a large urn that sat on top of a worktop in the small kitchenet. She'd made one for David, assuming he'd soon be joining her. A television sat in the far side corner of the windowless room facing two small, scuffed leather sofas. *This must be where family members came to take a break,* she thought wondering how long some of the other patients had been on the ward. A small kitchen table and two chairs sat along a wall covered in magazines. Tracy took a seat, sipped her tea, and picked up a magazine which was over a year old. She wanted to think and make a plan about what to do once they had left the hospital, but she couldn't think straight, she was too emotionally drained.

Five minutes later, Tracy had finished her tea and left David's tea on the side after reading a sign that read. *No hot drinks to be bought out onto the ward.*

She made her way back to Tony's cubical and as she got close, she could see a hype of activity around his bed. Machines were flashing and beeping in a high-pitched continual tone and doctors and nursing were fussing around him, whilst the doctor in charge shouted out orders.

"What's happening?" Tracy asked whilst trying to read the body language of the various medics.

"I need you to step aside." Said Samantha. The nurse who had calmly addressed her only minutes before, now spoke with a sense of urgency. "Unfortunately, Tony's vitals have taken a turn, the doctors are working to revive him."

Tracy stood back and watched as the medical team frantically worked to keep Tony alive. And for a moment she was taken back to that damp roadside when the two paramedics worked to revive Emma. The voices around her became muffled and she suddenly felt lightheaded. Samantha put her hand on Tracy's arm which bought her out of her flashback, and she noticed the machines connected to Tony had gone quiet.

"I'm really sorry, he's gone." Said the nurse.

Everyone left the cubical apart from Tracy, who was given some time alone with Tony to say her final goodbyes.

David arrived shortly after to find Tracy sat in a chair besides his dad. She looked up at him with red eyes and shook her head. She stood up and reached out to hold David, but he shrugged her away.

"I'll leave you to spend some time alone with him, I'll wait for you in the family room over there." She said and pointed in its direction.

It was nearly an hour before David joined her, she could see he too had been crying.

"I didn't get to say goodbye. Why did he have to go at that moment. I should have been with him."

Tracy said nothing and made him a fresh cup of tea. His hands were shaking as he took the cup from her, and they sat in silence while he drank it.

Tracy didn't know what to say. How could she leave him now, not today at least. She hated the man he had become, but nobody deserved to loose everything all at once, not on the same day.

CHAPTER 38

They didn't go back to their house that night. Daniel stayed with Tracy's parents and David insisted they stay at Tony's house. Tracy offered to make some dinner having found a few chops in the fridge, but David didn't much feel like eating. Instead, he found a bottle of whiskey in Tony's well stocked drinks cabinet and took to the sofa with the bottle and a glass that had number *one dad* engraved into it.

Tracy made herself busy by making up the bed in David's old bedroom and calling her mum to check on Daniel before joining David in the living room.

"Are you ok?" She asked, not knowing what else to say.

"What do you think?" He snarled, the whiskey starting to take effect. "You don't give a shit anymore; you're leaving me remember."

Tracy braced herself, expecting David to get angry, but instead he wept.

"Why does everyone have to leave me? First it was mum, then you and Daniel and then dad. I'm all alone. I have no-one. Why did he have to go and die?"

David sobbed uncontrollably and so she sat beside him, wrapping her arms around him and he let her.

"I'm sorry." He eventually said once the crying had subsided. "I'm sorry for everything and for the way I've treated you. I'm not surprised you wanted to leave. Please don't go. Don't leave me, not now."

Tracy felt her eyes well up and her own tears started to fall. "I'm sorry too, I'm sorry for what I did. I promise I won't leave you." But she didn't mean it, the reality was, she had no idea what she was going to do.

They sat and Tracy listened to David talk about his dad. She learnt more about his childhood that night then she had in the entire time they'd been together. Within a couple of hours, the bottle of whiskey was empty, and David was muttering incoherently.

"Shall I take you up to bed?" She said empathetically. David nodded with unfocused eyes, and she led him up the stairs.

Tracy was expecting David to wake with a hangover the next morning, but he didn't. Instead, he woke with a renewed sense of purpose. He seemed very focused.

"First thing we need to do is to make an appointment with the funeral director and start planning the funeral."

"Yes, agreed." Said Tracy.

"Then we need to make an appointment to see dad's solicitor. I can't remember who it is, but he'll have some paperwork around here somewhere, I'll search for it later. It should be quite simple, the mortgage was paid off years ago after mum died and as I'm an only child, everything will go to me."

"Ok."

"Then we need to pack up the house in Chesterfield Avenue. Good job you've already made a head start." He said with distain.

"I don't understand?" Tracy said, ignoring the sarcasm. Although, she suspected she did know where it was heading.

"We'll move into here of course. It's a bigger house and we can rent out or sell the other one. There's no way we're going to continue living next door to that interfering old hag. She's a bad influence on you and you're not to have anything further to do with her or that son of hers. Do you understand?"

Tracy nodded slowly.

"What we need now is a fresh start and this will be it."

Tony was a popular man and many people turned up to his funeral to pay their respects.

Tony had always wanted to be buried in the plot next to where his wife had been buried years earlier and David made sure to honour those wishes.

Daniel was deemed far too young to attend the funeral so Angela agreed to stay at home and look after him, and he was to stay overnight, so Tracy could focus her attention on helping David get through the difficult day.

In the days that led up to the funeral. Tracy could feel the all too familiar tension brewing in David. He had said he had forgiven her for trying to leave, and on the surface, all appeared fine between them, but she sensed he was harbouring resentment. Like a ticking time, bomb.

Following the church service and burial, the wake was held in Tony's local pub, where most of the mourners, including David spent the afternoon drinking to remember Tony.

It was early evening when they arrived home to Tony's house, now their house. Tracy couldn't get used to that, she still felt like a visitor. And they'd barely spoken a word on the short walk home.

"What do you fancy for dinner?" Tracy asked once they were back inside.

"Nothing. I'm not hungry." He replied, as he took another bottle of whiskey from the drink's cabinet.

"You've not eaten anything today, David. You need to eat, let me make you something."

"I told you, I'm not hungry." He said, taking a seat at the kitchen table and pouring himself a large measure of the amber liquid into the engraved glass. "I bought him this for Father's Day with my pocket money when I was about thirteen." And raised the glass before taking a big gulp.

Tracy sat down in the chair besides him.

"That was his favourite glass too." She said. "And maybe

one day, Daniel will buy you one similar."

"Yeah right." He scoffed, before taking another sip.

"What's that supposed to mean?"

"Number one dad. Do you even know who dad is then?"

"Not this again David. How many times do I have to tell you, Daniel is yours. There has never been anyone else."

Tracy stood back up, she was not going to argue with him, not today. She needed to take it today and allow him to grieve.

David didn't notice when she started making beans on toast from the other side of the kitchen. He just sat in silence, sipped his drink, and refilled his glass whenever it became empty.

Once ready, Tracy took two plates of beans and toast over to the table and placed one in front of David.

"What's this?" He slurred.

"I made us some beans on toast. It's been a long day and we need to eat."

"But I already told you. I'm not hungry."

"Well, I am, and I thought I'd make some for you, just encase you changed your mind."

Like a pressure cooker having its lid removed, the anger which David had managed to keep tightly sealed came unleashed in one quick movement. And he swiped his hand out in front of him, knocking away the plate of beans on toast in outrage. The force of it caused the plate to ricochet off the whiskey glass and both the plate and glass hurtled off the table and landed on the floor with a smash. David immediately realised what had happened and screamed in anguish, clutching his head in his hands.

"Look what you made me do!"

Tracy froze in fear.

"My dad's glass is broken. He cherished that glass for years, he's not even cold in his grave and because of you it's broken."

"I'm so sorry, I didn't mean to make you angry. I'll buy you another glass."

David stood up, reaching one hand on the table to steady

himself.

"You didn't mean to make me angry. Well, I am fucking angry, you stupid bitch. Don't think I have forgotten how you tried to screw me over and leave me."

"I wish we had gone David; I wish we left this shitty life behind." The words came tumbling out before she had a chance to stop herself.

Without warning David lunged at Tracy, knocking her to the floor as he placed his hands around her throat. She tried to beg him to stop but the words wouldn't come out. She couldn't breathe and fort to free herself. She tried to prize his hands away with her fingers, digging them deep into her own flesh, the need to breathe outweighing any pain she inflicted. She kicking out her legs, hoping to catch him and for him to let go. But the more she struggled, the harder he gripped.

"I will sooner kill you, then have you leave me. Do you understand." He was filled with such rage.

Lights flashed in Tracy's eyes as she continued to gasp for air. And then, everything went dark.

Tracy came to a short while later, on the kitchen floor surrounded by broken glass and baked beans. She sat up and took in a huge lungful of air, her airways hurt. The room started to spin, so she sat for a while until the feeling passed and she was able to piece together what had happened to her. She looked around the room, David was gone.

She rubbed a hand down her tender neck, stood up and walked over to the sink. She grabbed a glass from the draining board and filled it with tap water, she had to steady herself as her hands were shaking. She took a gulp of the water but that too hurt.

She took a few deep breaths through gritted teeth and wondered what to do next. David had hurt her many times, but he had never tried to kill her. She looked over at the table, searching for the whiskey bottle to use as self defence, encase she needed it, but that too had gone. So, she removed the breadknife from the knife rack and held it out in front of her as she slowly made her way around the house from room to room, in search of him.

Besides herself, the house was empty, he'd gone.

She looked out of the living room window; his car was still on the drive, so he hadn't driven off anywhere drunk. Had he panicked and made a run for it, thinking he'd killed her?

Tracy sat on the sofa in the dark living room, hiding the knife under a cushion and waited.

CHAPTER 39

Tracy woke on the sofa, having dosed off for a while. She did another sweep of the house, encase David had arrived home when she'd been asleep, but there was still no sign of him.

She passed the mirror hanging in the hallway and stopped to look at her reflection. She ran her hand over tiny red spots that covered her face, and her right eye was bloodshot. She looked down and saw that her neck was covered in bruises and scratch marks. How could he have done this to her?

She remembered that her parents were supposed to be dropping Daniel off late morning. She wouldn't be able to hide this with makeup and clothing. Or should she just show them. Show them what her husband was capable of and prove them wrong for doubting her?

The telephone rang, causing Tracy to jump.

"Hello." She answered with trepidation.

There was silence at the other end of the line.

"Hello." She said again. "Who is this please?"

She could hear the faint sound of crying down the line.

"David. Is that you?"

"You're alive?"

"Just about."

"Tracy I'm such a mess. I need help. I don't know what to do. Please help me."

Tracy was lost for what to say.

"I'm so sorry for what I did to you. I went too far......... Say something...... Please?"

She cleared her throat and eventually found her voice.

"You nearly killed me, David. What would you like me to say?"
She sighed, inwardly. "Where are you?"

"I'm at the old house. I walked there last night."

"Why David? Why did you do it?"

"I don't know." He sobbed, a little harder this time. "I'd had a lot to drink. I was upset. It had been an emotional day and I hadn't properly processed loosing my dad and then you… I'm sorry. I will get help. Anger management or something."

"I think we need some time apart, why don't you come back here and me and Dan can stay at the other house for a while. We'll see how things are, after you've gotten that help?"

"I need to see you. I'll call for a taxi and be back soon."

Tracy was cleaning up the debris from the kitchen floor when the front door opened. David walked into the kitchen and crumpled when he saw Tracy.

"I'm sorry." He whimpered.

"Stop feeling sorry for yourself and pull yourself together. Dan will be back soon."

David looked panicked. "They can't come here and see you like that. I'll go and pick him up, you stay here."

"I'm not going to hide away, I think it's about time that people saw your handy work, the real you."

"No, please. Give me one last chance to prove to you. Please?" He begged.

Tracy was too exhausted to object and so David left to collect their son.

David still had a couple of compassionate days left at work and wanted to use the time to pack up their old house and officially move back into his childhood home.

David wanted to rent out the house in chesterfield Avenue, seeing it as an investment for their future.

Tracy had wanted to go and pack up the house up on her own. She wanted to use the opportunity to see Maggie, but David had insisted they do it together. Tracy had given Maggie her keys when they left for the hospital that morning, and she and James had dropped off her belongings, dumping it all in the living room. Tracy had returned to the house a few times with David to grab the odd thing but most of their stuff remained untouched.

"We can leave the furniture and rent the house as furnished. My house is already fully furnished, apart from Dan's things so it won't take long to pack up."

Tracy hated the idea of living in Tony's house as it was, but surrounded by his things would only make it worse. It didn't feel like home to her, and she'd be handing yet more control over to David. If she could at least bring some of their furniture it would have made if feel a little more homely, but David was having none of it.

Tracy remembered the stash of money she had kept in the front pocket of one of the sports bags in the living room. She needed to find somewhere safe to store it, she couldn't risk David finding it.

"I'll start putting these bags into the car." She shouted up to David who was packing their bedroom.

She picked up the bag and walked up the path just as Maggie pulled up outside her house.

"Maggie."

Maggie looked up and saw Tracy's blood-streaked eye. She walked closer towards Tracy and gasped. "What has he done to you?"

"Tracy." Boomed David's voice as he hurried up the path. "Get back inside the house."

Tracy looked at Maggie, she felt conflicted. Maggie just shook her head.

"I have to go." She said and shoved the bag she was holding into the back seat of the car, closed the door and followed David up the path.

Several trips later, the contents of their home had been packed and bought over to the new house. Tracy tried to unpack and find homes for their belongings, but David kept interfering and insisting she leave things of his dads alone.

"David. I don't mean to sound insensitive, but if we are going to live here, we need to move some of your dads' things, perhaps we can put them into storage or the spare bedroom for now even?"

"I can't believe you'd even suggest such a thing. Absolutely not, no, it's dad's house and you leave his things alone."

"But David, it's our house now is it not? His record collection for example, it takes up a lot of room. And you don't even play records. I get you want to keep them, but they don't need to stay in the living room. And take the wardrobes in our bedroom, they're full of his clothes, your mum's clothes even. That's our room now, where are we supposed to store our clothes? I feel like I'm living in someone else home. We need to make this house ours. Have that fresh start we promised."

She had a point, he realised, but removing his things felt so final and he just wasn't ready for that. Not yet.

"Let me think about it." He said, as he took out a beer from the fridge.

Tracy took herself upstairs in search of a hiding spot for her cash. She needed to find somewhere safe, somewhere that David would never go, yet somewhere that she had easy access, encase she ever needed it. She decided on Daniel's bedroom as David barely ever stepped foot in there and was unlikely to start looking through his things. She found a shoe box, which she had kept as a keep's sake as it had contained Daniel's first pair of shoes. She stuffed the money into the shoes and kept the box at the back of Daniel's cupboard, hidden from view, behind a pack of nappies. She was just putting the nappies back in place when she heard David calling.

"Tracy, it's time to take your tablets."

Tracy was relieved when David finally returned to work. He needed the routine and structure, and she needed breathing space.

Despite his promise to Tracy, he still hadn't made that appointment to seek help for his issues and she was starting to believe he never would.

"Shall I make that doctors appointment for you?" She said a few days after the funeral.

"What for?" He replied, that wasn't promising she thought.

"To get that help you said about."

"I'm feeling better now, I don't think it's needed."

"But you promised." Tracy pleaded.

"Maybe if you stopped nagging at me, I wouldn't get so mad."

That meant conversation over.

Maggie was in her kitchen making herself a sandwich having just got home from a busy morning at the Post Office when her telephone rang.

"Hello." She answered, feeling slightly frustrated for the interruption as her stomach rumbled.

"Hello Maggie."

"Tracy."

"I'm sorry for rushing off the other day. I've been wanting to talk to you for a while. We haven't really spoken since that day with James and…" She trailed off, struggling to finish the sentence.

"But waiting for an opportunity when he's not at home, no doubt."

She understood only too well.

"I wanted to say thank you for all your support and I'm sorry for not. For not, leaving with James."

"What do you want me to say? You had the opportunity to leave, and you didn't. You've chosen option one. I can't sit back and watch him slowly destroy you, Tracy. It brings back too many bad memories for me."

"It wasn't that straightforward. David's dad was taken ill. He died."

"Tracy, it's never straightforward and there is never a good time to leave. And I'm sorry his dad died, really, I am, but you were not responsible."

"I know. You're right. Can we please keep in touch, here's my new telephone number." She rattled off the number slowly enough so Maggie could write it down. "I don't live that far away, so perhaps we can meet up some time? I know Daniel would love to see you."

"I don't know Tracy. Maybe contact me when you've left him and then we'll see. Goodbye."

And with that Maggie hung up the phone. And Tracy was on her own.

Tracy made subtle attempts to move Tony's things when David was out the house, even though he hadn't yet given her permission to do so. She replaced the odd photo on the wall with photos of Daniel and emptied the shoe cabinet of Tony's shoes, moving them into the spare room so that their own shoes were no longer pilled up next to the front door.

It was several days before David noticed any changes and it was the rug in the hallway which drew his attention to it. She'd replaced the existing rug which looked a bit tatty and had frayed edges with one from their old house.

"What is this?" David shouted as he removed his shoes.

"It's one of our rugs. I like it."

"Well, I don't and there was nothing wrong with the rug that was already down. My mum bought it during one of our holidays."

"David, if you want this to be my house, you need to let me make some changes."

"But it's not your house, it's mine. Yes, you live here because I allow you to. But let's just be clear, this is my house and I'll decide what rug we have in the hallway. Don't go making any further changes."

Tracy couldn't quite believe what David had said, and she couldn't get it out of her head. She felt as though she was back to square one, the independence she had fort so hard to achieve had been taken away from her.

She needed to try and reason with him and so tried again, a few hours later once Daniel was in bed and David was sat in front of the television, nursing his glass of whiskey.

"David, can we talk please?"

"What about?" He said, not removing his glare from the television screen.

"About our fresh start."

"What about it."

"I'm finding it difficult."

CHAPTER 40

February 2001

"Mummy. Can I watch TV?"

"Yes mate, I'll go and put it on for you and bring you in a snack. Go take your coat off and wash your hands."

"Ok mummy." Said Daniel, as he trundled off and Tracy put down the heavy shopping bags she'd been carrying. She switched on the television in the living room and then went into the kitchen to prepare Daniel's snack.

She returned a few minutes later holding a bowl of chopped apple and plastic beaker of milk, to find Daniel sat on the sofa watching Postman Pat, seemingly, without a care in the world. He was such a happy little boy. Well, he was at least when it was just the two of them.

Tracy went back to the kitchen to put the shopping away, leaving the receipt and the remainder of her weekly housekeeping allowance on the worktop for David to check when he got home. A rule that David had imposed a few years ago after Tracy had tried to leave him. He insisted on checking her receipts and counting the money she had left. He tallied every penny to ensure she wasn't secretly keeping any for herself. She had to plead her cause whenever she or Daniel needed new clothes and Daniel would soon be needing some, as he was having a growth spurt. Tracy's legging was also starting to look thread bare and the one pair of jeans that she owned had faded due to the constant washing, but she could forego her needs as long as Daniel was taken care of. She had been tempted on many occasions to use some of her own money, but David was sure to notice if Daniel suddenly wore a new pair of trainers.

Tracy had never been allowed to look at their bank account. And David kept all bank statements in a filing cabinet, which he kept locked. She assumed, that within reason, money wasn't an issue and imaged them to be fairly well off. Thanks to David's inheritance, rental income from their former home and the promotion to department head that he'd recently received.

They should be ok to afford the occasional splurge or family day out, but David never entertained the idea. The only place that he ever wanted Tracy and Daniel was at home where he insisted, they belonged.

Daniel was due to start school later in the year and should already be at playschool, however David declared that Daniel must stay at home until he became of age when school was a legal requirement.

Tracy knew it was because he didn't want to risk Daniel telling a teacher about his daddy loosing his temper. But she always conceded, doing anything she could to keep David happy and for them to live a peaceful life.

Tracy looked at the clock it was five thirty.

"Dan, your dad will be home soon. Go on upstairs and play with your toys and I'll call you when dinner's ready. Ok?"

"Oh, but mum, can't I watch the end of this?"

"No sweetie, I'm afraid not, you need to go up now. And take these with you." She said, handing Daniel the colouring book and pencils he'd played with earlier. Toys were forbidden downstairs.

"Something smells nice. What's cooking?" Said David when he arrived home, shortly after.

"Pie and mash tonight. Is that ok?"

"Sounds good." He said, looking slightly jaded as he took off his coat.

He grabbed a beer from the fridge and took a seat at

the kitchen table to read the newspaper, whilst Tracy rushed around to dish up dinner and lay the table.

"Dan, dinner's ready. Come down now please." She shouted up the stairs.

"How's your day been?" Tracy asked as the three of them sat around the table and ate.

"It's been another tough one. We're behind target on production for this quarter, we've been warned of consequences if we don't achieve, and we've only got two weeks to go."

Tracy didn't like the sound of that. If David was ever stressed at work, it would make him short tempered at home and he'd take it out on her.

"That does sound tough, do you know what's caused you to be behind target?" A genuine question she thought.

"Of course, I bloody know why. It's my job to know. What I'm going to do about it however, well that's another matter."

"Daddy. Can we go swimming one day?" Daniel interrupted.

"What?" Said David.

"I saw it on one of my TV programmes, some children went swimming and it looks like fun. Can we go?"

David rolled his eye and looked at Tracy disapprovingly, as though she should have prevented Daniel from asking the question.

"I think that television you've been watching is putting daft ideas into your head. Maybe you shouldn't be watching so much television."

"Daniel love, finish your dinner and then mummy will run you a bath."

Although only three, Daniel knew when it was time to be quiet and knew not to make his daddy cross. But it didn't stop him trying again, by asking Tracy when he was in the bath, knowing that David was downstairs.

It broke her heart. He wasn't allowed to be a normal boy, who socialised, had play dates and went swimming on a regular basis. When he was younger, it had been easy to please him, but now that he was getting older, he was starting to understand the world and like any other small child, he wanted to explore it.

"Maybe one day, we'll go swimming darling. For now, lets play with these." Pointing to a few small toys which Daniel had lined up alongside the bath. "And make them swim."

Tracy tried her best. She spent most of every day playing with Daniel, being imaginative and playing with the few toys he owned. She was his friend as well as his mother, but it was getting harder to please him and he was now starting to question things and challenge her.

"I'm bored." Daniel said a few days later. A phrase Tracy had not heard him say before. "Can I bring my dinosaurs downstairs and play with them in the conservatory. I like the plants in there, my dinosaurs like the jungle."

"Not today, Daddy's home remember. You'll need to play upstairs today. Mummy will come up and play with you in a minute. I'm just making Daddy something to eat."

"It's not fair." He shouted and stamped his feet, taking Tracy by surprise for the outburst.

"What on earth's that noise?" said David, as he appeared alongside Daniel.

"I want to play with my dinosaur's downstairs, but Mummy won't let me, because you're home."

David looked at his son. "I've been at work all week and I have a hangover. There is no way I'm spending my day listening to you screech at your toys. All I want to do is sit on the sofa and eat my bacon sandwich in peace. Got it."

"I hate you, Daddy." Said Daniel as he stormed off back upstairs.

"Are you going to let him speak to me like that?" David said to Tracy.

Although she thought it was, exactly what he had deserved.

"I'll go and speak to him."

Tracy sat on Daniel's bedroom floor, as Daniel led on his bed staring at the ceiling.

"I hate him." He said again. "He never lets me do anything and he never plays with me. He's just mean and horrible." A tear ran down his face and Tracy felt a lump form in the back of her throat. "And I don't like it when he shouts and makes you cry Mummy. I want a new Daddy."

Tracy didn't know what to say to him. Everything he had said was right, the problem was, there was nothing she could do about it.

So, she said the only thing she could. "Can I play with you?"

CHAPTER 41

Tracy and Daniel walked around the supermarket as they did most days, picking up something for dinner.

"Shall we have fishfingers tonight champ?"

"Yay, my favourite. Can I have ketchup with it?"

"You can indeed."

"Tracy." Came a man's voice from behind.

Tracy turned to see James holding a basket of shopping.

"Who's that Mummy?" Daniel asked.

"James, it's so nice to see you. What brings you here?"

"It's mum, she had a fall."

"Oh my god, is she ok?"

"Yeah, she is, well she will be. She fractured her ankle slipping on some ice a few weeks back. She's been a bit incapacitated, so I thought I'd pay her a visit. How have you been?"

"I'm ok." She lied.

"And this must be Daniel. Wow, you've got so big."

"Mummy, why does this man know my name?" Daniel asked quizzically.

"This is James and we used to live next door to his mummy."

"It would be great to catch up, can I call you sometime?" James asked.

"Probably best I call you."

"Arh. I guess, he's still around then?"

Tracy nodded and James wrote down his number on an old receipt found in his pocket and passed it to Tracy. She took it and thought that she must remember to stuff it into one of her socks in her drawer when she got home.

"Give my love to Maggie. I'd call her myself but..." She paused.

"It's ok, I will and speak soon." He said before walking away.

"Mummy, I like that man James, he seems really nice." Said Daniel on their walk home. "Is James your friend?"

"Yes, he is mate but probably best that you don't tell Daddy that we saw James today. We don't want to make him angry now do we?"

She hated having to have conversations like this with Daniel, it seemed so cruel.

"No mummy I won't. But I wish that I had a friend."

Daniel's requests weighed heavily on Tracy. She wanted to provide a life for him that meant he could be a normal child.

She resented having to make up excuses as to why he didn't do the same things as other children his age. For instance, he didn't go to playschool as they had run out of spaces. And they hadn't yet gone swimming as it would effect Daniel's eczema, which he suffered from occasionally on the backs of his legs.

She told all manor of lies to hide the truth and so no-one saw the reality of their life.

She considered taking Daniel places behind David's back but feared the consequences they would both face if he ever found out. And she couldn't risk Daniel being hurt in anyway. So, she decided on the casual approach and nonchalantly asked David one day if he would leave her some extra money, so that she could take Daniel swimming.

David's eyes narrowed. "Why?"

"Because Daniel keeps asking to go. He would enjoy swimming and it's good for children to get used to the water when they are young. And besides, at the moment it's often too cold or wet to go to the park."

"I don't think so. I don't like the idea of you parading

around in a swimming costume, with all those weirdo's about."

Or was it that he didn't want her to parade around showing off her bruises on her arms and legs? She wondered. Either way, that was the end of it.

James was back home in Manchester, having been assured his mum was on the mend and now more mobile. He often thought of Tracy and was pleased to have bumped into her in the supermarket that day.

He wasn't sure what it was about her than interested him so much. She was naturally pretty and seemed to be a genuinely nice person with a good heart. He felt compelled to help her, even though she had refused to help herself.

When he had told his mum that he'd bumped into her, she had warned him to stay away and not to get mixed up with her issues, but despite that, he had hoped she'd call.

Tracy had noticed changes in David. They were subtle at first but over time had become more obvious. He seemed more uptight and would anger far more easily and sometimes over such small and trivial things.

He would often change his mind and expect Tracy to comply, no matter how unreasonable it might seem. She tried her hardest to prepare and predict his mindset, but she wasn't always able to and would then be forced to suffer the consequences. She was convinced he did it on purpose as a way of exercising power. And he'd sometimes make out that she had forgotten and was going mad. He loved to play mind games and then use it as his reasoning to force her to take a diazepam.

Tracy hated taking them. She'd take one and then loose the ability to think straight or be on alert to protect Daniel. And she nearly always suffered a headache the next day. David's like for a drink was also seeming to become a nightly habit, it helped him to unwind so say, or wind him up, depending on his mood.

She wasn't sure what had caused the changes. She had thought to begin with that it might be the grief from loosing his dad, or the stress from his new job. Either way he continued to refuse any help.

Tracy had wanted to call James but was nervous to do so encase David found out.

Each month he checked the itemised listing on their phone bill to check she hadn't called anyone that wasn't on his approved list. A list which consisted of her mother and sister.

Once she called a number after seeing an advert in the local paper for someone giving away a tricycle. It was too late and had already gone by the time she rang, and she'd forgotten all about it. When David found the number having reviewed the bill some weeks later, he threw all manner of accusations, and she ended up with a fat lip.

So, for the first time since hiding her stash of cash, Tracy removed one hundred pounds from the shoe box and used it to buy a pay as you go mobile phone with credit.

She ensured to distract Daniel with a magazine so that he wasn't aware of the purchase. The packaging was removed and left behind, and she walked out the phone shop with only the phone and its charger.

David who had never before believed in mobile phones had recently bought one for himself. When Tracy asked if she too could have one, he refused. He reasoned that she didn't have a need for one and that the house phone was perfectly fine.

Once they were back home, Tracy placed the phone on charge in her bedroom. When Daniel was later engrossed in watching cartoons, she programmed James' number into the phone and decided to give him a call.

"Hi James, it's Tracy." She said when he answered.

"Hi Tracy, I'm glad you called. How are you? Really, I mean now that little ears aren't around."

"I'm ok, getting by I suppose."

"And how are things with David?"

All went silent on the line for a moment whilst Tracy thought of the best response to that question. But the silence in itself spoke volumes.

"Oh Tracy. You can still leave you know."

"I know. I used to think that he would change, and he did for a while and sometimes he can be so lovely, but I see less and less of that these days. And I'm too scared to leave."

It was James who now couldn't think of the right words to say, so asked "And how is he with Daniel?"

Tracy started to choke up. "If I'm honest, David doesn't have anything to do with him. He prefers it if he's not seen and not heard, if you know what I mean?"

"Poor little fella, he deserves so much better."

"I know." Her voice croaked.

"Has he ever hurt him?"

"No, he hasn't. He's always taken his anger or frustration out on me. How are you, James?" She asked, steering the conversation away from her.

"I'm good. I've set up my own business and now flying solo. It's been tough, but the best decision I've ever made."

"That's good to hear. Are you with anyone?"

"No. I've been on a few dates but never anything serious. I've recently bought myself a computer. It was intended to help keep records for work, but my mates keep telling me to get online and try internet dating."

"What the heck is internet dating?"

"It's where people register their details on a dating website and get matched with other like-minded people. It's a bit like the old lonely-hearts ads in the papers but more modern."

"Oh, I see." She sniffled. "We don't have a computer, so I don't really understand much about them."

"But you have a mobile phone now, I see?"

"I do, but I bought it myself with that stash of cash I had, well still have. David doesn't know about it. He checks the home phone you see and would know if I had called you."

"You bought a phone to call me? I feel honoured."

"Yeah, something like that." Tracy said, feeling embarrassed.

"Can I speak to you again?"

"Yes, that would be nice."

Tracy hung up the phone and sat for a moment reflecting on their conversation. She startled when she heard a 'ping' sound. She looked down at the phone and saw an envelope had appeared on the screen.

She clicked on it, and it read *'It was good talking to you. I guess this will be your first ever text message. Speak soon x. P.S Remember to switch the phone off x.'*

She read the message a few times, he had ended the message with a x, *was that a kiss?* Was that him just being friendly or did it mean something else? She typed a reply *'Yes, first ever text, thanks for the heads-up x.'* and hit send without trying to overthink it.

She deleted his message and switched off the phone. Then decided to hide the phone and charger inside a wash bag she had bought for when she went into hospital to have Daniel. The wash bag was kept inside a large sports bag on top of their wardrobe. And judging by the amount of dust which flew off it when she pulled the bag down, David was unlikely to go in there.

David had spent most of his afternoon in his director Gary Sutherland's office explaining all he was doing to catch up the shortfall against his quarterly target, and it was looking increasingly unlikely that it would be achieved.

It hadn't been his fault of course, he had been let down by one of his major suppliers, but that didn't seem to make any difference to Gary, who demanded the result.

David was in a foul mood when he walked though the front door. All he wanted to do was to have a drink and to block out his shitty day.

"Hi," Tracy said from the kitchen, with an almost sing song voice. The call with James having perked her up. "Dinner's nearly ready."

"What are we having?"

"Chilli Con Carne tonight."

"Not for me I hope." He said as he walked into the kitchen, making a beeline for the fridge to grab a cold beer. "You know I don't like Chilli."

"I thought you did like it?"

"Nope, I don't, and I've told you that before."

Tracy was adamant he had never mentioned this before, she was sure he had eaten it previously.

"So, what am I going to have?"

Tracy panicked, she didn't have anything else suitable that would make a meal, owing to the fact that she was forced to shop little and often, meaning the fridge was never well stocked.

"I could make you beans on toast or some pasta with cheese on top?" She said in an attempt to please him.

"That's not a proper meal is it!" He tutted. "Here's a fiver, go down the chippy and pick me up some fish and chips." And handed her the note.

"What now? But it's getting dark outside."

"Yes now, I'm fucking starving. I've had the day from hell and all I want to do is have a few beers and a nice, cooked meal. Is that too much to ask for?"

"David, you know I don't like the dark and dinner will be ready in a minute, Dan will be hungry."

"Dan can wait until you get back, it's not like he'll starve."

"Can I please at least have some more money to buy Dan something from the chip shop? He loves chips and he'll be upset if he can't have anything."

"No, you've made his dinner. He can wait until you'll back and eat the chilli."

Tracy reluctantly pulled on her coat and shoes and pushed the note into her pocket.

"Ok, I'll see you in a bit." She said with a defeated tone in her voice.

"Aren't you forgetting someone?" He called, from his

position in on the sofa.

"Can't Daniel stay here with you; he's happily playing upstairs, and it'll be quicker if I go on my own."

"No, he's not staying here. I want to relax without any interruptions."

Tracy called Daniel down the stairs. She asked him to put his coat and shoes on and was ready to battle the tantrum that came of telling a three-year-old he wasn't getting a chippy supper.

CHAPTER 42

March 2001

It was the last day of the quarter and David walked into work with a heavy feeling or foreboding. Despite his very best efforts to sauce alternative suppliers, he would be short of reaching his quarterly target, by almost twenty percent. Resulting in a considerable loss for the company.

Keeping his head down, he hurried to his office, fearing the imminent summons from Gary.

Tracy on the other hand felt cheerful. Spring was on its way, meaning she and Daniel could spend more time at the park.

It was her favourite place to take him as it allowed him the opportunity to play with other children, even if only for a short while.

She'd also been speaking regularly to James and they'd been texting each other most days. She had grown fond of James and looked forward to switching on her phone and seeing a nice but random text from him. More importantly though, the phone was hers and it was something that David had no control over.

They been to the park that morning and arrived home just before lunch. Tracy made Daniel a ham sandwich and sat him down in front of the television, before going upstairs to check her phone.

She switched it on and a few moments later the now familiar grey outline of an envelope appeared. She clicked on it and saw a text from James. *'It's nice and sunny here today, hope it is with you too. Speak later x.'*

Reading James's messages caused the pit of her stomach to flutter, a feeling she hadn't felt in a very long time. She typed a reply. *'It has been sunny here as well; we spent the morning at the park x.'*

The phone on David's desk rang. It was the call he had been dreading. He took a deep breath and picked up the handset.

"David, can you step into my office please." Came the voice at the other end of the phone before he had even had a chance to say hello.

A few minutes later, David stood in front of Gary's desk in his small yet functional office.

"You wanted to see me, Gary."

"Yes, indeed take a seat."

David did as instructed. Gary always seemed to wear a hard expression and today it seemed even harsher. Permanent lines were drawn across his forehead, which David assumed were not formed from too much smiling. And his poorly dyed hair, which had previously been the subject of many factory jokes, no longer seemed amusing.

"Tell me David, with only a couple of hours to go. Where do you anticipate finishing for this quarter?"

David swallowed hard and Gary's office suddenly felt very small.

"I am confident we will finish on eighty one percent," He hesitated. "Against target."

"Eighty one percent. I'm just checking, I heard that right?"

"Yes, that's right."

Gary squeezed his fists tightly into balls and placed them on top of his desk. This was not a good sign, David thought.

"Well, that's incredibly disappointing to hear. After my many interventions, I had hoped you'd pull it out the bag and cross the line, but it seems my optimism was proven wrong."

"I..."

"Let me finish please." Said Gary. "This will mean that

there will be no bonus this quarter, for your department." David had expected as much. "And I also need to consider if this role is right for you in the longer term. I appreciate you were only appointed six months ago, but I am now wondering if it was perhaps a little too ambitious to think that you could perform in this capacity. I need some time to think about your future and will call you back into my office in a day or two for a follow up chat. You may now leave." And gestured for David to stand.

David took a slow walk back to his own office. Feeling both angry and embarrassed at the show down that had just occurred in Gary's office. He had worked his bollocks off to salvage as much as eighty percent and doubted that anyone else would have done any better, given the circumstances he'd faced.

"Do you want to help mummy make pizza for dinner?"

"Yes please mummy, have you got any of that spicy ham to go on top?"

"Yep." She said with a smile.

Daniel loved helping to make pizza. Tracy bought ready made pizza basis, laid bowls with various toppings out on the table and let Daniel decorate them. He always made a mess, but she didn't mind, it was good to let him get involved.

"Mummy, look I made you." Daniel said proudly showing off his masterpiece. "Your nose is a mushroom; your ears are the ham, and your smile is the tomatoes."

"My nose isn't a mushroom, silly." Tracy said, poking Daniel jokingly.

He chuckled.

"I'll make daddy's now; I'll do a tomato for his nose."

"You do that mate."

The afternoon dragged. David looked over at the clock on his office wall for what was probably the hundredth time in the past hour. It was finally four forty-five and he let out a sigh of relief. The working day was officially over.

He pulled on his coat and left the office without stopping to say goodbye to anyone. And once in his car, he replayed the earlier conversation with Gary and felt a sudden rush of rage for the way in which he had been spoken to. He thrust his hands down onto the steering wheel in a frenzied motion and screamed. He wasn't discreet and didn't care if anyone passing by witnessed his breakdown.

After a few minutes David composed himself and pulled away from his parking space.

As he neared home, he realised he couldn't bare the thought of walking through the front door and playing happy families to his fussing wife, and her annoying kid. He wanted a drink. No he needed a drink. So, would stop at the pub on his way home. He thought with a but of luck, the boy would be asleep whenever he did decide to venture home.

"Mummy, where's daddy?" Daniel asked as he sat at the kitchen table swinging his legs in anticipation.

"I'm not sure, maybe he got held up at work. Why don't we go ahead and eat our pizzas, Daddy can eat his later."

She knew full well that David had not been held up at work but was determined not to let him ruin her good mood.

By seven thirty, Daniel was bathed and fast asleep in his bed. Tracy doubted that David would come home any time soon so went into her bedroom, pulled down the sports bag from on top of the wardrobe and retrieved her phone. She put the bag back in place, just encase he arrived home unexpectedly. Then switched on her phone and called James.

James answered straight away. "Hi, you don't usually call at night, is everything ok?"

"Yeah, it's fine, he's not home. He's done his usual, disappear to the pub without bothering to let me know. So, I thought, screw him, and called you. I wanted to hear your voice."

"His loss is my gain."

They both chuckled.

"Have you had a good day?" She asked.

"It's not been too bad; I finished a big job which I'd been working on for over a week. It was a total rewire and seemed to take forever. And I managed to finish early today, so went to the gym after work. How about you?"

Tracy imagined James at the gym lifting weights. Although she had never seen his chest, she had often dreamt about what it would look like and how it would feel to touch.

She stopped her mind from wondering any further and pulled herself back to the conversation.

"Daniel and I went to the park this morning, which was nice, we spotted signs of spring on our walk. Daniel likes to point out daffodils and buds on trees. Then we made our own pizzas for dinner. Daniel made my pizza, modelling it on me and apparently, I have a mushroom nose."

"Ok. I was just about to say clever boy, but I'm not sure I'd agree with the mushroom nose." She laughed again. "I wish I could see you again." He said in a serious tone.

"Me too and we will one day, I promise."

"I'll take you out for dinner."

"That would be nice."

They spent the next thirty minutes hypothetically planning dates which both knew would never happen. Not unless Tracy finally plucked up the courage to leave.

Tracy heard a key in the front door and was forced to cut James off midsentence.

"Shit, he's home. I have to go." She hung up the call before switching off the phone and shoving it into the pocket of her jeans in the drawer.

"Tracy." Came the yell from downstairs.

"I don't need to ask where you have been." She said as she walked down the stairs and sauntered past him, she could smell the stench of alcohol from upstairs.

"I'm hungry." He said as he swayed in the hallway.

"Of course, you are." She muttered silently to herself.

"Daniel and I made pizzas; he made one for you. Do you

want me to reheat it?"

"Yes please, thanks." He said and sat down heavily on a chair at the kitchen table.

Tracy couldn't be bothered to attempt a conversation with David. It was usually pointless when he was drunk so she ignored him and instead stood in front of the microwave and watched the timer count down, replaying the conversation she'd had with James.

"Aren't you going to ask how my day's been? Play the caring wife and all." He sniggered, breaking Tracy's concentration.

She turned to look at him. "David, sometimes you get angry when I ask about your day, so I never know whether I should ask or not. And I'm guessing by the fact that you went directly to the pub, instead of coming home, means you've either had a brilliant day, or a crap one. And just for the record, you never ask about my day."

He huffed loudly.

"How has your day been darling?" She asked sarcastically.

"Why are you such a bitch? Why can't you be like a normal wife?"

"You want me to act like a normal wife? I'm not allowed to be a normal wife. I am your possession, and you control absolutely everything that me and Daniel do. You don't treat us like a normal family, so what is it that you expect exactly?"

The microwave pinged and Tracy took out the reheated pizza, placing it in front of David before slowly backing away, realising she should have kept her mouth shut.

"Fuck you." He shouted and pulled himself up to standing, his leg buckled slightly causing him to stagger.

"I've had a Shitty day; I'm being thrown under a bus at work, and I'll probably end up loosing my job. So why don't you give me some appreciation for what I do. I work hard to provide for you both and you can't even be nice to me."

"I'm sorry," She said, feeling fearful. "I should have shown you more appreciation."

David leant down and picked up a slice of his pizza and took a bite.

"Did you say that Daniel made this?" He asked with a mouthful of pizza.

"Yes he did. He was proud of it too. Do you like it?"

"No, there's hardly any topping on it and it tastes like cardboard. You try it?" He edged forward, holding the half-eaten slice of pizza in his hand.

"No, you're ok. I had mine earlier."

"I said try it." And he held the slice of pizza in front of her nose.

She reached forward to take the smallest of bites, to appease him, and as she did, he thrust what was left of the slice hard into her mouth, slamming it into her throat and nearly chocking her in the process.

"Here you are. See how you like it?"

She struggled and tried to move away but David had clamped one hand on the back of her head and the other on the crust of the pizza that protruded from her mouth, forcing her to stay put. Her mouth was so stuffed with pizza, she gagged but there was nowhere for the pizza to escape. David eventually relaxed his hand and Tracy spat the contents of her mouth and stomach onto the tilled floor below.

CHAPTER 43

David woke fully dressed and on the sofa, having only vague recollection from the previous night. He wasn't sure of the time but could see dim light surrounding the edge of the curtains, it was getting light outside.

He sat up and as he did, the knot in his stomach tightened at the thought of another day at work. His head pounded and his mouth was dry. He stood up and staggered into the kitchen, narrowly avoiding the pile of vomit on the floor. He couldn't quite remember if it had belonged to him or not.

He poured himself a drink of water and had hoped to make it up to bed for a couple of hours, but guessed by how light it was, there wouldn't be time. He fumbled in one of the kitchen's drawers, in search of paracetamol, and when he found a packet with just two left, gave out a silent prayer of thanks.

As he knocked back the tablets he looked down at his watch and saw it was already seven fifteen. "Shit." He muttered to himself. He would have to call for a taxi or face being late for work. He couldn't afford to be reprimanded for that, on top of everything else.

He reached into his pocket and took out his mobile phone, it was flat, he'd forgotten to charge it. He walked into the hallway and used the house phone to make the call, urging it to arrive as soon as humanly possible.

He desperately needed a shower, he needed to wash away the sweat and stench from the booze fuelled evening but there was no time. He went back to the kitchen downed a second glass of water and splashed some water on his face. That would have to do. He felt sick, not sure if was due to nerves or from the hangover.

A few minutes later he saw a taxi pull up outside the house. He picked up his keys and ran out of the front door.

"Mummy. Wake up." Daniel said, shaking Tracy.

"I was a big boy and did a wee wee in the toilet, all by myself."

"Well done mate." She said, a little groggily, as she sat up. She saw from the alarm clock that it was nearly eight and then remembered that she had forgotten to set the alarm last night.

"Stay up here for a few minutes. Mummy's just going to quickly pop downstairs and check something."

"What's wrong mummy? I want my breakfast."

"Nothing's wrong my love and I'll make your breakfast in just a minute ok."

Daniel nodded and remained perched on the end of his parent's bed. Tracy cautiously went downstairs, having remembered what had happened the last time she'd had forgotten to wake David. She was both surprised and relieved to find no sign of him. *He must have got himself up and ready.* She thought. Tracy grabbed some kitchen roll and quickly cleaned up the vomit and forced fed pizza from the floor and then called Daniel down to join her.

David arrived at work just in time. Aware that he looked like shit and still wearing yesterday's clothes, he headed straight to the canteen to grab a large coffee before making his way to his office.

Once in his office and with his door closed behind him, he sat at his desk with the intention of catching up on emails. He stared at the screen, but the brightness made him feel queasy. *How on earth was he going to get through the day?*

Today was the start of a new quarter, and David had been instructed to present his plan for how his department would achieve its target, to the board of directors later in the week. He had blocked out most of the day in his diary, so that he could work on it. And following his failure to achieve last quarter, he knew there was even more pressure to achieve. But there was no way he'd be able to work on the plan today, he simply wasn't capable.

He picked up his takeout coffee and his hand trembled as he reached the cup to his mouth. He just hoped to God that Gary didn't need to see him today. He took several large gulps of his coffee, not caring that the hot liquid was scalding the back of his throat. He needed the caffeine hit.

Angela was by now in her final year of university, where she was studying to become a Human Rights Lawyer. She didn't see much of Tracy these days but kept in regular contact by phone.

Angela didn't have a lecture until the afternoon and woke late that morning. She'd arrived home late last night, following an evening at the student bar, where she worked part time to provide extra income. But she might as well had worked there for free, as most of her earnings were ploughed straight back into the bar's profits. For, she spent just as much time in there drinking as she did working. But that was student life for you.

Angela was preparing to take a shower when the phone in the living room of her shared house rang. Remembering she was the only one home, pulled on her dressing gown and headed down the stairs.

"Hello." She answered giving the impression to the caller that their call was most inconvenient.

"Hey sis, it's me. Have I caught you at a bad time?"

"Sorry no, I assumed the call would be for one of the others, it usually is. I was just about to jump in the shower. How are you?"

"I'm good thanks. I just wanted to pick your brains over something."

"Ok. My brain is a little scrambled this morning but go for it."

"Have you learnt anything to do with domestic violence

and the rights of the women inflicted?"

"A little. My degree covers many aspects of justice. And it isn't just women who suffer you know; you'd be surprised by how many men fall victim too. Why? David been knocking you about, has he?" She said, laughing.

"No, not David." Tracy lied. "A friend of mine is suffering from the hands of her husband, and I thought I'd seek some advice for her."

"What sort of thing has been happening?"

"He's a bully and controlling, and he lashes out if she doesn't obey, or if he doesn't get his own way."

"Has she got any evidence that she could take to the police? That would be my first thought, file a police report and have him arrested."

"I don't think she has and it's not that simple."

"It never is simple from the cases I've read. Why can't she just leave him then?"

"She can't. He knows something about her, something that would possibly land her in jail. He's threatened to tell the police if she ever left him. And they also have a child."

"Well, my advice would be, to be upfront and honest with the police, explain his threats and what's been happening at home. Providing whatever crime, she committed isn't too serious, and if it's not in the public's interest to prosecute, then it might not go any further. She would then be free to leave, and nothing would come of it, if he did follow through with his threat."

"Apparently the crime is serious."

"Do you know what happened?"

"Not exactly."

"Then it's difficult for me to give you an accurate prediction of what to expect."

"And what about if she killed him?"

"I'm sorry, you want me to advise on a potential murder?"

"Not murder, more self defence. If she retaliated during on of his attacks or tried to defend herself and he died as a result."

"Are you sure you're ok Tracy?"

"Yes, I'm ok, it's my friend who is struggling."

"Well, deaths like this are tricky, the defendant would need to prove that it wasn't a premediated murder. Self defence killings are incredibly difficult to prove. At best I would say she would face a manslaughter charge and serve a lesser sentence. But my advice would be to leave and seek professional help."

"Thanks Angela, that's really useful to know."

"Maybe next time you could call with something jollier to talk about."

"Sorry, will do."

Tracy ended the call, terrified of the punishment she might face for not waking David.

Tracy and Daniel were sat on the living room floor putting together a Postman Pat puzzle on the coffee table when David arrived home.

"Dan, come on, let's get you upstairs."

"Not until, I've finished this puzzle mummy." He said defiantly.

"Daniel, we can finish the puzzle later, but for now you need to go upstairs. Dinner won't be long and then you can come back down."

"No." Daniel said, crossing his arms and refusing to leave.

David, who had seen the showdown, walked across the living room, and kicked over the coffee table, causing puzzle pieces to scatter everywhere across the carpet.

"I hate you." Daniel shouted at his father. "I wish I could have a different daddy; you're mean and horrible. I wish mummy's friend from the supermarket could be my daddy."

"Is that right." David said, looking directly at Tracy and fixing his stare. "Daniel, you have three seconds to get up stairs before I drag you up."

Daniel did not need asking twice from his father and ran up the stairs as fast as his little legs would take him.

CHAPTER 44

What exactly had his wife been doing behind his back, whilst he was at work? David wondered.

"Who is he?" He shouted.

"Who?"

"The man from the supermarket?"

"It's just an old school friend, that I bumped into whilst shopping and Daniel said he was nice. I only ever saw him that one time. I promise."

"Is he Daniel's father?"

"What? No. Don't be so stupid."

"What did you call me?" He said, as he took a step closer towards Tracy. She reached over and grabbed the lamp from the side table, next to where she stood, without once taking her eyes off him. Even though the lamp was still plugged in and wouldn't stretch any further.

"What are you going to do with that lamp exactly?" He laughed menacingly.

Tracy chose to say nothing but stood guarded, clutching the lamp to her chest.

They both stood silent for a few moments, until David eventually said. "I've had enough of people taking advantage of me, stabbing me in the back and treating me like shit. You are just as bad as the rest of them."

"What are you talking about?" She asked.

"You, my parents, people at work, Gary."

"Who's Gary?" Tracy said feeling confused.

"That's just it. You don't know anything about me, or

anything about what I have to put up with."

"You never tell me David; you've never let me be part of your life."

David walked over to Tracy and removed the lamp from her trembling hands.

"Look at you, you're a mess. Who am I kidding, it's not like anyone would look twice at you anyway." He said, with pure hatred in his voice.

Tracy ignored the hurtful comment and walked past him, heading for the kitchen to dish out dinner. Hoping that sausage and mash, his favourite would at least be a safe choice.

"Daniel, can you come down now please?" She shouted up the stairs a few minutes later.

Tracy carried the plates to the table as a puffy eyed Daniel walked into the kitchen. She felt for her son, and knew what she had to do. So, through gritted teeth said.

"Daniel, you need to apologies to your father." Thankfully, he did as asked.

"Sorry daddy."

David took his seat at the table without acknowledging Daniel's apology. Once Tracy and Daniel had taken their seats, David stood up and picked up Tracy's plate and cutlery.

"David, what are you doing, that's my dinner?"

David carried the plate across the kitchen and towards the bin lifting the lid and scraping the contents of her plate into it.

"David, no." Tracy cried out, but it was too late.

He walked back towards the table and dropped the empty plate in front of Tracy. It clattered as it landed and he bent down so that his eyes were level with hers.

"You don't deserve any dinner for your behaviour today. And nor does he." David said, before repeated the action with Daniel's plate.

"But Daddy, I'm hungry." Daniel pleaded, but it was also too late.

David casually sat back down and turned his attention to Daniel. "Mummy is going to go upstairs, and we're going to have a little chat, whilst I eat my dinner. And maybe, you will both learn to behave in future."

"David, no, I want to stay." Tracy begged, too scared to leave Daniel alone with David.

David stood back up, grabbed hold of Tracy's arm, and pulled her from her seat, causing the seat to crash to the floor behind her.

"Ok, I'm going, I'm going. Just promise me you won't hurt him."

David smiled as Tracy walked slowly out the room and up the stairs.

"Now, I think it's time that we had that little chat, man to man." David said, once he was sure Tracy was up stairs.

"Tell me about the man from the supermarket?"

Daniel thought for a moment. "Um, well. Me and mummy were walking to buy fish fingers and the man shouted her name, Tracy."

"And?" He said, before taking a forkful of dinner.

"Mummy said hello, he said it was nice to see her and I... I can't remember what else. I just remember he seemed nice."

"Has mummy ever seen him again?"

"No daddy, she hasn't."

"Has mummy spoken to any other men?"

"No, I don't think so, she sometimes talks to people at the park, but I think they are all mummies."

"Ok, thank you. If mummy talks to any other men, I want you tell me, ok?"

"Ok. Can I please have something to eat? My tummy is rumbling."

David walked over to the bread bin and retrieved a slice of bread.

"Here you can have this," passing the bread to him, "take it up to your room."

Daniel took the bread upstairs, leaving David to eat his dinner alone.

Once upstairs, Tracy quietly tip toed into Daniel's bedroom

to questioned him on his conversation with David.

The next morning, Tracy woke earlier than usual, not wanting to risk sleeping in or David being late. She resumed the routine of making his lunchbox and waking him with a cup of tea. She hated doing this and never knew what mood he would wake up in.

"Morning, I've made you tea."

David woke and sat up reaching for his cup.

"I've been thinking." He said, without even a good morning or a thank you. "It's clear that you cannot be trusted when I'm at work. So, from now on, you are only to go to the supermarket, no where else and no more visits to the park. And before you say anything, you've bought this on yourself. And to be sure that you are doing as you're told, I will call you throughout the day. And you'll answer of course, as you'll be home."

"But what about if I'm out shopping."

"I've thought about that. You can go shopping, when it's needed, but at a time which I will allocate to you. And I will call you, at the time I expect you home, to ensure you have stuck to the it. This is a massive inconvenience for me Tracy, I hope you understand that, but like I said, you've bought this on yourself."

Tracy turned her head away. She could feel tears pricking the back of her eyes, and she would not give him the satisfaction of seeing her get upset.

"For dinner tonight, I want roast beef with all the trimmings."

She wanted to argue that it wasn't a Sunday and that it would take her hours, but it was no use saying anything. He enjoyed the power it gave him.

"You can go shopping today, between nine forty-five and ten thirty.

"But forty-five minutes won't give me enough time to walk there, buy the groceries and walk back."

"It will give you plenty of time, as long as you hurry and don't stop to speak to anyone."

Sure, enough as promised, and as the time approached nine forty-five, Tracy and Daniel were putting on their shoes, when the house phone rang.

"Hello."

"I'm just checking that you haven't snuck off early, I'll call again at ten thirty." And with that the line went dead.

"Let's go. We need to hurry today mate, so walk quickly please."

"Ok mummy, can we go to the park later?"

"Not today mate. We've got a lot to do."

Following a brisk walk, they arrive at the supermarket at ten o'clock. Tracy did a quick sweep of the shelves, grabbing items that were on her list, which included a joint of beef and vegetables, whilst Daniel's little legs struggled to keep up the pace.

David sat in his office watching the clock tick by, he imagined the frenzied state his wife would be in by now and smiled at the thought.

Tracy stood in line to pay for her groceries and was grateful that there were only two others in front of her. And they were both carrying baskets, not trollies. She glanced at her watch, it was ten past ten, she'd done well considering. It was then she realised she had forgotten to get flour, a key ingredient for the Yorkshire puddings which David had insisted on.

"Shit." She said out loud without realising.

"That's a naughty word mummy. What's wrong?"

"Sorry mate, I forgot something, and we need to leave the queue to go and get it."

Tracy picked up her basket in one hand, took hold of Daniel's hand with the other and walked as fast as she could without breaking into a run. She grabbed the flour from the shelf and headed back to re-join the queue. Cursing at herself when noticing someone had taken her place.

A few minutes later, with bags in had, they made their way through the car park. She looked again at her watch; it had just gone a quarter past ten.

"Right mate, fancy playing a game?"

"I love games. What is it?"

"This one is called monster chase. We have to pretend that a monster is chasing us and run home as fast as we can, ok?"

"Ok mummy, let's go."

They ran as fast as Daniel's little legs would allow, Tracy continually glancing down at her watch for a time check.

"Mummy, slow down, my legs are tired."

"Dan, we're nearly home. You need to run that little bit further and then we're safe from the monster, ok?"

Daniel tried to keep up a good pace but every few metres slowed to a walk. To any onlookers he looked as though he was skipping.

"Nearly there mate, keep going." Tracy insisted, at ten twenty-eight, and as the end of their road came into view.

"Mummy I can't run anymore; I don't want to play the game. Can we walk now?"

Tracy hesitated for a moment, she was aware she was panicking. "Daniel, mummy needs to run home as she is expecting an important phone call from daddy. If I run ahead, you can walk. I can see our house and I will be able to see you. There are no more roads to cross, so you just need to walk. Ok? Like a big boy."

"Ok mummy."

Tracy kissed the top of his head and ran as fast as she could. When she reached the front door, she could hear the phone already ringing. She dumped her shopping bag and hurried to turn the key in the lock. It opened and she picked up the phone just in time.

"Hello." She said panting.

"Good, you're home. And it sounds like you've been rushing about." Tracy bit her tongue and said nothing. "I will call again throughout the afternoon, so don't think about popping out again. And I'm really looking forward to my roast dinner later."

Tracy listened whilst pulling the phone cord as far as it would go, so that she was able to bend her head out of the front door and see Daniel approaching the house.

Through the handset, she heard the sound of a door opening followed by "Bye darling, see you tonight."

She realised that for David to end the conversation in that way, meant that someone must have walked into his office. David's actions had allowed her to put Daniel in potential danger. He'd gone too far, and she could not allow that to happen again. Years of put downs, telling her she was not a good enough wife. A good enough mother. Too fat. Dictating what she wore. Who she saw. Monitoring her movements. Forcing her to take pills that she no longer needed. The injuries she had sustained. The sex he had forced upon her. It was all too much, and she'd finally had enough. It was time for her to take back control.

Maggie was sat at her dining room table finishing off a jigsaw of a meadow which she had started a few days earlier. She had always enjoyed doing puzzles, but this one was particularly challenging, and she just wanted it finished.

She was glad of the distraction when she heard the phone ring.

"Hello."

"Hello Maggie, it's Tracy. Please don't hang up."

"Tracy, what do you want?" Said Maggie, her tone a little harsher than she had meant.

"I just wanted to say, I'm sorry again for what happened, and I need to tell you something?"

"Well, I know you haven't left him, and James has told me, that you two have struck up quite a friendship."

"No, I've not left him, but I have a plan and I needed to tell someone, but please don't tell James."

"Ok, enlighten me."
"I've decided to go with option two."

CHAPTER 45

Roast beef with all the trimmings as requested by David was almost ready when he arrived home from work. And the receipt for the groceries on the worktop ready for his inspection alongside her purse, which held the remainder of her weekly shopping allowance. Daniel was upstairs playing nicely, and the house was spotless. Tracy felt confident that David would be pleased.

"How was your day?" Tracy asked as she dished out the roast potatoes.

"It was ok, thanks." David said.

"Do you want to cut the beef or shall I?" She asked, trying to keep the conversation on safe territory.

"I'll do it, just let me wash my hands first."

They spent the next few minutes in companionable silence as David sliced the meat and Tracy dished out the remaining vegetables.

They sat and ate with little chatter between them. Tracy didn't have anything to say, and David didn't seem to be in a talkative mood or want to share much about his day either. That suited Tracy, who saw family dinners as a necessity rather than a social interaction.

Once dinner was over and three empty plates were all that remained on the table, Tracy began to clean the kitchen and Daniel went back to playing in his bedroom.

David went over to the medicine cabinet and took out two tablets, her antidepressant and contraceptive pill. Deeming it not an evening requiring diazepam, as Tracy had behaved. He poured a glass of water and handed her the pills. She took the contraceptive pill first and swallowed it with a large gulp of water before placing the antidepressant into her mouth to repeat the action. David smiled, feeling content that his job was done, turned to leave the kitchen. And once Tracy was certain he was out of sight, she spat out the small white pill and wrapped it in kitchen roll before tucking it into the pocket of her jeans.

May 2001

Tracy became used to David's cruel micromanagement style of matrimony. She tried innovative ways to gain Daniel's co-operation with the speed in which they shopped and walked, and planned each shopping trip to ensure she knew exactly where she needed to go. Only once had she missed David's call and it had resulted in a slap and her dinner once again being thrown unceremoniously into the bin. And she was made to sit and watch David and Daniel eat theirs. She was okay with that, providing Daniel wasn't forced to go without.

"I'm going out tomorrow night after work." David said once he had finished eating. And Tracy was surprised as it had been a long time since he had given notice of a night out.

"Ok. Would you like me to make your dinner, for when you get home?"

"Yes, please and I'd like you to make lasagne?"

"Will do." She said, with a helpless smile.

"The reason I'm telling you, is there's to be no phone calls whilst I'm out."

"But I usually call my mum or sister on an evening."

"I don't want you speaking to anyone when I'm out from now on. I'll call the phone periodically to ensure the line is free and I expect you to answer within three rings. The same goes for when I'm at work."

"But what if someone calls me?"

"You better hope they don't." He said, as he walked off to fetch Tracy's pills.

Daniel was playing happily in the bath, as Tracy supervised from her perched position on the toilet seat. That small boy with blond hair and big blue eyes was what kept her going and gave her the strength to carry on.

"Mummy's going to get your pyjamas out, I'll be back in a minute." She said as she stood up to leave the bathroom.

"Ok mummy."

Tracy stopped at the top of the stairs and listened for any sign of David approaching. All was quiet except for a faint noise of the television coming from the living room. Tracy went into their bedroom and pulled open the small top drawer from her chest of drawers, pulling it hard so that it popped out of the runners. Taped to the back was a small plastic sandwich bag containing pills and she reckoned there to be about twenty-five in total. She added today's before taping it back into place and replaced the drawer back on its runners.

The side effects from the sudden withdrawal of her medication had been difficult to cope with, she had suffered nauseousness which had lasted for days, a raging headache that she just couldn't shift and had been sick several times. Her nightmares had also returned and were worse than ever. She had read that stopping the medication, without gradually weaning off them, was not advisable. But needs must and she knew the side effects of a sudden withdrawal, would only be temporary.

"Mummy, I'm ready for you to wash me."

"Coming." She said and hurried back into the bathroom.

As advised, David stayed out after work the following evening. And Tracy made sure he had a plate of lasagne with garlic bread, dished out, ready and waiting, for when he got home.

Once Daniel was in bed, Tracy called James.

"How are you?" He said. "I've not spoken to you much these past couple of weeks."

"I'm sorry, I've not felt too well. I must have caught a stomach bug or something." She lied.

"Sorry to hear that, are you feeling better now?"

"Yes, I am, thank you. How have you been?"

"I've been really busy with work these last couple of weeks, I can't complain though, business is good."

"That's good, no date tonight, it's Friday after all?"

"No, I'm not sure that internet dating thing is really for me, after all?"

"Oh no, really, how come?"

"First of all, I might think I'm hooking up with a twenty-five-year-old attractive looking bar maid, but when we actually meet, it's a fifty-eight-year-old grandmother. Apparently, this happens all the time. People lie on their profile to get dates." They both laughed. "And besides, I'm not interested in dating right now."

"You can't let work get in the way of finding someone. You need to make time."

"It's not that. I've found someone. There's someone I have feelings for, but it's complicated."

"Isn't it always." She laughed.

"Tracy it's you. I have feelings for you, strong feelings in fact. I know I shouldn't have and it's wrong, but I can't help how I feel. There's something about you, I can't explain it." Tracy fell silent, unsure what to say. "Say something." He urged.

"I have feelings for you too James." Her voice croaked. "I didn't realise you had them too, I thought mine was just some sort of fantasy."

James sighed. "But I do understand it's useless, we can never be together."

She desperately wanted to tell James, to share her plans with him and ask him to wait for her, but she couldn't. She couldn't risk implicating him in anyway.

"Maybe we could be, one day." Was all that she felt able to say.

"I'd better go." He said, suddenly feeling awkward.

Tracy ended the call and laid on her bed for what felt like hours. Her heart was racing, and she felt giddy like a lovestruck teenager. She heard the phone in the hallway ring and remembering the three-ring rule, she quickly got up off the bed and rushed downstairs to answer it.

"Tracy." She heard David amidst a lot of background noise; chatter, music and shouting. The pub was obviously busy.

"Yes I'm here."

"Good girl, I'll see you later."

"Ok."

"And Tracy, and make sure you're wearing something sexy when I get home." He whispered down the phone before ending the call.

Tracy's giddy feeling suddenly changed to nausea and frustration. She went back upstairs, threw herself onto her bed and punched her pillow, allowing the anger she had been bottling to escape.

By the time David's taxi pulled up, the phone was back in its safe place, and Tracy had managed to compose herself. She wore her best bra and knickers and sat at the kitchen table waiting for him to arrive. She felt sick to her stomach at the thought of having sex with him, but she needed to keep him onside, and it wouldn't be for much longer, she told herself.

Tracy could hear David clumsily taking off his shoes and coat in the hallway, and cursing himself as he dropped his keys onto the carpet.

"I'm in here." She called out.

David soon appeared and realising that Tracy was wearing only her underwear, looked her up and down and smiled, his eyes heavy from all he had drunk.

He pulled out a chair and sat himself down next to Tracy. He instructed her to stand. She did as she was told and stood awkwardly in front of him. He rubbed his hands over her body, and she could see the bulge in his trousers, he was hard. She felt the urge to kick it but managed to stop herself.

"Dance for me."

She hesitated, she had never danced for him, or for anyone, for that matter and didn't know what to do.

She moved her hips from side to side and lifted her arms in the air, pushing her breasts out in front of her. Not knowing if that was right or not. She turned around, thrust her rear towards him and felt his hands clasps over her buttocks. She felt bile rise to her throat, and for a split second considered reaching for the block of knives. She could end him, right here, right now.

"Take off your bra." He ordered and she obliged. "And sit on my lap."

Rather that sit on his lap she straddled one of his legs. She turned her body to face him, as he fondled her breasts and sucked on her nipples.

"If you want to act like a hoar, I'll treat you like one." He said and grabbed a fist full of her hair. He pulled her head back and thrust his tongue into her mouth, so aggressively she didn't know how to respond. He grabbed one of her hands and held it over his bulge gyrating against it and groaning as he did.

She hated this man with a passion but was overpowered with frustration and decided to take advantage. She closed her eyes and thought of James. She imagined it was his lap she was sat on and that it was his wet cock she could feel through the material of his trousers. The thought of James turned her on. She rubbed herself slowly up and down against David leg, and letting out a groan of her own. He withdrew from the kiss and ran his tongue back over her nipple and sucked hard. And the more she groaned, the harder he sucked.

After a few minutes, he stood them both up and pushed away the chair. He pulled down her knickers and bent her across the table. He unbuckled his trousers, spread her legs wide, and forcefully entered her. She let out another groan which took them both by surprise and he still hadn't noticed that her eyes were closed. He plunged hard inside her, again and again. Her groaning increasingly grew louder, until she could hold it no longer and was consumed by a force of which she had no control. She wasn't expecting to climax, but she did, and it felt great. He wasn't to know that her orgasm wasn't for him. He thrust one final time and grunted before withdrawing himself.

David zipped up his trousers, pulled the chair back in place and sat down. Tracy pulled up her knickers and reached for her dressing gown, which hung on the back of one of the other chairs.

"I'm starving, did you make lasagne?" He asked. As if the last ten minutes hadn't happened.

"Yep, I'll go and warm it up for you."

He thanked her and licked his lips, drunkenly displaying signs of dehydration, as Tracy went to heat up his dinner.

"I'm thirsty too, can you get me some water? Oh, and you need to take your pills before I forget."

CHAPTER 46

Tracy switched on her phone, the envelope popped up and she saw she had three messages, all from James. She opened the first one, it read. *"I'm sorry for what I said the other night, I'd had a few drinks and it sort of came out. I'm falling in love with you and."* And what? she thought as she hurried to open the second message. *"I feel helpless as there is nothing that I can do about it, and I know you'll never be mine."* She read the message several times before opening the final message. *"It's messing with my head. So, I think it's best if I distance myself from you, for a little while at least. I hope you understand. James x"*

Tracy read the messages over and over as tears rolled down her face. She couldn't blame him for wanting to distance himself. She had never led him on, but to expect him to wait in the hope that she'd one day be available, would be unfair. She typed out a reply. *"I completely understand. I just wished things could have been different, I have feelings for you too. All my love Trace X"*

Tracy was sick of feeling like a hamster on a wheel. Constantly running, but going nowhere, as David barked his orders. To tell her what to wear, what to eat, what time to shop, when she could speak to her family and so on.

It was time to step up her plan.

David, now two months into another quarter, was sat at his desk checking various spreadsheets, to calculate his quarter end projection. The issue with the suppliers had long since been resolved, but a nasty case of norovirus had spread around the factory's shop floor and followed shortly after by the flu. The viruses had caused internal resources issues which affected productivity. And over the last few weeks, David had even found himself back on the shop floor, pitching in when needed.

His current projection was looking like he'd finish the quarter on eighty seven percent against target. It was better than the previous quarter but knew finishing on anything less than one hundred percent would not be acceptable. He didn't cope well with pressure at the best of times, but this was keeping him awake at night.

David came home from work in a yet another irritable mood. Tracy knew he was under pressure at work, but as usual, he hadn't shared any of the details with her. Instead, he turned to the bottle to find his escape. She always knew when he was stressed, as he opted for sprits over beer.

Ordinarily, Tracy would feel more on edge whenever David had presented these moods. But now. Now it played right into her hands.

David was in the living room nursing a large measure of a single malt.

"David, do you want to join us for dinner, it's nearly ready?"

"Keep mine in the oven, I'll join you in a bit." He replied, without even taking his eyes off the television. Tracy gulped, knowing the evening would end with some kind of altercation, and for her plan to work, she must not stand up for herself or retaliate in anyway.

A few hours later Tracy was up in Daniel's bedroom reading him a bedtime story, when she heard David calling up to her.

"Tracy, I'm ready for my dinner." Immediately followed by "Tracy."

"Sorry mate, we need to finish the story for tonight."

"Thay's not fair." Declared Daniel.

"I'm sorry, I'll read you an extra story tomorrow night,

ok?"

"Ok." He said. Clearly unimpressed by the interruption.

"Did you hear me?" David called, as Tracy approached the bottom of the stairs. She braced herself and poked her head around the living room door.

"Yes, I heard, sorry. I was just putting Dan to bed; I'll warm your dinner up for you now."

"He's old enough to put himself to bed, don't you think?"

Tracy ignored the comment and warmed up the plate of breaded chicken, chips, and peas, appearing a few minutes later with his plate of food before passing it to him, and then taking a seat on the sofa next to him.

"What the hell!" He shouted, having taken a bite of a chip. "The chips are disgusting and soggy."

"Sorry, they're reheated. Chips don't quite taste the same after they've been warmed up."

"Why the fuck did you give them to me then?"

It took Tracy all the strength she had, not to tell him it was his own bloody fault, for not eating his dinner, when it was freshly cooked.

"What would you like me to do?"

"I want you to make me some fresh chips?"

"Ok," she said and took the plate from him, before going into the kitchen and switching the oven back on. Half an hour later Tracy was holding a fresh plate of chips with twice reheated chicken and peas. And silently praying that the chicken would at least give him the shits.

"I'm going to go up for a bath and grab an early night, if that's ok?" She asked, once David had confirmed his dinner was ok.

"I don't want you to go up yet. I want you to sit and watch TV with me."

Tracy took a seat beside her husband. She wasn't able to relax and remained in an upright rigid position whilst she pretended to watch the programme playing on the television. Her mind going over how things had ended with James, until she felt her eyes water and wiped away a tear with the back of her hand, hoping David hadn't noticed.

Tracy woke David and the first thing she noticed was that he looked like he'd not slept.

"Bad night's sleep?" She said, handing him his cup of tea.

"I've had better." He replied, clearly not wanting to elaborate.

His low mood had lasted for days, and it was obvious to Tracy, that he had something on his mind. His pasty complexion and dark circles under his eyes, told of his troubles and lack of vitamin D.

In a normal marriage, in times of need, a wife would be concerned and would want to help her husband. A year a go Tracy may have also considered such. But she had since lost the ability to feel any empathy towards him and it was hardly a surprise, given all he had inflicted on her over the years.

Realising she was staring at him, Tracy smiled and asked. "How about I pick you up another bottle today? You can unwind with a few drinks this evening and me and Dan will pick us up a takeaway?" And for the first time, in a long time, the smile on her face was genuine.

"Ok, sounds good." He paused, thinking for a moment before adding. "Go shopping between one thirty and two fifteen today, ok?"

She nodded.

"And no phone calls during the day remember."

Tracy turned and headed out of the bedroom, without commenting.

The morning dragged and David had called the house three times to check she was at home. She guessed he had stepped up his check ins, since it was such a sunny day, and fearing she may have been tempted to take Daniel to the park.

Instead, Tracy set up a makeshift paddling pool in the garden from an old tyre which she'd lined with bin liners. It wasn't great but it just about held enough water and Daniel seemed to enjoy himself, none the less.

When lunch time came around, Tracy couldn't face eating anything, nerves had set in as she began making preparations for the evening.

Shey picked up the land line, hoping that David wouldn't choose now to call. She couldn't use her own mobile phone for this call, there needed to be an audit trail. And she dialled the number which she knew off by heart.

"Hello medical centre, how can I help you?"

"Oh yes, hello." Tracy said, peering around the door to check Daniel wasn't listening. But he was engrossed in cartoons and munching on a sandwich.

"I'm really worried about my husband, I think he needs to speak to someone, a doctor and get some help."

"Ok. Can you tell me a little more about what it is your worried about?"

"He's not been himself lately. He's been worrying about things for a while now, and is incredibly stressed at work. He's also been drinking a lot more recently. I'm worried he's suffering from depression and developing a drink problem to compensate." Tracy paused, to allow a small forced and rehearsed sob.

"I understand. Let me make an appointment for him to see a doctor. Do you think he'll cooperate and come into the surgery?"

"Yes, I think he will. I plan on having a conversation with him this evening. I'm going to tell him about my concerns, and hopefully we can have an open and honest conversation."

"That sounds like a good idea. Would he be able to make an appointment on Thursday morning at ten forty?" *In two days time, that's perfect.* Tracy thought to herself.

"Yes, I'll make sure he's there. Thank you."

Tracy then proceeded to supply David's details so that the receptionist could book him into the system, before ending the call.

"Daniel, are you ok?"

"Yes mummy."

"I'm just going to pop upstairs for a few minutes and when I get back down, we need to pop to the supermarket, ok?"

"Can we stop at the park today mummy?"

"Not today sweetheart, I'm afraid."

Daniel asked to go to the park almost every day and it broke Tracy's heart. She could hear the faint sound of Daniel's whining, as she climbed the stairs.

Once in her room, she closed the door behind her and climbed onto the bed to retrieve the bag containing her phone. She switched on the phone and had hoped to see a text from James. She waited for a minute or two and felt disappointed, when the envelope failed to appear. She scrolled down her contacts, she had only two, James and Maggie. And selected Maggie.

CHAPTER 47

Maggie answered on the third ring.

"Hello."

"Hi Maggie, it's Tracy. I'm calling because it's happening tonight, and I need your help?"

"What do you mean you need my help. I don't want to be implicated in your plan."

"No, not like that I promise. I need Dan to stay with you tonight please. I need him out the way, I don't want him. home when it happens."

"And how do you exactly plan to get Daniel out, without David noticing?"

"I've thought about that don't worry. Can you please meet us at six forty-five. At the post box, around the corner from my house? It's on Maple Drive, which is the first right off the High Street. I need you to take us both to get Dan some dinner, then drop me back off and take Dan back with you. I'll call you in the morning to make arrangements for getting him home."

"And what if your plan doesn't work?"

"What do you mean? It will work."

"But what if you end up getting arrested?"

"I won't."

"But what if you do?"

"Then call my parents, I'll give you their telephone number."

"Very well. Six forty-five?"

"Yes, that's right. And Maggie?"

"What?"

"Thank you."

At twenty past one Tracy and Daniel both had their shoes on and were ready to leave the house. And as expected, David called just before one thirty and again at two fifteen.

Once back home following another hurried trip to the supermarket. Tracy parked Daniel in front of the television which he was not pleased about.

"But mummy, I want to go back outside and play in the garden. I don't want to stay inside and watch my cartoons."

"I know darling, and we will go outside again real soon. I just need to do a couple of jobs, ok?"

"Ok." He said, unable to hide his disappointed and threatening tantrum.

Tracy placed the newly purchased bottle of whiskey towards the back of the drinks cabinet and removed the one that had already been opened. She held the bottle up to the light and realised there was still half a bottle in there. She poured half of its contents down the sink to ensure that only two, three glasses at most were left in the bottle.

She ran upstairs to retrieve her stash of pills, still hidden and tapped to the back of her drawer.

She didn't own a pestle and mortar, which would have been ideal for crushing tablets, so instead used a rolling pin to do the job. She laid the small, sealed plastic sandwich bag on top of the kitchen worktop, arranging the tablets and smoothing them, so that they were spread evenly. She picked up the rolling pin and ran it back and forth, applying as much pressure as she could muster.

Her collection had now grown to over fifty antidepressants and twenty diazepam. It took longer and more force than she had expected, but once the tablets had been crushed into dust, she cut a small hole in the corner of the plastic bag and carefully tipped its contents into the open bottle of whiskey. She re-screwed the lid and gave it a good shake, before placing the bottle back into the drink's cabinet, ensuring to place it in front of the full bottle she had just purchased.

"Mummy, can we go outside now?"

"Nearly mate, can you please just give me two more minutes?"

"Ok." He said impatiently.

Tracy pushed the empty plastic bag into the back pocket of her jeans, to dispose of later, and washed down the work surface, to ensure no traces had been left behind.

Tracy's nerves had started to get the better of her and when David returned home from work, she felt sick to her stomach at the realisation of what she was planning to do.

"Good day?" She asked as he walked through the door and into the kitchen.

He looked dishevelled. His shoulders were hunched, his shirt untucked, like a rebellious high school student and his tie loose around his neck. She also noticed stubble on his face, having neglected his morning shave.

"Nope." Was all he could be bothered to say.

"Want to talk about it?" She asked, unsure what else to say.

"Nope. I just want peace and quiet and to have a few drinks."

"Ok, I'll leave you be. I'll go upstairs and play with Dan for a bit and then we'll go out in about an hour to fetch that takeaway. What do you fancy?" She asked, knowing that there were several different takeaway shops within a mile radius, providing plenty of options.

"Not sure yet. Let me have a think about it and I'll tell you before you go."

"Ok." She said and began to climb the stairs, pausing after a few steps to listen to the sound of the drinks cabinet opening and liquid being poured.

"Hi mate, can I play with you, in your room for a while?" She asked Daniel when she reached his bedroom.

"Yes mummy, but I'm hungry, when's dinner ready?"

"I have planned a special dinner for you tonight, you just have to wait a little bit longer, can you do that for me?"

"But mummy, I am starving." Daniel said dramatically clutching his stomach for effect.

Tracy pulled out a folded piece of kitchen roll from her front pocket and unfolded it to show two chocolate digestive biscuits.

"Will this do for now?"

Daniel's face lit up. *It certainly would*, she thought to herself.

CHAPTER 48

They played for a while on Daniel's bedroom floor. His cars lined up in a row as he took charge and gave instructions to Tracy on where to drive the cars that she was in control of.

Forty-five minutes later, Tracy interrupted the game and said. "I'm just going to pop downstairs, I'll be back up in a second, ok?"

"Ok mummy, don't be long though, I'm still hungry." He reminded.

She crept down the stairs, not wanting David to hear her approaching.

She stood at the door to the living room and could see the whiskey bottle on the coffee table. She struggled to see how much was left in the bottle, given that the bottle and liquid was both brown in colour.

She took a deep breath and walked further into the room, where David sat holding a glass and watching the television. The glass was almost empty, and she reckoned given the time she had been gone, it must be his second glass.

"Any thoughts on dinner? I was planning on heading out shortly?" She asked, trying to act normal.

David turned his head to face her, his eyes were already heavy and bloodshot, and he let out an almost unintelligible slur which Tracy assumed to mean kebab and chips.

"Ok, I'll get Dan ready and head out in a minute. Can I have some money please?"

"Ten pounds, zin my wallet zon side." He just about managed to say, referring to the table in the hallway where he kept his wallet and keys. David rarely gave permission for Tracy to go into his wallet, he usually insisted on giving money to her himself. She guessed he was already starting to feel the effects of the tablets.

Tracy took the ten-pound note from his wallet and pushed it into the front pocket of her jeans, then headed back upstairs to get Daniel ready to leave.

She opened his wardrobe and retrieved a little green backpack which she had packed earlier in the day with pyjamas, his toothbrush, and fresh clothes. She reached further into the wardrobe for the shoe box containing her stash of cash, removing the cash from the box and placing it into the rucksack, pushing it down, so that it was concealed Daniel's clothes.

"What are you doing mummy?" Daniel asked glancing up from his cars.

"I am, um, getting ready for our little adventure, which starts with that special dinner I promised."

"Yay." He declared.

"Let's go downstairs and put our shoes on, ok?"

Daniel stood up excitedly and nodded.

"Let's go mummy."

Tracy put a finger to her lips to quieten his enthusiasm. He understood the gesture and so quietly made his way down the stairs and sat on the bottom step, waiting for Tracy to pass him his shoes.

"Ready?" She said in a hushed tone, once her own shoes were on.

"Yes mummy." He replied quietly.

She glanced at her watch; it was six thirty. She stuck her head around the door to the living room and saw that the lid to the whiskey bottle was sitting next to the open bottle on top of the coffee table. *He must have poured himself another glass,* she thought. And judging by what she could see of the glass he was holding, *was making good progress with drinking it.*

"See you shortly." She said.

"Hum." Was all that David could muster, in the way of a reply.

Tracy and Daniel left the house and made their way down the street holding hands.

It was a beautiful evening and the trees that lined the street were now out in bloom, with branches that were full of various shades of pinks and whites. She hadn't been able to stroll and appreciate its beauty in such a long time. Thanks to David.

"What are we having for dinner mummy?"

"You'll soon see." And feeling a sudden rush of adrenaline, said. "Tonight, is going to be a special adventure for you."

Daniel began to excitedly skip along the pavement, without letting go of Tracy's hand. They soon turned the corner, and she was relieved to see Maggie's familiar blue astra, parked halfway down the street, along side the post box as instructed.

"Daniel, you won't remember my friend Maggie. We used to live next door to her. She's really friendly and is going to take us for that special dinner I promised."

When they arrived at the car, Tracy opened the back door for Daniel to climb in.

"But Mummy, I don't have my boaster seat."

"Don't worry about that today. You're a big boy and will be fine." She said, pulling the seat belt over him before closing the door and walking over to the front passenger's side.

"Hi Maggie, thanks for doing this."

"Where do you want to go?" She replied.

"McDonalds please, this little man deserves a special dinner."

"Yay." Came Daniel's voice from the back seat.

Daniel had only ever eaten McDonalds once before on his birthday, when Tracy had convinced David to take them. David hated the place and the food, so it was never usually something Daniel was allowed to have. He'd only agreed to the meal on the condition that they did a drive thru. So, Daniel had never experienced the fun of actually sitting inside the restaurant.

Ten minutes later, Maggie pulled into the carpark and parked underneath an illuminated golden arch which span the length of several parking bays. Tracy climbed out of the car and opened Daniel's door to let him out. He'd already unbuckled his seatbelt, unable to contain his excitement. He had seen so many McDonalds adverts on the television and had always begged Tracy to take him. Maggie joined them as they walked through the car park and when they passed a bin, Tracy stopped, pulled out the plastic sandwich bag from her pocket and threw it in.

On a normal day, the smell of deep-fried food would have sent Tracy's taste buds into overdrive, but today, it made her feel queasy.

They searched for an empty table and as they made their way through the crowded restaurant, a spotty teenager wearing a uniform and carrying balloons, headed towards them and handed a red balloon to Daniel.

"Can I have it mummy?" Daniel asked, checking in with Tracy before accepting it.

"You certainly can mate; it's a special dinner remember?"

Daniel said thank you to the boy, skipped over to the empty table they had found and took a seat.

"Can I have a smiley meal mummy?"

Tracy chuckled. "Do you mean a happy meal?"

"Oh yes, that's right. I want chicken nuggets, chips, ketchup, and a milkshake please?" He said enthusiastically, requesting a repeat of what he'd had for his birthday meal.

Tracy looked quizzically at Daniel. "Strawberry or chocolate milkshake?" Unable to remember which one he'd previously had.

"Strawberry please."

"Ok. And anything for you Maggie?"

"Just a coffee for me please."

Tracy couldn't help but notice that Maggie looked

uncomfortable and was obviously struggling to keep her own nerves at bay.

"Stay with Maggie Daniel and I'll go and order the food."

Tracy shortly returned, balancing a Tray containing a happy meal, strawberry milkshake and two coffees. Daniel was happily colouring in a paper placemat that he had been given, along with a small pack of crayons from the same boy who'd given him his balloon.

"I love it here mummy. This place is the best." He declared, as Tracy handed him his dinner.

"How's it going?" Maggie asked, once Daniel was happily tucking into his dinner and oblivious to the grownups sitting in front of him.

"It's so far going to plan. And I'm confident it will be finished or thereabouts when I get home."

Although Maggie knew of Tracy's intentions, she did not know the details. She was surprised to hear that Tracy had gone through with it and had been convinced she'd change her mind at the last minute.

"Daniel." Tracy asked, as he shovelled a ketchup smeared French fry into his mouth.

"How do you feel about having a sleep over at Maggie's house tonight? Mummy needs to have an important talk with Daddy later and Maggie's promised you can have fun at her house."

Daniel hesitated and looked at them both, feeling a little nervous, which was understandable, given that Maggie was technically a stranger to him.

"Ummm." He said, dragging out the word, unsure what else to say.

Tracy silently cursed herself. She should have told him, rather than asked him and risk giving him an option to say no.

"Will you stay with me mummy?"

"No mate, but I will see you first thing in the morning and Maggie's house is really nice."

"But you said, I could have two stories tonight remember?"

"That's ok Daniel." Maggie replied. "I can read you two stories and I've also got Toy Story on video."

Daniel looked puzzled and Maggie realised he had no idea what Toy Story was.

"It's a film. I thought you could stay up late and watch it with me." She put her hand to the side of her mouth and whispered. "I also have biscuits."

"But Daddy doesn't let me stay up late."

"Daddy won't be there; we can keep it as our little secret. What do you say?" Maggie said, giving him a little wink as she spoke.

"Ok, sounds fun. But you promise mummy, I'll see you in the morning."

"I promise." She said and reached out to hold his hand.

"I've put my savings in Dan's overnight bag as a precaution. Although I'm not sure why."

Maggie nodded.

CHAPTER 49

It was nearly eight o'clock when Tracy walked through the front door, having asked Maggie to stop off at the Kebab shop to pick up a takeaway for David, just encase.

Pretending that Daniel was with her, she said out loud.

"Go on upstairs, put your pyjamas on and brush your teeth, I'll be up in a few minutes."

She walked into the kitchen and placed the wrapped bundle of food down on top of the worktop. She could feel bile rise in her stomach and her heart was beating so fast she thought she would faint. She took a few moments to compose herself before shouting.

"Shall I bring your dinner into you?" But there was no answer from the living room.

She took a plate from the cupboard a fork from the drawer and took slow footsteps as she carried the kebab into the living room, still wrapped in its paper.

David appeared to be asleep. His head slumped against the back of the chair, with his arms against his sides and his mouth open. She saw the empty glass still loosely gripped in his right hand and on the coffee, table was what looked like an empty bottle and along side it, the newly purchased bottle. *He'd drank it all* she thought to herself *and then some, by the looks of it.* She put the plate down next to the bottles and gently touched a hand on his arm, but he didn't move.

"David." She said shaking him slightly. Nothing. She stood back and looked at him; it was getting dark outside and the light in the room was fading fast. She walked over and closed the curtains, before turning on the light and going back to take a closer look. His pale face now looked grey and clammy, and his lips were a slight tinge of blue. She took the glass from his hand, placing it on the coffee table and put her hand under his nose to check for signs of breathing. After a couple of seconds, she removed her hand, she couldn't feel anything. She tried again, this time with her cheek. Like she had seen people do on those emergency rescue programmes, that David loved to watch. She was shocked to feel his breath against her cheek. It was faint, but he was still breathing and alive.

She took a step back and began to pace up and down the living room drawing in deep breaths to calm herself. She hadn't expected him to still be alive and didn't know what to do.

She picked up a sofa cushion and held it over his face, then quickly pulled it back. *No, she couldn't help him along.* If the police or forensic people got involved, they'd be sure to spot signs of suffocation. *Had she given him enough pills?* She had only guesswork and assumptions to go on, she had no way of being sure what a lethal dose consisted of. *Should she call an ambulance?* She left the room and walked into the hallway. She picked up the phone and froze for several seconds as she hovered over the numbers. *What would she say? And what if they made him better?* She slammed down the phone and ran clammy fingers through her hair in exasperation.

She continued to pace and realised that her mouth felt dry, so she walked into the kitchen and over towards the sink. She reached for a glass that sat on top the drainer, her hands were trembling. She filled it with water and took a large gulp. But that only seemed to make her nausea worse, and she retched into the sink, bringing up only liquid, her stomach empty from loss of appetite. She turned on the tap to rinse the sink and took another mouthful of water. This time to rinse her mouth.

She sat down at the kitchen table and cradled her head in her hands. All was quiet in the house, except for the faint murmur coming from the television which continued to play in the living room and the ticking from the kitchen clock on the wall.

She hadn't planned on him still being alive, she had assumed he'd be dead when she returned home. She ran through the options again in her mind. *Call for help? Help finish him off? or wait it out and see what happens?* Either way she couldn't undo what had already been done. If she called for help and they managed to reverse the damage, he'd know she had tried to kill him and would make her life even worse that it was already. *And what we he does to Daniel? What if he went to the police and they believed him? Daniel would grow up without her.* A similar outcome, she imagined if she finished him off and the police found out.

"Fuck it," she said out loud. Cross with herself for repeating the same thing over and over. She glanced at the clock on the wall, it was now nearly nine. She decided her only option was to wait it out. She would go up to bed and if he was still alive in the morning, she would have no choice other than to call for help. She walked into the living room one last time and checked again, still breathing.

She contemplated tidying up and stopped herself, she needed to leave things as he had left them, she didn't want anything to appear staged or having been interfered with.

Daniel had made himself at home at Maggie's house and was curled up on the sofa watching Toy Story. Maggie observed him from her own position in the armchair. He was such a lovely little boy, and it angered her to think of the things he had been denied or had bared witness to. She felt reassured, knowing that Daniel had settled in her company. *If only she could settle,* she thought to herself, fearing what Tracy was up to back home.

"My Daddy never lets me watch TV at night or when he's at home?" Daniel suddenly said, out of nowhere.

"Does he not?" Maggie replied. "That doesn't seem very fair."

"He's not fair, he's mean."

Maggie wasn't sure how best to respond, so went for a safe option. "Well let's make tonight extra special then. Would you like a hot chocolate to go with your biscuits?"

"Yes please." He grinned; all thoughts of home temporarily forgotten.

Tracy laid on top of the bed covers, not wanting to climb inside and get too comfortable. They smelt of David, the faint woody scent of his aftershave. The same fragrance he'd always worn. More recently that scent had made her retch, but she remembered back to a time when it had resembled comfort and happiness and of the man she had once loved.

She couldn't pinpoint when things changed exactly. Maybe he had always been a monster and the first few months had simply been an act?

She thought back to those early days in the garden of her parent's house when he had saved her from such a dark place. And she'd kept the letters he had written, in a box under the bed. She reached under the bed for the box and began to read them, allowing herself to grieve for the man she had once loved. Light sobs came at first, which intensified until she was howling.

Unsure what was driving the emotion, was it grief? Was it sadness for how things had turned out? Or was it anger, at how he'd taken advantage of her vulnerabilities when they had first met. *Yes, it was anger*, she told herself. *Anger and frustration.* She had already spent years grieving for the man he had once been and would not shed another tear.

Her thoughts drifted to different memories. Ones that had involved kicks and punches, of lost friends, rape, and slavery. Being removed of her independence and freedom and of the basics rights that any adult human being should be allowed. He had denied her of those. And finally for the experiences and opportunities that Daniel had missed out on.

She recalled many of the traumatic events that he had

inflicted on her over the years and vowed to herself, that once this was over, Dan would have the most amazing childhood. She would see to that.

Her legs felt jumpy, and she couldn't relax laying down. She got up, put the letters back in their box and under the bed, and walked over to the window. She pulled back the curtain to look out into the darkness. Since the accident, she had always feared the dark, but tonight it seemed so calm and almost soothing. The half moon prominent in the clear sky kept a watchful eye as it shone down on the world below. The moon combined with distant streetlamps provided a faint amount of light and she could see the outline of neighbouring houses and trees. It was all so quiet and so peaceful.

She thought of Emma. It was nearing the anniversary of her death. Seven whole years since that fateful night. As she looked out into the night's sky, she felt the burden of the guilt she'd been carrying for all these years suddenly lift. And she forgave herself. She'd served her sentence, her comeuppance for what she did. Only her prison bars were invisible.

By three a.m. she was certain she had done the right thing and it was finally time to head downstairs and check on David.

She didn't want to draw attention to the house so didn't switch on either of the lights in the hallway or on the landing. She took the stairs slowly, creeping down them in the dark and not wanting to make a noise.

Nerves took hold once more as she pushed the door to the living room, opening it slowly and was glad that she had at least left the living room light on.

David sat motionless, slumped in his chair where she had left him and with his head bent to the side. She moved closer towards him, convinced that any second he would wake and take his revenge on her. She tilted his head straight, his earlier grey complexion now looked mottled and lifeless and his lips dry and blue. She repeated the same breath check that she had done several hours earlier, and this time could no longer feel the faint breath against her cheek.

She let go of his head and it immediately lolled forward, his neck no longer supporting it. She placed two fingers on her own neck to find where to feel for a pulse and when she found it, it was beating hard and fast. With one hand on David's forehead, she moved his head back and placed two fingers from the other hand on his neck, in the same place she had felt her own heartbeat. And she felt nothing. The earlier clamminess she had felt on his skin had gone and he now felt cold to touch. He was dead.

CHAPTER 50

Tracy immediately let go and took a step back, clasping her hand over her mouth. Although this was the result she had wanted and was expecting, it still came as a shock.

She hesitated for a few moments, before the adrenaline took hold reminding her that she still had one final thing to do, before making the call to the authorities.

She decided to unwrap the kebab, and make it look as though she had given it to him, with the intention that he would eat it. The sight of the cold congealed meat and stench made her gag.

Next, she went in search of the empty blister packets she had kept. Having previously fished them out of bins when David was out of sight, and hiding them upstairs along with the empty packets of diazepam from the cupboard, which David had assumed were unopened. She scattered them on the coffee table, next to the bottles and glass.

She surveyed the scene and rehearsed in her head the words she would say to the paramedics, police, family, and anyone else who needed to know.

She suddenly remembered that the empty bottle would contain traces of the medication, and if examined, may determined the death to be suspicious. She picked up the bottle, took it into the kitchen and washed it thoroughly several times, before drying the outside with a tea towel. She carried the clean bottle back into the living room, pouring in a tiny amount of whiskey from the other bottle and swilling it around.

"That'll do" She said to herself.

Tracy looked down and realised she was still fully dressed. She darted upstairs, hurried to remove her clothes, and changed into a fresh pair of pyjamas. Too fresh, she considered and quickly removed them, opting instead for a pair out of the washing basket. She put the fresh pyjamas back in her drawers then rumpled the bed, so that it looked as though someone had slept in it. Finally, she tilted her head forward and ruffled her hair.

Once she was certain she had everything in place she made her way back down the stairs, picked up the phone and dialled 999.

"Emergency, which service do you require?"

"Ambulance. It's my husband."

"Just putting you through." Said the operator.

"Ambulance service, is the patient breathing?" Came a new voice.

"No, I don't think so."

"Ok, can I have your address please?"

Tracy rattled off their address followed by their telephone number, sounding hurried and out of breath.

"Please hurry."

The operator asked Tracy to check a number of things. She stretched the phone as far as it would reach, making her actions seem authentic as she dashed back and forth to the phone. She was asked to lay David onto the floor which she did after moving the coffee table to provide more room. It was a struggle, and she was left out of breath, *but at least all seemed genuine,* she thought.

She confirmed to the operator that she didn't think he was breathing, and neither could she feel a pulse. She was asked to perform CPR while instructions were provided to her down the phone. She did not follow these instructions of course but made sufficient grunts and heaves for the benefit of the operator, who could just about hear in the distance.

Several minutes later Tracy could hear sirens in the

distance and was momentary bought back to that roadside where she hugged Emma tightly. Panic set in as the sirens got louder and flashing blue lights could be seen through the curtains.

She ended the call with the operator, hurried to open the front door and quickly ushered the two paramedics into the living room.

A middle-aged lady with greying hair pulled into a bun, immediately knelt to assess David, and had what looked like a portable oxygen tank in her hand. A second paramedic, a younger looking man with short cropped dark hair, spoke softly to Tracy.

"Can you tell me what's happened this morning?"

"I woke up, realised the time, and saw that David's side of the bed was empty. I came downstairs to tell him to come up to bed and found him. I thought he was asleep at first, until I saw the empty pill packets." Pointing to them on the table. "I've been worried about him; he's not been himself lately." Aware she was speaking quickly, she paused for breath before continuing. "I've been worried about him, so arranged for our son to stay with a friend last night so that we could talk. I bought him home a takeaway. He had asked me to bring him one. But when I got home, he said he wanted to be left alone and didn't much feel like talking. I tried and tried to get him to talk." She let out a wail. "But he refused, saying he needed some space to think. He poured himself a drink, told me to go up to bed and said he'd join me shortly."

The male paramedic picked up the empty blister packets, examining them.

"Where these full?" He asked.

"I don't know, I think so." She nodded.

"I'd estimate a full packed of diazepam and two packets for SSRIs." He directed to his colleague.

The female paramedic shook her head "We're too late." She declared.

Tracy wailed and knelt besides her husband, shaking him

to wake him.

"No, he can't be. You must be able to do something."

The male paramedic placed a gentle hand on her shoulder whilst the other paramedic left the room. She could be heard speaking to someone on her radio but was unable to hear what was being said. She reappeared a few minutes later. Tracy still cradling her husband and keeping up the façade.

"I've called it in, and they have dispatched the police and a coroner to collect your husband."

"Why?" Tracy asked, realising she may have been a little too hasty in asking?

"It's standard procedure. The police will want to talk to you and understand more, before deciding if an investigation needs to take place. And in circumstances when a death is unexpected and unnatural, the coroner will need to be involved, they will collect your husband and ultimately decide the next steps. Is there someone I can call to be with you? You shouldn't be alone right now."

Tracy hadn't considered this and hesitated before whispering. "My mum and dad."

Peter and Jean were not expecting the early morning telephone call. The paramedics had offered to make the call, but Tracy insisted on making it herself.

Peter answered and it was obvious from the sound of his voice that he had been woken by the telephone. To be expected given it was only five fifteen.

Tracy launched straight into an almost unintelligible ramble as soon as she heard her father's voice.

"Dad. Dad, it's me. He's dead."

"Who's dead?" Asked Peter

"David is."

"What! I don't understand. What do you mean David's dead?"

"He took an overdose, he took his own life and now he's dead. Can you and mum come over?"

"Yes of course we can."

"I found him dad." She sobbed. "He'd taken my pills, I couldn't wake him, so I called for an ambulance, but they said it was too late. Come quickly please. I need you."

"Oh sweetheart, I don't know what to say, I'm shocked. Are you alone right now?"

Tracy could hear rustling coming from the other end of the phone as Peter pulled on his clothes.

"The paramedics are still here, and the police and coroner are on their way."

"And Daniel, is he still asleep?"

"He's not here. Long story. I'll fill you in when you get here.

"Ok, sit tight, we'll be with you in twenty, thirty minutes tops."

The police were the first to arrive. Two uniformed officers, both male, one looking incredibly young, a rookie she suspected and an older officer.

By now Tracy was sat on the sofa rocking back and forth and holding a sweet tea that had been made for her by one of the paramedics, she wasn't sure which one. The police stayed in the hallway for a few moments speaking to the two paramedics and being briefed on the situation before going into the living room to survey the scene and speak to Tracy.

"Tracy." Said the female paramedic. "We are going to hand you over to these two police officers and head off now, ok?"

"Ok." She whispered quietly. Shock had now set in. Not for his death but for the realisation that she once again had blood on her hands. This time however, it was premeditated.

"I'm really sorry for your loss."

Tracy couldn't work out which one of the four in the room had said that and she remained silent.

Shortly after the paramedics had removed their equipment and left, Tracy's parents arrived. Both were tear stricken and immediately hurried to sit besides Tracy and envelop her in a hug, whilst they all sobbed. The police officers stepped back, allowing the three family members to grieve as

David remained on the living room floor.

It was nearly nine am before David had been collected and the police finally left Tracy and her parents alone. Jean went into autopilot, making useless cups of tea which almost always remained undrunk. She offered to make Tracy some food, but she just shook her head. She needed to call Maggie to arrange collecting Daniel.

Maggie seemed genuinely shocked when Tracy told her what had happened. She confirmed that Daniel had been a little superstar and it was agreed that Peter would collect him and take him back to their house. And Jean would stay with Tracy, insisting that she tried to get some sleep and would field any calls that came through.

Tracy had wanted to see Daniel, to keep the promise she had made him. But had he seemed happy to go with his grandad.

As Tracy laid in bed, this time allowing herself to get comfortable. She couldn't believe that her plan had worked.

She knew the next few days would be difficult. It was now up to the coroner and police to decide if they believed David's death to be a result of suicide or if they suspected foul play.

One thing was for sure, the abuse was over. And she would never again encounter any such cruelty, for as long as she lived.

CHAPTER 51

June 2001

Tracy contemplated restarting her daily antidepressant but felt for the first time in many years she didn't need them. It had been a turbulent couple of weeks as expected but following a few enquires and a post-mortem, the police were happy to rule David's death as a suicide. And the inquest which would follow would simply be a formality.

Tracy was surprised that Daniel cried when she told him of his father's death. She didn't go into any detail and merely said that he had been poorly. Tracy then had to reassure him that she wasn't poorly and was not going to leave him. And after she had, he seemed ok.

Once the family had started to give her and Daniel some space, Tracy was able to tear up David's antiquated book of rules and introduce her own. And hers began by enrolling Daniel into swimming lessons and bringing the toy box downstairs.

The funeral was fast approaching which Tracy was dreading but knew that once it was over, she had the rest of her life to look forward to.

Peter took the morning off work and accompanied Tracy to see the Wright's family solicitor. The same firm that had not that long ago supported the family after Tony died.

She was surprised to learn that David didn't have a will, given the control freak he was, but it made no difference. There were no other living relatives to contest so Tracy being his wife inherited everything.

At nearly twenty-five years of age Tracy was now in possession of two mortgage free properties and a substantial amount of money which David held in various investments, from money he had inherited from his father. Money which Tracy knew vaguely of but wasn't aware of its value. And there was also David's pension from work, which was automatically paid to Tracy as his next on kin.

Tracy left the solicitors not believing quite how wealthy she had become. It had never been about the money and part of her felt that she didn't deserve it. But another part of her thought to hell with it. It meant she was now able to comfortably provide a life and stability for her son.

There was always something eating away at her though. It may have been caused by guilt; she wasn't sure. All she knew was that she wanted to help others, other sufferers of domestic violence. She wanted to do some good, *pay it forward,* she supposed, just like Maggie had done for her. She just needed to work out how.

Tracy was adamant that she no longer wanted to live in Tony's house, it bought back too many bad memories, as did the house she had rented out in Chesterfield Avenue, next door to Maggie.

She put both houses on the market and gave some serious thought into where her and Daniel would live. And she needed to decide quickly before Daniel started school in September.

The house phone rang. Tracy had become used to this happening a lot more since David's death. She answered it expecting it to be her mum, who had taken to calling several times a day. She didn't mind though, as her mum didn't punish her for not picking up or for leaving the house.

"Hello." Tracy said, feeling cheerful.

"Hi Tracy, it's James."

"Hi, I wasn't expecting to hear from you." She said feeling surprised.

"I know. I had tried to call your mobile a few times but couldn't get hold of you."

"Sorry, I've not really had a need to use my mobile, so it's been switched off."

"I just wanted to call, mum told me what had happened, and I wanted to check in, to see if you are ok."

"Thank you, I'm doing ok. Better than ok actually.

EPILOGUE

April 2002

Tracy stood at the school gates and waved to Daniel as he disappeared inside the school building. She felt a tear prick the back of her eyes, the same feeling she had felt every morning since he had begun school some seven months earlier.

Daniel loved school and had already made a group of friends, some of whom he'd had play dates with after school.

He was such a confident little boy and took everything in his stride.

Daniel often spoke of his father and although it pained Tracy, she felt it was best to let him. She would try to guide his memories to happier times, despite there not being many. In a hope that he would grow up to forget the cruel man and only remember him as being a good father. A decision she had thought long and hard about and was doing purely for Daniel's sake.

Tracy climbed into the waiting jeep.

"Did Dan get off ok?" asked James.

"Yep. He didn't even look back this morning. He met one of his friends in the playground and that was it."

"Good lad. So, what have you got install for me today?"

"The outside security lights need installing." Tracy replied, with an eager expression on her face.

"Let's just hope the weather holds." He said, leaning forward to get a good look at the dark grey skies through the windscreen.

"Well, there's only a seventy percent chance of rain today apparently. So, you might get lucky."

"Great." He said sarcastically. "And what do I get in return?"

"Satisfaction that you are helping a great cause." She paused "And, maybe I'll throw in dinner. Do you like turkey dinosaurs?"

"Depends. Do they come with chips and peas?"

"That can be arranged."

"Then it's a deal." Said James, and stuck out his hand to shake Tracy's, before pulling away and driving them both to Elmtree House.

Elmtree House was a small, abandoned hotel which Tracy happened to stumble across when on a woodland walk with Daniel. She saw it was sale, saw it needed some renovation and fell in love with it straight away. She immediately made an appointment to view it, and within twenty-four hours had made an offer, and had had the offer accepted.

The sale went through in early January and Tracy was hopeful to have the renovations complete by early summer. If all went well, she'd be in a position to launch her initiative, into the community soon after.

That was all thanks to help from James and the various tradesman who had offered to either donate their time, or work at reduced rates to support the cause.

The ten ensuite bedroom property with large reception area, kitchen, dinning room, and lounge. Also boasted additional facilities such as a games room, laundry room and office. It would be the perfect safe haven for victims of domestic violence. Although Tracy never liked to use the word victim, she preferred to say survivor.

The name Elmtree House, which Tracy had decided to retain from the original hotel, would welcome and provide temporary accommodation to survivors. Both male and female, and with or without children; depending on their circumstances. They'd have a place to stay. A place they could be safe.

But it was to be more than just a safe space. She wanted to help survivors overcome the challenges one might face when leaving an abuser. To help those rebuilding their life's and provide practical advice, with the help and support from external experts. Whether that be navigating the justice system for criminal matters, custody battles and divorce. Obtaining a job, finding childcare, learning how to budget, rebuilding confidence and life skills. Or in those extreme cases, to help a survivor escape and create a new life, far away.

It was something Tracy felt very passionate about and had been set on making happen, ever since she first moved to Manchester, back in August.

Tracy purchased a modest two-bedroom end terraced house for her and Daniel, deeming it perfectly suitable for just the two of them. She kept enough money back for them to live off and then allocated the remainder to kick start the Elmtree House initiative.

She had it all planned out. She would need to recruit volunteers and apply to the government to secure funding to support Elmtree House's ongoing running costs. Something she had been told should not be an issue, given that she had generously funded the start up.

"Why Manchester?" Her parents both asked. Unable to understand the fresh start, she so desperately craved. Those not in the know, might have seen it as cashing in and running, but she didn't care what people thought.

Her relationship with her parents was great, on the surface at least. And she would forever be grateful for the support they had given to her, in her late teens. But as an adult, when she had reached out to them for help. She was denied it and instead, forced to go back with her abuser. She knew deep down that it was because David was a manipulator and had her parents believing his every world. But it still hurt, and she could never truly forgive them. Peter and Jean, however, would always remain oblivious to this.

James never questioned Tracy about David's death. He had his suspicions, but regardless of the truth, it didn't matter to him. He would have even finished the bastard off himself if he had the opportunity and could have got away with it.

He knew that with Tracy he needed to play the long game and he was ok with that. She had been very clear and honest about it when agreeing to move near to him. Daniel was her number one priority and she needed to take things slowly. Also, only James and his mother Maggie, knew the real David and what went on behind closed doors. To anyone outside the circle, they would quite rightly question the matter, if Tracy immediately jumped into another relationship.

James was just grateful that Tracy chose Manchester to settle. It enabled him to help her, which he did, by offering free labour a couple of days a week. Although he had to repeatedly stress to Tracy, that he was an electrician. And not a plumber or a plasterer. The skills of such trades differed significantly to that of his own. But Tracy exploited him all the same, and in all honesty, he loved being able to support her. And he loved how passionate she was about the cause.

And even if, for whatever reason, the government's funding to support the Elmtree House initiative didn't come through. He knew she had the determination to make a success of the venture regardless.

Who knew what the future would bring? The only thing that Tracy was sure of, was that she would never suffer the hands of another human being in the same way she had suffered with David, and neither would Daniel. She would spend her life ensuring that! And if she could use her experiences and fortune to help just one survivor, then it would all be worth it.

She just needed to be careful how much of her own story she retold in the process...

ABOUT THE AUTHOR

Meg Hallam

Meg Hallam is a British novelist living in Oxfordshire with her family. She spent her career working in a corporate environment whilst juggling the demands of being a working mum. An illness in her early forties forced a career break, and as a keen reader of fiction and listener to audio books, began writing her own books.

Twitter: @MegHallamAuthor

Printed in Great Britain
by Amazon

23766370R00189